where butterflies go

debra doxer

Where Butterflies Go
Copyright © 2020 Debra Doxer
All Rights Reserved

Edited by Pam Berehulke of Bulletproof Editing
Cover Design by ©Sarah Hansen at Okay Creations
Formatted by Stacey Blake at Champagne Book Design

No part of this book may be reproduced in any form or by any electronic or mechanical means including information storage and retrieval systems—except in the case of brief quotations embodied in critical articles or reviews—without permission in writing from its publisher, Debra Doxer.

This is a work of fiction. Names, characters, places, brands, media, and incidents are either the product of the author's imagination or are used fictitiously. The author acknowledges the trademarked status and trademark owners of various products referenced in this work of fiction, which have been used without permission. The publication/use of these trademarks is not authorized, associated with, or sponsored by the trademark owners.

For all the Tovahs

Based on a true story

where butterflies go

part I

chapter 1

Warsaw, Poland, 1932

My family was poor, but the city was rich with sounds and smells. Each afternoon, children played in the streets, laughing and shouting, until wagons filled with goods for sale scattered them to the sidewalks. We bought much of our food from those wagons, my mother always bargaining for lower prices. There was the meat man, the man who sold vegetables, and my favorite, the bakery wagon with its warm bread and cookies.

There were other men too, who stood on the corner and argued about the meaning of life. For hours on end, they would ponder the philosophical questions of the universe. Papa said they had too much time on their hands. I thought they were interesting and eavesdropped every time I passed by. But no matter the hour, day or night, the city was always alive—breathing, changing, and growing.

We lived in a part of the city called the Jewish Quarter. It existed inside of Warsaw, a city within a city, a cultural island where we had our own businesses and synagogues, theaters and symphonies. We had our own shops and markets with signs written in both Hebrew and Polish. Everyone who lived on our street was Jewish. I might have mistakenly thought the whole world was Jewish if it weren't for the local newspapers making it clear that the city was filled with too many Jews for most people's liking.

My family lived in an apartment on the first floor of a two-story brick building, sandwiched between two taller apartment buildings that always seemed to cast a shadow and block out the sun. My older sister, my younger sister, my parents, and I all lived there. Sometimes it seemed the perfect size for our family. At other times, it seemed much too small, like tonight.

"Meira! Change your clothes. Your sister's young man will be here soon."

"He's not her young man," I muttered under my breath.

Mama huffed, and I knew she'd heard me.

Avrom was intended for my older sister, Zotia. The fact that they barely knew each other made no difference.

"None of that hair spray and lipstick tonight, Meira. Let your sister shine."

I held my tongue, but if Avrom were truly smitten with Zotia, my wearing a little lipstick and hair spray shouldn't matter.

Mama smiled to herself as she drained the potatoes in the sink, certain her eldest daughter would end the evening engaged, or close to it.

For this monumental dinner with Avrom and his parents, we were serving roast chicken with boiled potatoes, and green beans that I'd washed and cut myself. That was all the help I was allowed to offer in the kitchen since my attempts at cooking had all been disasters. Mama said there wasn't enough money in the bank to pay for all the food I'd ruined. The kitchen wasn't where my talents lay. Unfortunately, I had yet to discover what my talents were.

I did know one thing, though. I had to bury my feelings for Avrom, push them down so deep that they ceased to exist at all, which wasn't going to be easy since I'd admired him forever.

My stomach did a little flip each time I saw him around the neighborhood. There was no mistaking the way his coat stretched across his wide shoulders, or the confident way he walked. Avrom wasn't too tall or too short. He was the perfect height for a man, and when he spoke, his hair flopped onto his forehead.

Avrom laughed a lot too, and he made others laugh. He was what Papa called a "jokester," and Papa didn't mean it as a compliment. But since Avrom's family owned a popular jewelry store on Belzys Street, Papa could overlook Avrom's shortcomings.

I didn't think Avrom's sense of humor was a shortcoming. I liked his ready smile and the row of shiny white teeth it revealed. I also liked how deep his voice was, and the way it rumbled in his chest. The fact that he turned his smile on me more often than anyone else was something I spent too much time thinking about, especially late at night, when I was alone in my room.

But Avrom couldn't be interested in me if he was meant for Zotia. She was the eldest, although barely. She was only one year older than me, and Papa intended to have her married off first. I would be next and then Leah, the youngest at only nine years old. She still cared more for dolls than boys.

"Meira, get dressed. They'll be here soon."

Zotia's heels clicking on the floor alerted me to her entrance in the kitchen. She had on her best shoes, the gray dress she wore to synagogue, and her dark blond curls were captured by a thick gold barrette at the nape of her neck. Zotia's body bristled with nervous energy as she stood for Mama's inspection, and I couldn't help wondering what I would wear if I were dining with someone who could be my future husband.

Our clothes weren't fancy, but that didn't mean we had to look drab and colorless the way Zotia did. If I were her, I'd tie a red scarf around my neck and match it with red lipstick. Of course, Mama would tell me to take it off, and I'd agree for the moment, but then I'd have it back on when my future husband arrived, and Mama wouldn't dare say a word about it in front of him.

The fact that I cared more about my appearance than Zotia did about hers was no secret. From the time we were little, my parents would give us very different compliments. I was pretty and precocious, while Zotia was smart and responsible. As much as I liked being called pretty, I wouldn't have minded being called smart once in a while. Just like Zotia would have appreciated being told she was pretty.

For the most part, Zotia and I got along, but there was an undercurrent of competition between us. I wasn't sure when it started or why, but it was there, and it prevented us from becoming too close.

Avrom's family was punctual, and that impressed Papa. He was always going on about my lateness and lack of proper planning. As a tailor, all his measurements had to be precise and his alterations delivered on time, or he'd be out of business. I couldn't recall how many times he'd mentioned those facts to me, insinuating that I was neither precise nor on time.

Our small parlor became crowded as Avrom and his parents came inside. I stood back, holding Leah's hand to keep her from disappearing upstairs to play or color. She fidgeted beside me, not understanding the importance of this moment.

Avrom is here! In our house.

Papa took their coats and hats, and I caught glimpses of Avrom from where I stood off to the side, noticing the way he removed his arms from his overcoat and smiled brightly at my mother.

Don't smile so much, I thought. He'd never win my father over by smiling. Papa didn't trust happy people.

Avrom's gaze scanned the room, and when his eyes met mine, they came to a halt.

My stomach flipped and then settled at the warmth I saw looking back at me. *Avrom's deep brown eyes remind me of hot chocolate on a cold night.*

The moment I thought that, I was swamped with guilt and quickly looked away. I shouldn't feel that way. I was a horrible sister. Then it occurred to me, where was Zotia? Shouldn't she be out here staring into Avrom's gorgeous brown eyes?

Glancing over my shoulder, I spotted her in the kitchen, wringing her hands. Catching her eye, I silently gestured for her to come out.

After a few moments, Zotia made an appearance in the parlor with great reluctance, as if she were going to a funeral.

"Smile," I whispered to her.

Zotia tried to take my advice, but her grin was tight and forced, and all wrong. If I were in her shoes, I'd be beaming like the sun, dying to show myself off to a handsome young man. It wasn't often that you were the center of attention around here. It was a moment to be savored, not dreaded.

When our guests noticed Zotia, I steeled myself for the sight of Avrom turning his smile on her. I would be happy for her, or would at least pretend to be. If I pretended long enough, it might actually be true someday.

But Avrom didn't smile when Zotia was presented to him by my mother like a prize he'd won at the fair. In fact, his expression fell and filled with confusion as his gaze darted away from Zotia's and back to mine again.

I sucked in a breath. *Why is he looking at me that way?*

My mother was talking to Avrom's parents, filling the room with compliments about Zotia like she was being sold at the secondhand store, but Avrom kept darting glances at me.

"Keep Leah occupied," Mama hissed in my direction as she showed everyone into the back room, where she had two tables set up. We didn't have one dining table large enough to accommodate everyone.

Leah clutched my mother's skirt, begging for cookies, and I avoided looking at Avrom as I detached her from my mother and led her out onto the front stoop.

My stomach sank, as if I'd done something wrong.

Was smiling at Avrom when I saw him on the street wrong? I smiled at lots of people. I was outgoing and friendly. Everyone said so.

Was admiring Avrom from afar inappropriate? If I'd never even spoken to him, how could it be? But why was Avrom here with his family if he didn't want to meet Zotia? Had anyone else noticed the way he'd looked from her to me?

My head hurt, and I turned my attention to my little sister, who was still insisting that cookies had been promised to her.

"Before dinner?" I asked skeptically.

"Yes," she answered firmly.

With her brown curls and big blue eyes, Leah and I resembled each other most. We took after my father's side of the family, while Zotia was a miniature version of our mother. The only similarity between Zotia and me was that we were both blondes, while Leah was a brunette.

"If you come inside with me now and eat your dinner quietly, with no mention of cookies, I'll save you an extra helping of dessert and sneak it up to you later."

Leah contemplated this for a moment. "Promise?"

"I promise."

At those words, she happily marched into the apartment.

In the back room, everyone was seated except for Mama and Zotia, who were wearing out a path in the rug as they served all the food. Avrom and his parents were at one table, where there was one free chair, and my father was seated at the other. Leah went and sat down beside Papa while I went into the kitchen to help.

"The window was smashed at Pearlman's Bakery yesterday," I heard my father say from the other room.

To my surprise, Avrom's father laughed. "Let the Poles smash our windows and have their meetings about how to 'solve the Jewish problem.' It's only because we're doing better business than they are."

I glanced at my mother and wasn't surprised to see her expression tighten. She didn't like this subject brought up in front of us, especially Leah. She tried to shelter us, but there was no avoiding the newspapers and new signs on Jewish businesses.

Each day, newspapers printed articles about how to solve "the Jewish problem," the problem being that there were almost three million of us in Poland now. That was three million too many for some Poles. They'd passed a law that all Jewish businesses had to put the owner's last name on the sign so people could tell it was run by a Jew. Once that happened, Pearlman's Bakery wasn't the only store with a smashed window.

Avrom's last name was Sokolow, and I wondered if his father had put their name on the sign for their jewelry store. Since I didn't think so, I also wondered what the penalty was for ignoring the law.

"I hear there's a new film at the Yiddish theater," my mother said, changing the subject and giving my father a pointed look.

Avrom's mother cleared her throat. "I don't approve of those films. I heard the censors considered shutting the last one down."

My father looked over at their table. "It was about Polish nationalism and how we should try to integrate more. The Jews wanted it censored, not the Poles. Perhaps we *should* integrate more. It might make us less of a target."

Mama turned her scowling expression on Papa now. On this point, they vehemently disagreed. Mama wanted nothing to do with the Poles.

"I saw the film," Avrom said. "Pretending ideas you don't agree with don't exist doesn't make it so. Better to be informed, don't you think?"

Avrom's mother pressed her lips together in disapproval, and I forgot myself and smiled at Avrom. I'd only been to the cinema a few times, but what he said made perfect sense to me.

Throughout dinner, conversation continued about politics and the goings-on in our neighborhood. Soon my mother steered the talk back to Zotia, informing everyone of how smart and accomplished she was, while my older sister blushed furiously and remained silent.

Mostly it was the parents who talked while the rest of us exchanged awkward glances between bites of food. On the bright side, Leah was a perfect angel with dreams of extra dessert floating in her head.

The dinner was unsuccessful, in my opinion. I'd never been to a dinner where two virtual strangers were meeting for the purpose of spending the rest of their lives together, but I'd gotten an earful from my friend Rivka when her sister went through the same thing. According to Rivka, her sister and the boy talked and laughed all night at their dinner.

That was hardly the case here, and a part of me was glad. I didn't want Zotia and Avrom to get married. The guilt I already felt grew, forming a tight ball in the pit of my stomach, and a part of me wanted to fall right into that pit. I was a terrible sister.

When our guests finally left, it was obvious that Zotia and my mother were both unhappy.

"You should have spoken to him more," my mother told Zotia as she dropped a dirty pan into the sink.

"He could have spoken to me too."

"That's true. He could have. We'll have another dinner. We'll think of some topics to discuss in advance. You'll have a nice chat, and soon you'll be engaged."

Zotia swallowed hard at the prospect of another dinner, but said nothing. Arguing with Mama was a one-way street. While you talked, Mama remained frustratingly silent as she waited you out, but she never changed her mind.

"I don't like the parents," Papa grumbled as he went to the phonograph and put on a record. It was Prelude in C Minor, one of his favorite Chopin recordings.

"Oh no. Not Chopin again," Mama said as the slow progression of chords began.

"Chopin relaxes me, and after the high expectations of this evening, I need some relaxation." He poured himself a small glass of red wine and settled into the recliner in the parlor.

"What did you think of Avrom, Papa?" I asked, settling on the floor beside him.

Squinting into his glass, he sighed. "No one is good enough for my girls, but I suppose he'll do."

Despite the knot in my stomach, I chuckled. Coming from Papa, that was a high compliment. Not that it mattered to me. I intended to quash my feelings for Avrom once and for all. I didn't know how I was going to do that, but I didn't need that kind of guilt on my conscience.

As the music played through the house, I went back into the

kitchen. "Go upstairs and rest," I said to Zotia. "I'll help Mama with the dishes. Could you take this plate up to Leah? I bribed her into good behavior with promises of extra dessert. This cake should do the trick."

With the strain of the evening showing on her face, Zotia took the plate from me and smiled her thanks.

Once she was gone, I helped Mama clean up, insisting on washing all the dirtiest pots and pans myself as punishment for my selfish feelings. My guilt lessened as the pile of dishes slowly got smaller and smaller.

chapter 2

Buttoning my coat to ward off the chill, I waited on the sidewalk for Mr. Blacker to pass with his fruit cart before I jogged across the street.

A little over three weeks had passed since Avrom came to dinner with his parents. In that time, my mother let it slip to her friends that they were a perfect match and would soon be engaged, much to Zotia's embarrassment, since she hadn't spoken to Avrom at all.

Oddly, I hadn't seen him either. We usually passed each other on the sidewalk when he was on his way to work, and I was on my way to watch the Solomon children, which I did three mornings a week. It was on those mornings that I got the most smiles from him. We never spoke, but his smiles made my day, and I missed them.

Maybe he was avoiding me, or maybe he was angry at my whole family because he knew my mother told all her friends he was going to get engaged to Zotia. The thought of Avrom being angry at us, especially at me, was upsetting. I could try to explain, only I never saw him anymore. But I knew where he was, or at least I had a good idea.

I told myself I was only going to walk past the jewelry store owned by Avrom's family to see if they had added their last name to the store sign. I didn't want them to get into trouble, and I was simply checking for Zotia's sake. I told myself that so many times as I approached the store, I almost believed it.

My heart hammered in my chest because it knew I shouldn't go there, but I walked quickly. I kept my gaze on the store signs, not on the windows or the sidewalk, which was why I didn't see the large man walking in the other direction until I'd already bumped into him. Down went his brown paper bag filled with apples, which he'd probably just purchased from Mr. Blacker's cart.

"I am so sorry," I said as I bent to grab the fruit before it rolled into the street.

"Stupid girl," the man muttered.

As I loaded the apples in my arms, another set of hands joined mine, scooping the fruit off the pavement. To my surprise, it was Avrom, grinning as he shook his head at me and stood to pour his armful of apples into the paper bag held by the disgruntled stranger.

My cheeks heated as I grabbed hold of the last few and handed them to the man. "I am so sorry," I said again, but he only grunted before he walked away. Now that there was no fruit left to gather, there was nothing for me to do but look directly at Avrom.

"Thank you for your help," I said, meeting his warm brown eyes. "You'd think I would have seen a man of his size coming."

Avrom chuckled, but then schooled his smile and cleared his throat. "Good to see you, Miss Sojcher. What brings to you this side of town?"

My cheeks heated as I looked up at the store sign, my excuse for coming here today. To my relief, the name Sokolow was painted in white letters at the bottom.

Avrom glanced up also. "Papa painted it himself last week, scowling the entire time."

"I was a little worried after what he said the other night. I'm glad he's following the rule, even if it is a terrible one."

Avrom watched me, his expression unsure now. "Would you like to come inside? I can show you the store. It's only me here today. My father is out on other business."

The two of us would be in the store alone. I should probably say no. "All right. Just for a minute."

A tiny bell rang when Avrom opened the door and held it for me. After the brightness of the afternoon sun, the interior of the store was dark, and it took a moment for my eyes to adjust. Soon my surroundings came into focus, and I saw glass display cases arranged along the sides of the room, each filled with items I was sure were too expensive for my family to afford.

"You're Meira, not Zotia," he said after the door closed behind us. "You're not the eldest daughter of the Sojcher family."

I tried not to smile as my suspicions were confirmed. "You thought I was Zotia, and that you were coming to meet me that night."

Looking a lot less happy than I currently felt, he nodded. "I knew who your family was, and I asked around, trying to learn your name, but obviously I got it wrong."

"A lot of people make that mistake." Since we were so close in age, Zotia and I were often confused for each other.

Avrom shifted on his feet, and some of his hair flopped over onto his forehead. My fingers twitched, wanting to push it back for him.

"Your mother spoke to mine about another dinner, but I told her no. I don't... I don't think it would be fair to your sister."

Familiar guilt washed over me again, and suddenly I felt the need to defend Zotia. "Maybe you could like her. She's a wonderful person, kind and smart. And she's a fantastic cook. I couldn't bake a *challah* if my life depended on it."

Avrom's eyes narrowed in confusion. "I can buy a *challah* if I want one. Are you saying you want me to like your sister?"

Even though that's exactly what I should be saying, I said, "No. It's just that my mother is telling everyone that you and Zotia are engaged."

"That's unfortunate, because she isn't the Sojcher sister I'm interested in."

My chest squeezed tight. *Avrom feels the same way I do.*

Then why hadn't he spoken to me on those mornings when we passed? Why hadn't I said hello? This whole mess could have been avoided if only one of us had said something.

"I can't hurt my sister, Avrom."

He nodded solemnly. "Family is important. I understand."

He understands. I swallowed past the lump in my throat, wishing he didn't sound so resigned. "Maybe in time, after she finds someone else."

"Maybe," he said.

Why does he have to be so agreeable? To my surprise, my eyes filled with tears.

"Oh, Meira." He took a step in my direction.

"I am being silly." I wiped at my cheeks. "We don't even know each other. Not really. I must be crying for Zotia, not myself."

His hands rested on my shoulders, and I could feel the warmth of his touch through my coat. "If thinking about you all the time counts as knowing you, then I think I do know you."

My heart soared at his words, but at the same time, my shoulders tensed in frustration. If he thought about me all the time, why was he so willing to give up on us? Didn't our feelings count for something?

Desperation made me bold as I reached up and laid my palm against his cheek. It was scratchy, like Papa's, but touching Papa never caused my skin to tingle with awareness. Our eyes held, and there was so much in Avrom's gaze—sadness, longing, and maybe hope too. I still had hope. Did he?

His hand covered mine, and his fingers closed around it as he turned his head and kissed my palm. Butterflies rioted in my chest. I'd never felt like this before, and I was afraid I never would again.

The bell over the door rang, and a woman walked into the shop. Just as her eyes widened at the sight of us standing there, Avrom and I sprang apart.

"Can I help you?" Avrom asked, running a hand over his suit jacket, trying to pretend everything was normal, even though his cheeks were flushed.

My face flamed too as I turned away, not wanting to be recognized.

The woman asked Avrom a question, but before she finished, I muttered a good-bye and moved toward the door.

"Wait," Avrom called after me.

I glanced over my shoulder, and even though he said nothing, there was determination in his eyes. *This isn't impossible. It can't be.*

I stepped out into the cold afternoon with adrenaline rushing through my veins and a new secret hope buried deep in my heart.

Another week passed without Avrom's family agreeing to come to dinner, but the rumors of Zotia's engagement to Avrom continued, catching fire and spreading further. Then, yesterday, another rumor reached my mother's ears. Avrom had been seen in close contact with a girl who wasn't Zotia, in his very own store.

My heart leaped into my throat when I overheard Mama telling Papa and Zotia about it.

Was that rumor about me? Had the woman who interrupted us in the jewelry story talked to someone? If so, she didn't seem to know the girl was me, or Mama certainly would have said so.

Thank goodness for that, at least.

This scandalous news had Mama and Zotia talking frantically into the night, wondering if it were true and what they should do. When they finally they decided it wasn't true, I breathed a sigh of relief, even though I had no business celebrating the fact that I hadn't been discovered.

After yet another restless night, I knew I couldn't handle the guilt anymore. The obvious person to talk to was Papa. He would at least try to understand, while Mama would do nothing but lose her temper and shout at me. Even though I didn't know what would become of Avrom and me, Mama and Papa had to know that Avrom wasn't going to marry Zotia. At the very least, I could put a stop to the engagement rumors.

My father's tailor shop was located in a space at the back of a small textile factory a few blocks from our neighborhood. The factory made clothing for big department stores, like Jabłkowski Brothers, but also for smaller shops. When customers needed something altered or custom-made, stores would send them to my father.

Papa had no sign and did no advertising, but he didn't need to. He had his good reputation, and that was enough to provide him with more business than he could easily manage in a day. As a tailor, he didn't make as much money as a shop owner would, but he was respected and could do his work alone while he listened to music, which suited him fine.

When I walked inside and heard the Minute Waltz playing, I knew he was there alone and in a good mood. Unfortunately, the fast-paced music did nothing to calm my nerves.

Some of the girls I knew were afraid of their fathers. Warsaw could be a dangerous, judgmental place, and strict fathers meant safer children, but my father wasn't that way. He wanted us to be safe, but he trusted us and knew we could think for ourselves. He also listened to us, more than Mama did. She spoke *at us*. Papa might use fewer words, but he spoke *to us*.

The thought that I'd betrayed his trust by hurting my own sister was eating me up inside. That secret hope I held was too sharp sometimes, and cut deep every time I spoke to Zotia.

But if nothing ever happened between Avrom and me, why hurt everyone by confessing? If neither of us acted on our feelings and forever wondered *what if*, wouldn't that be punishment enough? I didn't know what to do, but the fact that I was wrong, no matter what I did, sat like a rock in my stomach.

I stood watching Papa work for a moment before making my presence known.

With his thick gray hair and long beard, and dressed in a white shirt with the sleeves rolled up, he looked much like many of the older men in the Jewish Quarter. His hands moved quickly and efficiently, measuring fabric, marking it with chalk, and cutting it quickly before moving on to the next swath.

Since I was little, I'd asked him to teach me his trade. Often, he'd let me sit and work with him, but only in secret, when no customers were scheduled for appointments. They wanted Samuel Sojcher to sew their clothes, not some girl they'd never heard of. That was okay. I didn't want to be a tailor. I only wanted an excuse to spend time with Papa.

"Hello," I finally said, hearing the slight tremor in my voice.

He glanced up and grinned before going back to his task. "Are you here to help me today, *bubelah?*"

My palms dampened, and I rubbed them over my dress as I moved closer. I only held half of his attention until I reached over and lifted the needle off the phonograph. The music abruptly stopped, and the room quieted except for the sounds filtering in from the street.

Papa stilled his hands and eyed me curiously.

"I have to talk to you about Avrom," I said.

"What about him?" There was a wary tone to Papa's voice. He was tired of all the gossiping about Zotia and Avrom.

I drew in a shaky breath, hoping he would understand. "He's not going to ask Zotia to marry him."

Papa nodded. "I don't think so either. He barely spoke to her at dinner."

"No. I mean I *know* he's not going to ask her, because I talked to him."

"When did you talk to him?" Papa put his hands in his lap and sat up straighter to listen.

I took a shallow breath and tried to get my thoughts straight. "The other day. You see, I knew Avrom a little before he came to dinner that night. I'd never spoken to him, but we'd see each other around the neighborhood. After a while, we smiled when we passed, in sort of a silent hello. After a while, I looked forward to seeing him each day. It felt like something passed between us when our eyes would meet."

I cleared my throat, feeling foolish for saying it out loud, and to Papa, of all people. "Avrom asked around about me, trying to learn my name. Someone had told him I was Zotia. When the idea of him coming to our house to meet Zotia was presented to him, Avrom agreed because he thought that was me. He thought he was coming to meet me."

Papa didn't move a muscle, but he managed to look cross anyway. "How do you know he thought that?"

Sweat broke out on my upper lip. "I know I shouldn't have done it, but I went by his family's store and spoke to him. He explained everything."

His eyes narrowed. "You spoke to him? Alone?"

"Yes. Alone." My vision blurred with tears. "I just meant to walk by the store to see if he was there. I didn't plan to go inside, but then I did go in. I'm so sorry, Papa."

My father pushed to his feet. "Stop crying. You girls are all making too much of this. If it was a misunderstanding, he should have said something that night."

"How could he? He didn't want to hurt Zotia's feelings."

"There's no avoiding that now, is there?"

I sniffled quietly. It wasn't easy to just stop crying like Papa wanted me to.

"Do we have to tell her the truth? Can't you just say you decided against Avrom or make something else up?" When Papa's brows slammed down in disapproval, my gaze dropped to the floor. "That would be wrong. I know. It's just that they're not going to end up together. Telling Zotia the truth won't change that."

"How are you and Avrom going to *end up* together unless you tell the truth?"

I blinked, wondering if I'd heard him correctly. "Papa, you would allow that?"

He sighed. "You care about this young man?"

I nodded.

"I only want you to be happy, Meira, although I don't see what's so special about him. It seems to me there's dozens like him. Ones who won't get you and your sister mixed up."

I cringed. "It's not his fault. You know how often people confuse Zotia and me for each other."

Papa scowled and picked up his scissors again. "If you have your mind set on Avrom Sokolow, I can't pretend that the security he can provide you with won't be a relief to me. His family is well off. That fact alone will probably bring your mother around, despite how this will embarrass Zotia."

This news should have made me happy, but I was afraid we were getting ahead of ourselves. I cared for Avrom, but I didn't *know* him, not yet, and we were about to create quite an uproar.

"Papa, since this also embarrasses him and his family, we can't assume he would still want me."

"He's a fool if he doesn't. Either way, Zotia needs to know this boy isn't interested, and why."

I wrung my hands and tried to imagine that conversation. All I could see in my mind were the angry faces of Zotia and Mama looming before me.

"America?" Papa spit out the word as if it left a bad taste in his mouth. "She does not have to run all the way to America because of some boy."

Mama pursed her lips in disapproval. "This is what she wants."

"Because she's embarrassed and upset, and wants to punish us all. You should talk some sense into her."

Even with tears pooling in her eyes, Mama looked formidable. "After what happened, can you blame her?"

"Yes, I can blame her, and I blame you, Esther. You told everyone they were engaged. All this could have been avoided if you hadn't lied in the first place."

At those words, Mama crumpled, collapsing into a chair and burying her face in her hands.

I was crying too from where I sat in the parlor. Upstairs, Zotia was locked in the bedroom we shared, and Leah cowered on the staircase, fear and confusion clouding her eyes. However badly I imagined this going, the reality was so much worse.

After I'd confessed everything to Mama and Zotia, my words running on and on in a tear-filled outpouring, Zotia ran from the house, fleeing to her friend Yuri's flat. When she came home hours later, she declared that Yuri's cousin in America needed a wife, and she was going to travel there to marry him. It felt like a tornado had hit our house and debris was flying through the air, injuring all of us in one way or another.

Zotia was so much more than embarrassed. She was utterly mortified and wanted only to disappear. She was so scared of everyone believing that Avrom had broken off their engagement and jilted her in favor of her younger sister, that she ran to our bedroom and declared she wasn't coming out until her ship set sail for America.

Days later, the dust still hadn't settled.

"She'll change her mind," Papa said firmly as he sat across from Mama at dinner. He'd said those words many times already.

"I spoke to Yuri's mother. This boy is doing very well for himself. He owns his own business and has his own flat. I know she'll be far away, but so much is changing here, Samuel. The anti-Semitism gets worse every day, and now Germany is trying to send all its Polish Jews back to Poland. What happens if Poland tries to export us to some other country? I read that the Germans made them leave their homes with only what they could fit into one suitcase."

"The Polish government wouldn't dare kick us out. There are too many of us."

"You don't know that." Mama sat straighter in her chair. "It breaks my heart to see her go, but maybe Zotia's leaving is for the best."

"Best for you or for her? Zotia going to America gives you bragging rights too, doesn't it? There's a certain status associated with it. If she sat around here all day, you'd look just as foolish as her."

Mama's mouth dropped open as her eyes glistened. Papa shoved back from the table and stormed out of the house. Obviously, the thought of one of his daughters leaving him and going so far away was almost more than he could bear.

Our family was being torn apart, and it was all my fault. Papa seemed to only blame Mama, but she and Zotia blamed me. They both hardly spoke to me, and Mama spent all her time upstairs with Zotia.

This was all over a boy I hardly knew. It was so foolish. What if I got to know Avrom better, and I didn't like him so much, or what if I did? If I was going to lose a sister over him, Avrom had to be the best husband a girl could ever ask for.

What frightened me was that I wasn't sure he would be. I wasn't sure of anything anymore.

chapter 3

In the silence that fell over the house after Zotia was gone, her last moments here with us played over and over in my head.

At the train station, she'd hugged everyone in our family except me. When I tried to embrace her and she refused, I fell to pieces. What if we never saw each other again? Was this how she wanted to leave things?

Papa scowled at her, and even Mama seemed unhappy with how she was behaving. But since Zotia was leaving, no one wanted to make things worse by trying to reason with her.

"Will we ever see her again?" I asked Papa when we returned from the station. Zotia was traveling with Yuri's aunt and uncle to London, and from there they would all board the ship that would take them to New York City so Zotia could meet Eli Katz, her new fiancé, a complete stranger.

"Of course we'll see her. If this young man is as well off as they say, they should be able to come home for a visit." Papa's voice was strained, as if he wasn't sure of his own words.

Despite how angry he was at the idea of Zotia leaving, he couldn't say no when her prospects there were so much better than the life she would have here. In Poland, we would always be poor. In America, there was more opportunity. It was the type of opportunity Papa couldn't give any of his daughters himself, and in the end, he couldn't say no. He wanted to go with Zotia and meet Eli, but there was only enough money for one ticket.

Papa still blamed Mama for the situation. He was so heartbroken over the whole thing that he'd hardly spoken a word to anyone in weeks. Our family was shattered.

After everything that had happened, I could hardly bring myself to look at Avrom when he passed me on the street each morning. With Zotia gone, we went back to our regular schedules, which included me watching the Solomon children three mornings a week and taking the route that put me in Avrom's path. He still smiled at me like always and often paused to talk, but I had a hard time smiling back, and I kept on walking.

At this rate, Avrom would be a memory, and Zotia would have left for nothing. The sinking feeling I carried with me each day made it feel like the sky was always dark with clouds, even on the sunniest afternoons.

As far as the neighborhood was concerned, Zotia had jilted Avrom before she ran off to America, and not the other way around. Zotia had started the rumor herself, although I didn't know how many people believed it. Girls like us didn't suddenly move to America. To his credit, Avrom said nothing to contradict her story.

At home, poor Leah was quiet and withdrawn, knowing all the facts but not really understanding them. I tried to cheer her up by drawing silly pictures and offering to play dolls with her, but nothing would put a smile on her face.

"I didn't think I'd miss Zotia this much," she told me one night.

I patted her on the cheek and dropped a kiss on top of her head. I felt the same way.

Zotia had been gone for almost a month when I pulled my coat on one morning and stepped out into the light layer of snow that had fallen the night before. I was on my way to my babysitting job when I approached the block where I usually saw Avrom.

Steeling myself for the encounter, I let my gaze wander over the faces that passed, most of which were shielded by scarves or hats pulled down low. Up ahead, I recognized Avrom's wide shoulders and confident gait. Unbothered by the snow, he wore nothing covering his hair, which fell over his forehead like always.

With a tight smile on my lips, I nodded curtly as he reached me, and our eyes met. When I continued on, a hand wrapped around my upper arm to stop me.

"Meira, please. Can we talk?" Avrom's voice was soft but insistent.

I nodded and let him direct me to a corner away from the foot traffic.

"How are you?" he asked, bending to catch my eye.

"Fine."

He cocked his head as if he didn't believe me. "I'm sorry your sister left. You must miss her."

I nodded. "No letters yet, but I'm sure she'll write soon."

Avrom sighed as he looked at me. "I wanted to let enough time pass so no one would think badly of you if they saw us out together, but I'm afraid I may have taken too much time and given you the wrong idea. Do you still think about me, Meira? Because I think about you." He watch me closely, looking a little nervous as he waited for my answer.

My heart still took notice when he was near, beating a little faster, but so much had happened. "I do, but—"

"I understand," he said sadly. "Your sister's gone, and it's my fault."

What? He was blaming himself too? His words couldn't have surprised me more.

Avrom believing it was his fault seemed to shift something inside me. There was so much blame being thrown around. We all wanted to own it or place it elsewhere, but most of the blame belonged to one person.

"It's not your fault, Avrom, and I'm not sure it's mine either or my mother's. We all had a hand in it, but Zotia's pride was the main problem. When everyone learned what happened, she might have been embarrassed for a little while, but it would have blown over. People around here have enough to worry about. They would have forgotten about this eventually. She didn't have to leave the continent, for goodness' sake."

A smile broke out on his face, and I held up my hand to cover my own grin.

"I do miss her, though," I said, "and I hope things are going well for her."

"Of course you do. So do I," he said. "But I've wanted to spend time with you for a very long time, Meira. How about we make a fresh start? Hoping to catch your eye as we pass on the street isn't enough. I want to do things right this time. Should I ask your father if I can take you out on a date? Do I have your permission to do that?" His warm brown eyes smiled down at me.

"Yes. You have my permission." I grinned at his formality.

"Is he going to say yes, or has he had about enough of me?" he asked anxiously.

If Papa never heard Avrom's name again, he would be very happy, but I wasn't going to tell Avrom that. Besides, Papa would say yes if that's what I wanted.

"Don't worry about Papa."

Smiling now, Avrom straightened his shoulders and reached into his breast pocket. "I made you something." He bent his head closer to mine as he held out his hand. In the middle of his palm was a small gold pin. "I melted down some cuff links and turned them into this for you."

Surprised he'd done anything for me, especially make a delicate piece of jewelry, I carefully picked it up and saw it was a flower. Looking closer, I realized it was a rose with small golden petals.

"You made this yourself?"

He nodded.

"It's so beautiful."

"So are you."

My gaze leaped to his, and my breath hitched at the admiration I saw there. Nerves skittered down my spine, and my cheeks were suddenly on fire. To cover my awkwardness, I tried to pin the rose on the lapel of my coat, but I only made it worse because I couldn't keep my hands steady.

"Let me." Avrom took the pin, lifted my lapel, and fastened it into place.

"Thank you," I said, running my fingertips over the cool metal and smiling at the fluttery feeling in my chest.

"I'm glad you like it. I should let you get on with your day. I hope you have a very nice day, Meira." He stood looking at me, humor twinkling in his eyes, probably because my face was beet red.

"You too." With that, we both gradually turned and walked in opposite directions.

"Do you like *kreplach*?" Avrom asked.

"Um . . ." Picturing the meat-filled dumplings my grandmother used to make, I giggled.

"What about *golabki*?"

"Isn't that made with boiled cabbage?" I wrinkled my nose in disgust, and he laughed at me. "You're choosing odd things on purpose."

"Chicken soup, then? You must like chicken soup."

With a grin, I nodded. "I do like chicken soup."

"Then I'll tell my mother to make chicken soup when you come for dinner."

"Am I coming for dinner?"

We were seated on a park bench because we were early for the cinema. After getting Papa's permission, Avrom had already taken me to a dance at the synagogue last week, but it was loud and crowded, and our friends were filled with questions about why we were there together after all the rumors about Avrom and Zotia. Although we didn't answer any questions, we had fun, but we didn't talk much or have any time alone.

Tonight was different. It was just the two of us alone, under a starlit sky. Avrom's voice was low and rumbly when he spoke, and mine was high and breathy with anticipation.

"If you want to see me again after tonight, I expect my mother will believe it's serious and invite you to dinner," he said.

"What if you don't want to see me again?" I was flirting with Avrom, and it was fun.

"Not possible." He flashed a smile my way. "I've spent the better part of a year trying to catch glimpses of you. I'll never stop wanting to see you, Meira." His gaze traveled over my face like he was watching to see how his words made me feel.

"Why do you do that?" I asked.

"Do what?"

"Say sweet things, as if you're afraid I'm not going to like them."

He looked surprised. "Do you like them? I'll admit it's hard to tell. I know they embarrass you sometimes."

"Of course I like them, but I'm not used to it. I never had a boy say those kinds of things to me. Did you think I didn't want to hear them?"

Avrom smiled and took my hand in his. "Maybe. I also thought you might be shy, but I wasn't sure. I'm glad you like them."

I squeezed his hand, wondering why it was hard for him to see how I felt. Because I did have feelings for him. They might have been bittersweet because of what happened with Zotia, and maybe that was why I was holding back, but they were there, and they weren't going away. I didn't want him to doubt me, and my hand gripped his tighter.

"Avrom, I want you to know that when I'm with you, it's the only place I want to be. When I'm not with you, all I do is think about you. I might get embarrassed because I'm not used to compliments, but I do like hearing them, and I like you too."

He looked at me for a long moment before he smiled and squeezed my hand back. He only let go of my hand to pay for the tickets, and then he held it again all through the movie. It made it hard to concentrate on the screen. All my attention was centered on the place where my skin touched his.

When the movie ended and we filed out of the theater, he pulled me to the side away from everyone else and said, "I want to kiss you."

My stomach did a nervous flip as I nodded, and a fleeting smile touched his lips before he pressed those lips against mine. My body grew warmer as I kissed him back, thinking how soft his mouth was and how good he smelled, like soap and mint. His strong arms came around me, and I melted into him, knowing I'd never before felt anything as exhilarating as kissing Avrom.

When the kiss ended with both of us breathing a little harder, I looked into his eyes and saw something that made me feel special and wanted, like I was important to him. I'd never felt important before.

We were married six months later, beneath the *chuppah* in our synagogue. The entire community came, and both our families were in attendance.

Only Zotia was missing, and since she was married and expecting her first child by then, I didn't believe there would be any hard feelings when Mama wrote to her with the news about Avrom and me.

chapter 4

Warsaw, Poland, 1939

Tovah's exaggerated sniffles and coughs were comically loud.

"I already told you there's no school today. No need to put on such a show," I said as I finished washing the last of the breakfast dishes.

Since it was announced on the radio that the German army was marching into Poland, our lives had changed considerably. The Polish army was holding them back, or at least slowing them down, but to prepare for possible air raids, the government ordered a citywide blackout each night. If we didn't black out our lights, we could be arrested.

Tovah was only six, but that was old enough to be scared of the Germans and to become fearful at night when I lit the candles and closed the curtains. To ease her fear, I did my best to act as if everything was all right and maintain a normal schedule, but I gave in far too often when she wanted to stay home from school. Having her with me eased my own fears about her safety. If something unexpected happened, it would be better if we were together.

"Is anyone coming to have their hair cut?" she asked, looking hopeful.

"Maybe Mrs. Wolowitz," I said, hoping it was true. There wasn't much we could count on these days. Sometimes the market would open, and other times it wouldn't. Papa and Avrom both continued to work, but often went all day without seeing a customer.

Smiling at Tovah, I tried not to let her see the worry that always simmered just below the surface. Normally, I'd have a couple of ladies coming to have their hair cut before I went to help Papa at the tailor shop. His arthritis was making it difficult to hold his needles and thread. With my help, his customers hadn't noticed the difference yet.

Due to how little business the jewelry store did these days, my cutting hair earned just enough money to prevent things from getting too tight. Although if the store closed altogether, I wasn't sure what we would do. Avrom had lost all his gentile customers, and the Jews who had enough money to splurge on jewelry were instead using it to emigrate elsewhere, like Paris and Belgium, where there were no anti-Semite laws preventing them from making a living. Avrom's parents were talking about moving to South America. His uncle had traveled to Uruguay and said the streets were paved with gold. You could go there and do anything you wanted.

Avrom and I discussed leaving, but we never considered it seriously. Our families were all here. Mama and Papa had talked about all of us going to visit Zotia and Eli in America and not coming back. But that required more money than we had, and the truth was, a journey such as that was becoming riskier.

The Germans were moving in, and no one had much confidence in the Polish army. They couldn't stop the Germans the first time, and there was too much bad blood with the Soviets to allow the Red Army into Poland to help fight. Some thought the Soviets were planning to invade also, and the two forces would divide Poland in half. Either way, our lives were going to change again soon. But inside our flat, I tried to keep things as normal as possible for Tovah.

"I want you to cut my hair to look like Norah Ney's." Tovah tossed a blond curl over her shoulder and stuck out a skinny hip.

I laughed. "How do you know who Norah Ney is?"

"I heard people talking about her. She's in the movies. She must be beautiful if everyone wants to look like her."

I leaned down to kiss her forehead. "I think you're beautiful."

She grinned, displaying the empty space where one of her baby teeth used to be. "You're beautiful too, even though you're not a movie star."

I narrowed my eyes. "Thank you very much."

My daughter was me all over again. Avrom commented on it daily, and I had to agree. She was a smaller version of me with her blond curls and curious blue eyes. On the one hand, that filled me with pride, but on the other hand, it hurt my heart a little because I wanted her to be bolder than I was and to have more confidence. I wasn't unhappy with my life, but for her, I wanted more.

I crossed my arms and looked down at her. "I suppose you can stay out here and watch me cut Mrs. Wolowitz's hair, and then you can decide if you want to look like Norah Ney."

"Yay!" Tovah clapped, and I shook my head.

Once she saw how short Norah Ney's hairstyle was, Tovah would change her mind.

Mrs. Wolowitz was what Avrom called a "colorful character." Despite the news about Germany, she was more concerned about silly things like the latest styles and the best dinner parties.

"What color dresses did you see the last time you went into town?" Tovah asked her, not wanting to miss this chance to chat with a woman of the world. Even though Mrs. Wolowitz was hardly that, as far as Tovah was concerned, she was exotic compared to Avrom and me, who hardly ever left the neighborhood.

Mrs. Wolowitz turned to Tovah. "Would you believe I saw a dress that was red? Bright red with red fox fur wrapped around the collar."

"No!" Tovah giggled. All our clothes were gray, black, or brown.

"Yes, my dear. Red as a ripe apple."

"Would you ever wear an apple-red dress, Mama?"

I snipped a quarter inch off the bottom of Mrs. Wolowitz's hair. As expected, she wanted a bob like Norah Ney's. "Probably not. Too showy for me, but I wouldn't mind a blue dress."

"A blue dress! Yes, Mama, blue would look so good on you."

"She's such a darling," Mrs. Wolowitz said, smiling fondly.

"Why don't you just make yourself a blue dress?" Tovah asked.

"Well, I'd have to buy the fabric, and I'm afraid blue, like red, is very expensive. Brown, on the other hand, is not, and brown is the same color as the earth, which God created. So I will very proudly continue to wear my brown dresses."

Tovah scrunched up her face and plopped down on the sofa. "God created red apples and the blue sky too, Mama."

"She has a point," Mrs. Wolowitz muttered.

Yes, she did. "Well—"

As I tried to think of another answer for Tovah, a loud explosion sounded that shook the building, sending Tovah scurrying in my direction.

"What was that?" she asked, gripping my skirt.

"I don't know." Looking toward the windows, I pulled her close.

There was another explosion, this one violent enough to rattle my teeth. I gripped the chair Mrs. Wolowitz was seated in and bent my body over Tovah.

"It's the Germans," Mrs. Wolowitz cried, standing abruptly. "They must be dropping bombs."

"Is that right, Mama?" Tovah gripped me tighter. "Is it the Germans?"

I swallowed the panic rising in my throat and didn't answer.

"I'd better get home." Mrs. Wolowitz stood and headed for the door.

"Shouldn't we all go down to the basement like they tell us to do on the radio?"

Mrs. Wolowitz shook her head. "If a bomb hits, we'll be crushed down there. You take that precious baby and sit in the stairwell. There are no windows, so you can't get hit with broken glass. I have to get home to my husband."

I didn't think she should go outside, and I said so, but she wouldn't listen. The sounds of screams on the street traveled into the flat when she pulled open the door. Clinging to me, Tovah pushed her face into my dress.

"Shh, it's okay, little one." I brought her with me out into the stairwell as the explosions continued, reverberating through the building.

My throat tightened as I thought of Avrom and my father out there in danger. Down the road, Mama and Leah were probably home, and I hoped they were staying put, keeping themselves safe. The stairwell began to fill with people from the building, and we all sat helplessly, staring at each other, our wide eyes with fear.

Tovah trembled in my arms, tensing each time a bomb sounded in the distance. I clenched my teeth and fought the urge to run outside to see what was going on. I couldn't leave Tovah alone here, and I couldn't bring her out there.

What if our building gets hit? My body was rigid with fear, my fingers digging into Tovah's back as if holding her tighter would make any difference if a bomb hit us.

Please stop. Please stop. Didn't they realize there were innocent people in the city, people who cared nothing for politics and power? And there were children, so many children. What had our children ever done to them?

It felt like hours, although I know it was probably only minutes that passed before the terrifying noises stopped. An alarm sounded outside, signaling the end of the air raid, but none of us moved.

Tovah lifted her head and saw David Lesner, the boy who lived upstairs, sitting on the stairwell above us. He was a year older than Tovah and always looked a bit disheveled, like he was left to his own devices most of the time. His dark hair was always tousled and in need of brushing, and his clothes were just a smidge too small, short in the arms and legs.

"Hi, David. Were you scared?" she whispered up in his direction.

He shook his head, trying to appear brave, but the worry lines etched into his forehead told a different story.

Frieda, our downstairs neighbor, called up to me. "Can we go back inside our flats?"

"We'd better stay here a little longer in case they come back." My muscles were so tense, I didn't know if I could move without effort.

More time passed before Avrom's voice called for us from the bottom of the stairwell.

"Papa!" Tovah yelled, and several people shushed her.

Relief swept through me as Avrom rushed up the stairs and pulled us both into his arms.

"You're fine," he said beside my ear. "You're both fine." He was breathing hard, like he'd run the whole way home.

"Is it over?" David asked from his perch above us.

Avrom nodded. "The sirens signal when the planes are gone. If you hear the sirens again, it means they're coming back."

"Does that mean it's safe now?" someone asked.

Avrom hesitated before answering. "Yes."

What did the word *safe* even mean anymore?

"Our parents," I said as he ushered us back into the flat.

"I'll go down to the post office and telephone everyone."

"No." I gripped his arm at the thought of him leaving us again.

"I'll come right back." He looked into my eyes, urging me to trust he would return.

"Can I stay with you?" David asked, standing hesitantly in our doorway. "My parents aren't home."

"Of course," Avrom replied. Then he kissed me and kissed the top of Tovah's head before leaving the flat. We didn't have a telephone, but the post office did, and the family who lived next door to my parents also had a phone. They would know if my family was safe.

"How about a snack?" I asked with an overly bright smile.

My role as a mother was to pretend everything was fine, even as my insides quaked with fear. The problem was that neither child believed me.

"Many of the men are traveling to the front to help the soldiers," Avrom said when he came to bed after checking on Tovah.

After spending several long, sleepless nights sitting in the stairwell of our building with half the other tenants, we decided to take a chance and sleep in our own beds again. The air raids had been occurring more frequently, causing some people to take up permanent residence in the stairwell, and it was beginning to fill with the odor of spoiled food and too many perspiring bodies.

"You're not going," I told Avrom. It wasn't the first time he'd brought up joining the Polish army. "The Poles have been trying to run us out of the country little by little, and now you're going to risk your life to go fight with them?"

"They're the devil we know, Meira. We don't know what the Germans will do if they push into Warsaw."

I swallowed against the growing lump in my throat. "You can't go. Who will get us food when the market doesn't open for days? Who will protect us when the Poles try to steal the little food we do get?" The Germans had stopped supplies coming in and out of the city. Food and resources were growing scarcer by the day, making people desperate and dangerous.

"You and Tovah will move in with your parents."

"What?" I sat upright in bed and glared at him. "How long have you been planning this? So quickly you already have a solution for what we'll do when you leave? You're not going, Avrom. One more person won't make a difference to the army, but it will make a difference to us. We need you more than they do."

My words sounded selfish, even to my own ears, but I had our daughter to think of. I couldn't protect her the way Avrom could.

He pressed his lips together, anger and frustration brewing in his eyes. I understood that he was torn. He felt helpless and wanted to do more, but I couldn't let him go. I wouldn't support that decision, and without my support, I knew he wouldn't leave us.

The next day when the sirens sounded again for the third time since dawn, we didn't have the energy to panic. Instead, we wearily trudged into the foul-smelling stairwell and sat there as the ground shook and plaster dust fell from the ceiling, coating our skin. Wide, frightened eyes scanned the darkness, and Tovah cried in my arms the way she did each night now, breaking my heart into little pieces.

How long can this go on?

It had been almost a month since the bombing began, and because there was no longer any telephone service, we'd been cut off from our families for weeks. Avrom made quick trips to check on our parents. He brought them all food and shared news of Tovah and me.

I leaned on him. His strength was all I could count on these days. When adversity struck, some people rose to the occasion and others shrank back. As much as I loved Avrom, I couldn't have predicted the steely resolve he'd shown in the past few weeks. He did whatever was needed, no matter the danger. Avrom was a lifeline, both for us and for our families.

Just when we thought we would have to live in that awful stairwell forever, the bombings stopped. Not just for an hour, but for several hours. Long enough for us to cautiously go back into our flats. Avrom and a few of the other men went outside to see what was going on.

"We should go back into the stairwell," Tovah said, afraid to even be in her own home.

"We'll see what Papa says when he gets back. Would you like to play paper dolls?"

Tovah had lost interest in her toy dolls, but enjoyed cutting two-dimensional ones from old newspapers and stringing them across the ceiling. We'd spent hours in the stairwell, making paper dolls as a distraction.

When Tovah finally wrinkled her nose at the thought of more paper dolls, I racked my brain to think of something else to do. I'd barely had time to brainstorm when Avrom came running back inside, out of breath.

"What is it?" Hope bloomed in my chest that maybe it was finally over.

"We surrendered. The German army is coming."

I was struck by a combination of relief and fear. There would be no more bombings, but what would the Germans do when they got here? Maybe once they took over, there would be food in the markets again, and customers for Avrom and Papa.

"What do we do now?" I asked.

He shot me a worried look. "We stay put until we know more."

When the Germans marched into Poland, it was a terrifying sound. Their nail-studded boots clapped loudly against the pavement, the sound meant to frighten us. Their dramatic entrance intended to prove that they were a fierce occupying force not to be challenged.

As those first weeks unfolded, the relief I initially felt evaporated. It quickly became clear that the Germans wanted to do more than just rule over us. They wanted to frighten and humiliate us.

The curfew we lived under during the bombings wasn't lifted. Instead, it was now enforced by penalty of death. Food became even scarcer, and a new declaration indicated that the Germans disliked the Jews even more than the Poles did. All Jews over the age of ten had to wear an armband on the outside of their clothing with a blue six-sided Star of David on a white background. That way Jews could be identified on sight, and more easily segregated and discriminated against.

"The Germans should be ashamed, not us. I will wear it proudly," Papa said as he sewed armbands onto our clothing. If you were Jewish and found not wearing an armband, they warned of a terrible punishment.

With our armbands on our clothing, we tried to go about the

business of living in our new reality. Britain and France had declared war on Germany. We didn't know what that meant for us, but there was no time to dwell on it.

Avrom and Papa went out looking for food each day, and I taught lessons to Tovah because the Jewish schools had closed. Many of the Jewish men, including Avrom, were forced by the Germans to clean up the rubble created by the bombings. He came home exhausted on those days and in a state of quiet shock, astounded by the destruction of the city we hadn't fully understood until then.

Sometimes, without notice, the Germans would put signs on residential buildings that read Nur für Deutschen, *for Germans only*, signaling that anyone who wasn't German had to vacate immediately, native Poles and Jews alike. The people who lived there had very little time to gather their things and go.

When the Germans took over the entire block next to ours, we didn't wait for an order to leave. We packed our bags and moved in with Mama and Papa. Avrom and I settled into the parlor, while Tovah took my old bed and roomed with Leah.

One night, Avrom and Papa came back to the house just before the sunset curfew. Breathless, they rushed inside and locked the door behind them.

"The Poles are breaking into Jewish homes and taking everything," Papa said as he shrugged off his coat and took the glass of water Mama offered.

"The Germans are encouraging them to do it," Avrom said. "Telling them Jews are fair game, and there will be no consequences for any crimes committed against them."

"And the Poles are listening?" Mama asked, her eyes wide and disbelieving.

"Are you surprised?" Avrom asked. "Do you think they needed much encouragement?"

"We'll look for extra wood tomorrow and shore up the windows and doors," Papa said.

Leah stepped forward with her arms crossed. "They grabbed Heinrich off the street today and forced him to work for them. They had him and hundreds of other men building a wall around the Jewish Quarter."

Heinrich was Leah's boyfriend. He stayed with us sometimes too, sleeping on the floor in the parlor. Tonight he sat at the kitchen table and stared at the broken skin on his knuckles.

"They're moving Jews from the countryside into the city," Heinrich said. "They want us all in one place."

"Why?" Mama asked.

"If it's to keep us away from them, that's fine with me," Papa said.

Avrom said nothing as he stood and walked back into the parlor. When I went to follow him, I spotted Tovah sitting on the kitchen floor, playing with Mama's spoons. It was all she had to play with since we'd been forced to leave all her dolls and games back at our flat. It made me angry at everyone and no one that we had to leave our home with so little. Sometimes it felt like anger was all that fueled me. Anger and the need to make things okay for Tovah and Avrom, to remind them that things would get better, and to try to believe it myself.

Going back into the parlor, I saw Avrom sitting on the couch with his head in his hands. "What is it?"

He turned to me. "We found no food today. Nothing. There were no markets open, and the streets are filled with hungry people ready to kill you for a crust of bread."

I sat down beside him, hoping he was exaggerating. "We'll be okay. We have enough, and maybe the markets will open tomorrow or the next day."

He looked at me as if I were naive or delusional. "I met a Polish man today on his way out of town. Some of the Poles are leaving for Russia, and the Germans are letting them go."

"They're not letting Jews leave."

"No, but you don't look Jewish, and neither does Tovah. With your coloring, you look more like Poles than Jews. We could get you both papers, forged documents, and you could—"

"Avrom, no!" A volatile mixture of anger and fear surged through me.

"Yes." He grabbed my shoulders. "We have to think about it."

"No, we don't. You're suggesting we leave without you. Without Mama, Papa, and Leah. I won't do it. Besides, it's too dangerous. Forging documents and trying to escape the country? You can't be serious."

"I am serious. If there's a way for you and Tovah to go—"

"No. I don't want to hear another word about it." With that, I stood and stormed out of the room.

I could hardly comprehend what Avrom had suggested. Risk my life and Tovah's trying to escape to Russia? Leave him and my whole family behind? I was insulted that he thought I would ever agree to something like that. He was overreacting. Everyone was panicking, letting their fear get the best of them. I was determined to stay rational and make measured decisions. But my determination was tested later that night.

As we lay in bed, a barrage of gunshots sounded out on the street, followed by screams. Avrom jumped up and rushed to the window.

Seconds later, there was a knock at the door. We looked at each other, our eyes wide, afraid to answer the door and afraid not to. Our indecision was settled when Papa walked down the short hall and pulled the front door open.

"Move this man off the street!" This was shouted into the house by a German soldier standing in our doorway, holding a handgun by his side.

Avrom moved past me, and I watched out the window as Avrom, Heinrich, and Papa went out into the street and picked up a limp body off the road. Several doors down, a woman was yelling something at them, her voice high and hysterical. They brought the body to her door, disappearing inside for a moment before coming back out again.

Their eyes were downcast as they filed back inside, filling the parlor. Tovah stood behind me, clinging to my nightgown as Mama came in and turned on a lamp. When it illuminated the men, we could see their shirts were soaked with blood. Mama gasped as Avrom pushed past us toward the bathroom. Papa put his arm around Mama and led her away.

"What happened?" I asked when I found a trembling Avrom yanking his blood-soaked clothes off his body. Tovah still clung to me, and I maneuvered her behind me as I leaned in closer to him.

"It wasn't a man," he said under his breath. "It was a boy caught outside after curfew. His body was nearly machine-gunned in half."

I gasped as I fixated on Avrom's bloody shirt discarded on the floor, trying not to picture what he'd just described. They shot a boy for being out after curfew? They'd murdered him.

I should have comforted Avrom in that moment. He was in shock, on the verge of breaking down, but I couldn't let Tovah see him that way. I had to stay strong for her sake. Instead of going to Avrom, I backed out of the room and took Tovah into the parlor, where I embraced her and inhaled the sweet smell of her hair. To me, she still represented innocence and hope, while Avrom's eyes only reflected the horrors he saw outside the walls of the flat.

I wanted this to be a nightmare that would go away when the sun rose in the morning. But I knew it wouldn't go away, not tomorrow or the day after that.

Maybe Avrom wasn't overreacting when he suggested sending us away, but I still wouldn't leave. It was much too dangerous, although I couldn't pretend it wasn't just as dangerous here. At least here, we were all together.

I was still wrestling with the images of that boy in my mind when Avrom returned to the parlor and collapsed onto the couch beside me, his knees buckling as his head fell onto my shoulder. I pulled him closer, wrapping my arm around him. On my other shoulder, Tovah cried softly, a sound I was becoming too accustomed to hearing.

Tears trickled down my cheeks too as I hugged my family tighter. They weren't the only ones breaking down tonight. I was falling apart too—slowly, quietly falling to pieces. We all were, and there was nothing to do but keep breathing and deal with each day as it came.

chapter 5

Warsaw Ghetto, Poland, 1941

The dream always began the same.

Papa stood in the middle of the road in the dead of night. I called to him from the open doorway, pleading with him to come inside. He was out after curfew, and soon the soldiers would find him and shoot him. But he couldn't hear me. He never heard my voice, even though it was so shrill that it hurt my own ears.

To my horror, bright red flames flared to life beneath Papa's feet. I called out to him until my throat was raw, but he never moved. I tried to run to him, but I couldn't move. My feet were glued to the ground.

Papa stood there as the flames licked their way up his body, leaving ashes in their wake.

It wasn't until the fire reached his face and singed his beard that I woke up screaming, sweat pouring off my skin. Avrom would take me into his arms and say comforting words, but there were no words that would erase the image of Papa burning to death in my mind.

I blinked into the darkness, not sure at first where I was. Across from me, the wall of our bedroom came into focus with the framed *ketubah* hanging in the middle. Avrom had framed our marriage contract and hung it there when we first moved in. It was a custom many people followed. I blinked again and the *ketubah* was gone. In its place was an empty wall dotted with old yellow water stains. The damp smell of mold hit my nostrils, and a dark cloud fell over me as I remembered exactly where I was and who was no longer here with me.

When Papa died, he took the music with him. At first, I went looking for records, asking those who lived nearby if they had brought anything by Chopin with them, but what was Chopin compared to the daily struggle of survival?

With Papa gone, I thought it was the end of everything. I didn't know how I would go on, but it was only the beginning of the end. A long good-bye to the life I'd known before. A painful letting go of someone I loved, and feeling guilty because I wondered if he were better off than I was. Going was so much easier than staying.

I'd finally written the letter I knew would be the hardest letter I would ever have to send. My teeth chattered and my hands shook from the cold as I signed my name and folded the paper before sliding it into an envelope.

"What are you writing, Meira? What are you saying there? You know the Germans read every word."

Louisa, Avrom's mother, called to me from the bed where she lay day after day, constantly talking, constantly complaining and criticizing. The ghetto was hard on people like her, people who'd been well off and never had to work hard in their lives.

"I'm writing to my sister in America," I said, pulling my sweater tighter around me.

She laughed. "You think that letter is going to get all the way to America?"

I stood without answering. The Judenrat, a council made of Jews, was appointed by the Nazis to make sure their rules were followed in the ghetto. The Judenrat did their best to both please the Nazis and make things easier on us when they could. They were able to get letters out, and I hoped this one would find its way to Zotia.

Twelve of us lived in this small three-room flat. Other than Louisa, we tried to help each other by sharing what little food we had or could trade for with the smugglers, most of whom were children who managed to crawl through spaces in the ghetto wall.

The wall, which was thirteen feet high in most places, made of brick and topped with barbed wire, completely sealed us off from the rest of the city. The German soldiers drove us from our homes and forced us to live within these walls, walls that they'd forced us to build ourselves. Hundreds of thousands of Jews, all packed together into what was once the thriving Jewish Quarter. The Germans said it was for our own safety, which was ludicrous. Our well-being was the least of their concerns.

David Lesner, the boy who had been our neighbor in the old flat, was one of the smugglers. Lucky for us, he had a soft spot for Tovah.

Mama walked over and placed her hand on mine. "Careful what you say in that letter."

Dark circles ringed her eyes, and her hair hung limply over her shoulders. Unless I got her dressed and did her hair, she didn't bother. Unless I made her eat, she wouldn't bother with that either. She wanted to die and join Papa. For my own selfish reasons, I was determined not to let her. I couldn't lose her too.

"I wrote to Zotia about Papa. She deserves to know."

Mama scoffed as she grabbed the letter and tore it in two.

"Mama!" I grabbed the pieces from her hands.

"They'll confiscate it and come here looking for us. Do you think they want the world to know what they've done here?"

The stinging pressure of tears built behind my eyes. "I didn't tell her how he died, just that he was gone."

She blinked and stared at the pieces of paper in my hand. "Why does Zotia need to know that? So she can feel as sad as we do? Just let her be."

"Mama." I reached for her arm. "Maybe it's better he's not here suffering. Do you think the Nazis would care about his arthritis? They would have put him to work on the wall like everyone else."

Anger twisted her features. "Do you think he didn't suffer in that church? Locked inside and burned alive? Do you think he wasn't suffering then?" She turned away from me with familiar devastation clouding her expression, and sank back onto the pile of blankets that served as her bed on the wood floor.

Squeezing my eyes closed, I pushed away the images from my nightmare. I could hardly bear them in the darkness; I didn't want them with me during the day too. Before the Germans forced us into the ghetto, the Poles went on a rampage, looting Jewish homes and killing Jews in the street.

When Papa and Avrom's father didn't return from synagogue one afternoon, the neighbors came and told us why. A gang of Polish men grabbed them on their way home, as well as all the other Jews out on the street, including women and children. They forced them into a church, locked the doors, and set it on fire. They shot anyone who broke a window and tried to escape. Everyone inside died.

A part of me died too that day. Even though I woke up each morning, it didn't feel as if I were here on earth anymore. I dwelled more in my thoughts and memories. My mind couldn't comprehend the evil around me, and there was no part of me that wanted to.

If it weren't for Avrom and Tovah, I might have stopped eating too. But I couldn't, and neither could Mama. We had to be strong for each other. That was the only way to survive.

"Mama," I whispered. "Avrom and Heinrich will be back soon. Let's do your hair and go listen to the violins later. They're playing in the theater on the corner."

"That theater has a hole in its roof," Mama muttered. It had been hit in the bombings, like so many other buildings in the ghetto.

"Then we can listen to the music and look at the stars. I know Tovah would like to go." I often used Tovah to persuade Mama to do things. Even if she'd given up on herself, she knew it was important to put on a good face for Tovah.

"It's not the music I want to hear," she said quietly.

She meant it wasn't Chopin. She used to hate when Papa played Chopin all afternoon, but now she craved the sound, just like I did. Her eyes fell shut, and since she hadn't protested too strongly, I picked up a brush and walked toward her.

We were always hungry and scared, yet we woke up every morning, and because our broken hearts still managed to beat, we tried to live some semblance of a life. What choice did we have? There was still a makeshift school for Tovah and the other children to attend, and concerts given by talented Jewish musicians.

That night, when Avrom came home, he smiled because he'd managed to get a loaf of bread that day. The bread, along with the potatoes we received from our German rations, would make up dinner. Tovah and Avrom had become so thin, it hurt for me too look at them too long, and I knew I looked the same. But we still ate what we had and trudged out of the flat to the concert hall.

As the haunting violin music filled the air, I closed my eyes and tilted my head back. After taking a deep breath, I looked up and gazed at the stars through the jagged hole in the ceiling. Those pinpoints of light were so beautiful.

How could anything be beautiful anymore? It hurt to look at such beauty in the midst of so much that was ugly.

It pierced through me like a knife to think the universe went on just the same, all while there was so much suffering on the ground beneath it. It was as if the universe didn't care about us anymore. Just like the rest of the world didn't care what happened to us.

Because we were Jewish. That was all. There was no other reason.

Tovah took the bent, rusty nail she'd found on the street and scraped it against the damp wooden floor of the flat. I tried to take the nail from her, afraid she'd cut herself, but then she showed me she only wanted it to draw with, and I couldn't bring myself to take it away. She used the nail to carve designs into the wood for hours each day, and one morning I realized there was a shape to her scrapings.

"Butterflies," I said, tracing my hand over the carvings. "You're drawing butterflies."

She nodded. At nine years old, the last two years of her life were filled with horrors I wished I could erase, yet she drew butterflies. The tenderness that filled my heart made me want to cry.

Tovah nodded. "I saw one."

"Really? Where?"

"On my sleeve, when I was coming back from getting our rations with Papa. It landed on me, and when I tried to touch it, it flew away."

I ran my hand over her hair, gathering the unruly locks that had fallen into her eyes. "What color was it?"

"Yellow, and it was black on the tips of its wings. I thought maybe it was Zayde saying hello. I don't know why I thought that. Probably because I never saw a butterfly here before, and I haven't seen once since."

Zayde was what she called my father. It was the term for grandfather in Yiddish. *Bubbie* was the Yiddish word for grandmother.

My throat tightened. "Maybe it was Zayde giving you a little butterfly kiss."

"Maybe there are lots of butterflies where Zayde went. If I die, Mama, I'll come back and give you a butterfly kiss too."

"Oh, baby." I squelched the sob that rose in my throat. "Don't talk that way. It won't always be like this. Wars don't last forever. We just have to hang on. It will end someday." I said those words to myself as much as to Tovah. Although if it hadn't been for Tovah, I don't know if I could have hung on myself.

"Why don't we just say we're sorry?" Tovah asked.

"What do you mean?"

"If we did something to them, why don't we just say sorry, and maybe they won't hate us anymore."

If only it were that easy. "We didn't do anything to them."

"Then why do they hate us?"

"I don't know. Sometimes hate has no reason. Sometimes people who hate are sad in their own lives and want to blame others for it."

"Is that why they hate us? They're sad themselves?"

"They must be very sad and unhappy to hurt so many people."

I'd lived with anti-Semitism for so long, I didn't even ask why anymore. It just *was*. Because it always *had been*. But it had never been like this, and I could hardly comprehend the horror of it.

Tovah bit her lip and looked across the room at Mama. She watched us from a dark corner.

There were fewer of us in this flat now. Louisa had died from the lethal combination of starvation and hopelessness, refusing to eat any food offered to her. A young couple staying here left one day and never came back. We assumed they'd been shot or shipped out of the ghetto to a work camp. Hundreds were shipped out each month. The Judenrat made lists of names for the Nazis. If your name was there, you were taken away on a train.

That evening when Avrom came home, he was drenched in sweat from head to toe. He'd begun pushing a rickshaw in exchange for food or whatever money he could get. Vehicles were banned in the ghetto, and so the Jewish woodworkers had begun building rickshaws for transportation. Those rickshaws were also good for smuggling goods through the ghetto, like bags of flour and wood for fires.

He held a pile of clothes in his arms. "More orders for you, Meira."

Between the two of us, we managed to keep Heinrich, Leah, Mama, Tovah, and ourselves alive. Avrom was always finding ways to get us food or whatever else we needed, and the skills I'd learned from Papa were also helping. I sewed until my fingers were numb, making clothes for people from whatever materials they brought me. With enough cloth and thread, I could salvage even the most threadbare trousers, and create a shirt from nothing but a burlap bag.

Avrom frowned as he gingerly lowered himself into a chair. "No food today. We have to go to the soup kitchen."

Despite my rumbling stomach, I didn't voice my disappointment. The soup kitchen had saved us from having nothing to eat many times. Run by Jews, with no contributions from the Nazis, the soup kitchens managed to operate each day, and only if you had nothing else to eat did you go there. People stood in line together for hours to get one bowl of soup.

Later that night, the three of us trudged out of the flat along with Mama to get into the soup line. Avrom stopped abruptly and held out an arm to halt us we when we came upon three German soldiers harassing a young girl on the sidewalk.

Sucking in a breath, I put my arm around Tovah and tried to go back the way we came, but a German officer barked at us, ordering us to remain where we were. So I stood stock-still with my arms wrapped tightly around my daughter.

One of the soldiers grabbed the girl, who couldn't have been more than fifteen, and pushed her against the wall face-first. I stifled a gasp when he bent to reach up underneath her dress and rip off her underwear.

The girl screamed, and I pushed Tovah's face into my side so she wouldn't see. Avrom tensed beside me as if preparing to intervene, and I grabbed his arm, silently pleading for him to stay with us and not do anything foolish.

My stomach lurched as I watched the soldier undo his pants. Everything inside me screamed to go help, but the street was filled with soldiers, all watching, all daring us to try.

The soldier lifted the girl's skirt, gripped her hips, and pushed up against her. Her mouth opened in a silent scream as her eyes squeezed shut.

Instinctively, I backed away with Tovah when someone yelled, "Stop!"

Fear tore through me when I realized it was Mama. She'd screamed out at them. Then she did it again.

"Stop!" she yelled and rushed toward the girl.

"No!" Releasing my grip on Tovah, I reached out for Mama, but a strong arm grabbed me around the waist and pulled me back.

It all seemed to happen in slow motion as the soldier raping the girl barely spared Mama a glance before another soldier stepped forward with his handgun and shot Mama in the chest. Her body jerked and time seemed to stop, suspended for the longest moment, until she fell backward onto the street and a small red dot on her shirt blossomed into an ever-widening circle.

A scream ripped from my throat. I tried to move in her direction, but Avrom held me in place and then forced Tovah and me back into the flat, leaving Mama out there to die. I struggled to free myself from Avrom's hold, turning away from the sight of Tovah crumpling to the floor in tears.

"She's gone," Avrom said softly into my ear. "There's nothing you can do except get yourself killed too. I'm sorry, Meira. I'm so, so sorry."

"Does the world know what these monsters are doing to us? Does it even care?" I cried out as I struggled with everything I had, but Avrom's arms wouldn't let me go. They banded around my body, anchoring me to him, while screams sounded in my head, threatening to steal away every bit of sanity I had left.

chapter 6

Tovah squeezed my hand and turned her head as we passed a decomposing body on our way back to the flat. She held her breath, and I rushed us on. Dead people in the streets was too common an occurrence to outwardly traumatize either of us or even slow us down. We lived with death each day.

Tovah was quiet most of the time now. Too quiet, but I didn't make her talk when she didn't want to. I also couldn't stop to worry about how my beautiful little girl was dealing with the traumas she experienced each day. If this ever ended, could she go on to have any normal kind of life, or was she ruined forever? It was too far-fetched to contemplate, because surviving was all any of us had time for. If we survived, there might be time for simpler worries again, like whether rain would ruin plans for an afternoon outdoors. I longed for worries as simple as that.

We were in a new flat now with many more people, most of whom we barely knew or spoke to. As more Jews died each day or were sent off on the trains, the boundaries of the ghetto shrank, giving us less and less space.

David's father and mother had both been killed, and so he stayed with us now, giving Tovah someone to play cards with when he wasn't sneaking outside of the walls and returning with whatever he could carry. It terrified me each time he left, but he was only one of many Jewish children, small and wiry enough to fit through the tiny breaks in the ghetto wall. Each night, they went scavenging the streets of Warsaw for whatever food could be sneaked back inside. If it weren't for David and the other children, we would have all starved to death.

One day when most of the men were out on a work order given by the Nazi soldiers, I put out a small portion of bread and rice I'd saved from the night before for Tovah's lunch. As she sat down to eat, a woman who lived with us in the flat dashed across the room and grabbed the bread.

Most of us now ate with our backs turned and a protective arm around our plates, but this woman took food right out from under my daughter's nose, and I wouldn't stand for that. Before she could shove the bread into her own mouth, I grabbed her arm and ripped the bread from her fingers.

She screamed at me and raked her nails down my cheek. Mustering all my strength, I shoved the woman against the wall. With my hands digging into her shoulders, I slammed her into that wall over and over again, until blood dripped down from behind her head.

From where she sat, Tovah cried and called out to me.

Out of breath, I stepped back and warned the woman. "If you take food from my child again, I will kill you."

The bread now lay on the floor. I picked it up and gave it back to a horrified Tovah. Tears trailed down her cheeks as she looked up at me.

"It's okay," I said quietly. "Eat it."

But Tovah could barely get the food down her throat after what she'd seen. I told her that I was only angry, and I didn't mean what I said to the woman, but I'd meant every word. Each bite of food was necessary. I hoped that woman was afraid of me now, because if she stole one morsel from Tovah again, I'd have no choice but to kill her.

That night Avrom saw the cuts on my cheek. I told him what happened, but the woman whose head I'd bashed in said nothing, not to anyone. She huddled silently in the corner. Perhaps shame kept her lips sealed. Taking food from a child was nothing to brag about.

The next day, Avrom spoke to the other men in the flat, and soon the woman was gone.

"You made her go?" I asked Avrom.

"We found another place for her to live."

"Another place? So easily?"

He brushed aside my questions. I was too relieved to see her gone to wonder if Avrom had told me the truth, or if they'd done something else with the woman.

Late one night, many weeks later, a loud knock sounded at the door. Nothing good came of unexpected visitors at night.

Avrom and I sat up in alarm. We were pressed against each other in the small space we'd commandeered in a corner. Tovah was at our feet where she always slept, partially splayed over one of my legs.

Across the room, Heinrich grabbed a brick from our small fire pit. He and Leah would have been married by now if things had been different. Heinrich's mother lived in another flat nearby, but his father and both his brothers had been taken away on trains.

"I'm looking for the seamstress." This was said from behind the closed door in a combination of German and broken Polish by what could only be an SS soldier.

Knowing he meant me, everyone turned their heads in my direction.

"Say nothing," Avrom whispered, grasping my hand tightly.

Ignoring him, I pulled a blanket around myself and nodded at Heinrich to open the door, knowing if he didn't, the soldier would force his way in. Knowing this too, Avrom gripped me tighter.

Heinrich slowly pulled open the door to reveal one of the SS soldiers with his gun hanging from a shoulder strap. We often saw him patrolling the streets near our flat. He was one of the younger ones, tall and youthful looking.

"I need these buttons sewn on. I was told a seamstress lives here." He held out his uniform, along with the gold buttons that had apparently fallen off the jacket pockets.

Avrom released my hand, stood, and walked toward the soldier. "Leave it here, and she'll sew it for you."

He shook his head. "I cannot leave my uniform here. She will come with me and—"

"No!" The word burst from Avrom, and we all held our breath. You didn't yell at the SS. "She needs to do her work here," he said, rushing to explain. "All her things are here."

Pressing his lips together, the soldier forced the door open further and took a step inside to look around the room. His face wrinkled in disgust when he saw how we were all crammed together in one room. "Who is the seamstress?"

Tovah gripped my arm tightly. Her worry for me was palpable, but if I didn't volunteer myself, someone else here would likely do it.

"I am," I said, my voice stronger than I thought possible.

"You will do it now, and I will wait," he said, his gaze drilling into mine.

There was no question of arguing or disobeying. Avrom was lucky the soldier hadn't already shot him.

Under the watchful eyes of the soldier, Avrom took the coat and buttons and brought them to me. I took hold of them with trembling hands. Lighting a candle on the closest table so I could see, Avrom offered me an encouraging nod.

Taking a deep breath to calm myself, I gathered the heavy material in my hands. I'd seen too many of these uniforms, but I'd never touched one. It symbolized power and fear, and what I wanted most was to burn it in the fire pit. This one still held the scent of the man who wore it, and I recognized the spicy smell of cologne. While we bartered and begged for the tiniest sliver of soap, this man was showering and applying cologne. That fact nearly paralyzed me with loathing.

Swallowing my emotions, I walked over to the table where my supplies were. With everyone's eyes on me, I sat down slowly and picked up a needle and thread, which I struggled to hold steady. After pulling in a shallow breath, I began to work. I pricked my own fingers many times before I managed to sew on the two small buttons that had fallen off. When I finished, everyone silently watched as Avrom took the coat from me and returned it to the waiting soldier.

As he watched me, the soldier tugged on the buttons to make sure they were secure. Then he nodded a silent thank-you and left.

"Oh dear God," Leah said, pushing her hair back with a trembling hand and falling back onto her blanket.

With an expression of relief, Avrom blew out the candle and slipped back under the blanket with me. Soon, Tovah shuffled over and crawled between Avrom and me. Together, we all lay awake until the fear and adrenaline drained from our bodies.

Over the coming months, that soldier was not the last to inquire about my sewing services. And as I patched holes and sewed more buttons onto uniforms, I silently stewed over the help I was providing. SS soldiers could get themselves into trouble if their uniforms weren't perfect, and I was secretly helping them.

"This is good for us," Avrom said. "Being useful to them is good."

I couldn't agree. Being useful to them made my stomach turn, but I couldn't refuse them either.

One morning, a German soldier stood in the road with a megaphone.

"Report to Stawki Street for resettlement in the east. If you come voluntarily, you will receive three kilograms of bread and one kilogram of jam each."

"What does it mean?" I asked Avrom as my gaze wandered to Tovah, who slept curled up in a ball on a blanket on the floor.

I no longer allowed her to leave our flat. It was too dangerous. People were too hungry and desperate, and the SS were more trigger-happy than ever. It broke my heart when Tovah didn't protest at all. She didn't care about being confined in the dark, dank flat all day. She was too hungry and too tired to do much more than sleep, and maybe read a little in the afternoon.

"It's a trick," David said, coming to sit with us. "There's no settlement for Jews in the east. Why move us east when we're already here? They mean to kill us, not resettle us."

I searched Avrom's expression for a hint of his thoughts. We'd survived this long because of the chances he and David had been willing to take, and the instincts that told them what rules we had to follow and what rules could be disobeyed without consequences.

Heinrich and Leah came over to listen, as did most of the other adults who lived in the flat with us. Their eyes shone in the light of the tiny fire we kept burning in the fire pit, which was nothing more than a pile of sawdust and paper lodged between two bricks.

"We've been buying guns," David whispered. "There are sympathetic Poles outside these walls, and they sold us weapons, handguns mostly."

Guns?

Avrom tensed beside me, looking around to see who might have heard. Times were desperate, and it wasn't unheard of for Jews to inform on each other in hopes of gaining favor with the Germans.

"What are you planning to do with those guns?" Avrom asked.

With a gleam in his eyes, David said, "I plan to fight. They can try to take me out of here, but I won't go quietly. There are others here constructing bunkers beneath the ghetto. We can make a stand and show them that we won't go easily."

Avrom scoffed. "That would be suicide."

"It's death on my own terms."

His words were shocking. David was just a child, but he spoke like a man. And I knew he meant what he said. His thoughts weren't those of some naive boy. He would fight to the bitter end.

Avrom stood. "We'll wait and see what happens. If death is certain, the end will be the same either way, and I'd rather my family go quietly than in a gunfight with the devil."

David's expression softened when he glanced at Tovah. "I understand, and I can't blame you for that. But think about it. We need everyone we can get."

A few days later, Tovah and I sat on the floor working on math equations that Mr. Oblisky had written out for the children. Mr. Oblisky was a civil engineer, and he resided in the flat with us, along with his brother. Both of their wives died of typhoid last year. Typhoid, starvation, and bullets were the most common killers in the ghetto these days.

I pretended to understand when he explained the problems to Tovah, David, and another boy named Isaac, but I was out of my depth.

"What do I need to know this for?" Tovah asked me.

"Well, it's math." I thought for a moment and laughed. "Honestly, I don't know."

"So I don't have to do it then." She started to push to her feet, but I put my hand on her arm.

"You most certainly do. It's good to exercise your brain, Tovah." To my relief, she didn't ask what the point of learning new things was when the future was so uncertain, whether she was thinking it or not.

Avrom came in a little while later with a cloth bag in his hand and a smile playing on his lips. "Look what I have," he said to Tovah as he withdrew something from the bag and held it out to her in the palm of his hand.

Curious, she stood and walked over to him. "What is it, Papa?"

He glanced at me. "Chocolate."

Tovah's eyes got big and round, but she didn't reach for it.

"Go on." Avrom lifted his hand closer to her. In it was one small piece of candy wrapped in gold foil.

Carefully, she lifted it from his palm and stared at it. "Chocolate, really?"

He nodded.

"How much can I have?" she asked, knowing that everything we got had to be sensibly divided and made to last as long as possible.

"All of it," Avrom said. "You can eat it all now and enjoy every minute of it."

Tovah eyed him skeptically, wondering if he was teasing.

"Go ahead, Tovah. It's all yours, little one."

Excitement lit up her eyes, but she still hesitated.

When he nodded at her again, some invisible barrier in her mind let loose, and Tovah tore into the candy. Crumpled pieces of foil fluttered to the floor as she put the whole thing in her mouth. Her eyes closed, and she made a pleasant humming sound as she slowly chewed. Then she looked at Avrom and me, and grinned with melted chocolate staining her teeth.

I sputtered and laughed out loud at the sight, even as I tried to hold back tears. A strange pressure built in my chest. Seeing such joy on Tovah's face caused me the most exquisite pain. One small piece of candy shouldn't mean the world to her, but in that moment, for a girl who had nothing, it meant absolutely everything.

"Where did you get the chocolate?" I asked Avrom later that night.

He shook his head as if he didn't want to say.

I squinted at him in the dark. "Did you steal it?"

"You know I steal everything I get for us."

Fear for him crawled up my spine. "What did you do, Avrom? Are you going to get in trouble?"

He watched me for a long moment. "No. No trouble. The person I got it from can no longer say anything to anyone."

I asked no more questions after that. If Avrom killed for the chocolate, I didn't want to know. If he got it from one of the children smugglers who then got caught and killed, I didn't want to know that either. All I wanted to know was that for a few minutes today, Tovah was happy.

I looked over at her sleeping form, wondering if was possible to have a conscience in a place like this. Mine was slowly slipping away, recalibrating itself based on what was necessary for survival. Could we do awful things here and go back to living a normal life out there? I didn't know, but it didn't matter, because if we didn't survive in here, we would never know. I pressed my hand against the dull ache that grew in the center of my chest.

As my eyes started to close, Avrom turned to me with the

strangest expression. "You should know why I wanted Tovah to have that piece of chocolate tonight."

"Why?" I asked, even though I feared the answer.

"The soldiers came and cleared out three blocks by the west section of the wall this morning. They ordered everyone out into the street, and if you didn't come out, the soldiers went inside and forced you out or shot you where you stood. Once everyone was in the street, they marched them to the Umschlagplatz train station for resettlement." He swallowed and looked over at Tovah. "I don't know what or where resettlement is. I only know that we will also be forced to leave soon, and I wanted Tovah to enjoy something before it was too late."

"Too late for what?"

His shadowed eyes held mine in the darkness. "I don't know. Why resettle us? Why move us somewhere else? Maybe they have something else in mind."

Avrom's words frightened and angered me. I was angry at him because he ruined the picture of Tovah smiling that I had worked so hard to hold in my head, dashing it away. I went to sit up and leave the bed, but he caught me around the waist and pulled me to him. Instead of pushing him away, I burrowed against him, hating him for telling me that, but also loving him for making Tovah happy, even for a moment.

As I lay there in his arms, I wondered how much worse things could get. Maybe there was nothing at the end of the journey other than the end. If so, there would be no more constant hunger and fear. I could be with Mama and Papa again.

But then the thought of Tovah's life ending with mine broke me like nothing else could. For her life to be so short, with so much horror and heartache, was too cruel to fathom. My child knew nothing about what a real childhood should be, and I couldn't help but blame myself for not leaving like Zotia had when there was still time to go.

If I'd made different decisions, Tovah's life would be different. Because helplessly watching her suffer was the hardest part of all.

It took another month of the SS soldiers clearing the ghetto of its inhabitants, block by block, before they finally reached our section. We were ready, resigned to get on the train without knowing its destination.

David wanted Avrom to join his fight. He said they needed men to shoot the guns they'd been smuggling inside, but Avrom wouldn't leave us. Since fighting meant certain death, I did nothing to change his mind. Perhaps resettlement meant exactly that. We decided the odds were better if we took our chances on a train out of Warsaw.

When the order came to vacate, we took the meager possessions we still had—some extra clothing, cups, and eating utensils—and put them in a sack. Leah and Heinrich stood beside us as we walked out into the street and presented ourselves to the SS.

Once the block was filled with people ready to leave the ghetto, the SS officer in charge picked up his megaphone and warned those who remained inside that this was their last chance to come out peacefully. They would be searching the buildings, and anyone left inside would be shot.

In tense silence, we all watched and waited. Soon, a few stragglers made their way out onto the street to join the rest of us.

"Time is up!" the officer shouted.

Holding their rifles and pistols in front of them, the SS soldiers marched into each building on the block.

Tovah, Avrom, and I held hands the entire time, wincing as shots rang out, echoing in the silence, each crack of sound signaling the discovery of a hiding place and the end of a life. We startled every time a weapon was fired, and by the end, Tovah's face was pushed against me as I did my best to cover her ears.

Once the buildings were cleared, the officers made their way down the line, inspecting us before sending us to one of two lines. Most people were sent to the line on the right. When the officer reached us, he stared at me for a long time, and I realized that he was the young man who first asked me to sew the buttons onto his uniform.

"Go to the left," he told me.

My heart pounded as I reached for both Avrom and Tovah, watching as the same soldier inspected Leah and Heinrich.

"What is this line for?" I whispered to Avrom as we went to the much shorter line on the left.

"I don't know." His voice was tremulous, filled with fear, just like mine.

When Leah and Heinrich were sent to the other line, I bit my bottom lip to stop it from trembling. My eyes held Leah's until both lines were complete, and she was led away from us.

My hand pressed against the hollow ache inside my chest. *Leah. My little sister.* Would I ever see her again? I watched as she moved farther and farther away until I couldn't see her anymore. When she was gone, it felt as though another part of me was gone. I couldn't run after her, just like I couldn't stop the tears from quietly falling down my cheeks.

We stood in line for what seemed like hours before the order came to move toward the train station. It was eerily quiet as we walked away from the littered street that had been our home.

"I don't see David anywhere," Tovah whispered. "He didn't come out. Do you think they shot him?"

I scanned the area, but there were too many of us to spot one single person. I hoped that if David decided to hide somewhere, he hadn't been discovered.

"If there's anyone who knows how to hide and be sneaky about it, it's David," I said, trying to reassure Tovah, but I believed every word. Two years in the ghetto had hardened the boy, making him clever in ways no child should ever need to be.

A commotion came from the end of the line, and I turned to see a man break away and run back toward the buildings. My fingers dug into Avrom's arm as two soldiers ran after the man. Avrom pushed Tovah's face into his side, hiding her eyes so she couldn't witness what was sure to come next.

After a moment, one of the soldiers stopped, raised his rifle, aimed, and fired. The man jerked to a stop and went down into the street face-first.

Gasps came from the line, and some people cried out.

"Keep moving!" another SS soldier shouted, waving his rifle at us.

We moved along faster as Avrom held Tovah firmly at his side.

On the train, we found there were no seats in the car. It was a simple rectangular box, and all we could do was sit on the floor and try to see through the spaces between the wooden slats that formed the walls.

If we were traveling to our deaths, you'd think we'd say profound things to each other, express last words of love, but we said nothing. Everyone in the railroad car was silent and sullen as we traveled toward whatever new hell the Nazis had in store for us.

chapter 7

Poniatowa, Poland, 1943

The town of Poniatowa, located west of Lublin, had several factories and fields where Jewish workers were sent. Signs posted on the buildings read Arbeit macht frei. That meant "work will set you free," and we all worked hard each day.

I was sent to a factory that made uniforms for the soldiers. Avrom was sent to the fields to clear land and farm, and Tovah spent the day inside the small living quarters that were assigned to us. It turned out that the soldier in the ghetto had sent me to the left line because of my sewing skills. The left line was for workers who had talents the SS army needed, including sewing uniforms for the hundreds of Ukrainian men who had volunteered for the SS civilian police force.

When we arrived at the settlement at Poniatowa, we heard that the right line led to certain death. The Germans had two types of camps for the Jews: work camps and death camps. Leah and Heinrich were sent to a death camp, along with thousands of others.

A part of me didn't want to believe it was true. *Death camps?* But another part knew it likely was true, and Leah was already gone. Mama, Papa, and Leah, all of them were taken away over time, like rocks carried off the beach by a relentless ocean tide.

When I first heard of the death camps, I cried anytime Tovah or Avrom couldn't see me. Then a strange sort of numbness set in, and the tears stopped.

I stopped asking how the world could let this happen, and stopped wondering why. Instead, I asked myself, *How do I survive this day and* make sure my family does too? Because I didn't intend to lose anyone else. The answer was to work hard and follow orders.

"You saved us," Avrom said as he embraced me that first night at the work camp.

Papa saved us by teaching me to sew, I thought.

At Poniatowa, the conditions we lived under were better than they'd been in the ghetto. We had larger food rations, beds to sleep in, and our own small space in barracks, a dormitory-type building. There were still soldiers with guns who watched our every move, and rules that had to be followed, such as the mandatory morning and evening head counts.

Each day, a count was taken of all the prisoners before breakfast, and again when we returned from our jobs. In the evening, when the count was finished, we could pick up Tovah from the room where the children stayed while the adults were gone all day. Then we stood in the long line for food and returned to our bunks to eat it. Each day was the same, but it was predictable and without the terror that had run through our veins in the ghetto, where death was a part of each day.

That's how it was until the end of the summer when a new group of SS soldiers and commanders arrived in Poniatowa. Their displeasure at the leniency they saw at the camp was obvious, and they began to make changes immediately.

A count had already been taken one morning, when there were orders to line up again only an hour later. I sent Tovah off to the children's area before Avrom and I went outside to present ourselves.

The SS and the Ukrainian police stood by watching as we filed into the yard, the same as always. One of the new SS men made a point of looking up at the sky as if he were bored. Then he blew out a heavy breath and began firing his pistol into the air.

"Faster!" he shouted. "I want you out here faster!"

The leisurely procession turned frantic, with people running into the yard half-clothed, pulling on shirts and shoes as they came.

The new SS officer who had fired his gun into the sky, and whose name I would soon learn was Commandant Amon Glostnik, took the count, inspecting us all as he did so. When he finished, he looked at a small notebook in his hand. "You are one short."

One of the prisoners stepped forward. "My wife is ill. She is too sick to come out."

We all lived so close together, when someone came down with an illness, it spread quickly. Oftentimes, the roll call was short by more than one person due to that reason, and the soldiers would either let it go or send people inside to find whoever was missing and finish the head count.

It was clear by the firm set of the new commandant's jaw that leniency was not part of his makeup. He barked an order in German, and two soldiers ran back into the barracks. Soon a gunshot rang out, and the soldiers exited, dragging the body of the ill woman. She'd been shot in the head.

I stared at the dead woman, her eyes open and lifeless. Avrom gripped my hand and whispered that he wanted to check on Tovah, but there was no time. We were ordered to our jobs, and we didn't dare disobey.

Tension was thick in the factory that day as we worked in silence. I tried to focus on each stitch and not on the dead eyes that haunted my thoughts. That evening, as we filed out of the factory building, an SS soldier pulled certain people out of line and ordered them to move to the side. It seemed to be the older women who were chosen.

They let me pass, and took a woman behind me who had broken her finger yesterday when she tripped on a tree branch in the yard. A horrible sinking feeling grew in my stomach as I watched the group form and quickly walked in the direction of the barracks.

"They're taking them out into the woods. They won't be coming back," Liza whispered as she fell into step with me.

She worked in the factory too, and sometimes we spent our lunch breaks together. Because the soldiers didn't like the prisoners talking to each other or mingling too much, all I knew about Liza was that she was here alone. Her husband and son had been sent to another camp.

Before we reached our barracks, we were startled by the sound of gunshots echoing through the camp. I tensed as Liza grabbed me.

"I told you they wouldn't be coming back," she said in a tremulous voice.

I ran all the way to the barracks and didn't take a full breath until I was holding Tovah in my arms.

That night, I said to Avrom, "You cannot injure yourself in the fields. If you can't work, they'll shoot you. You have to be careful."

"You think they need a reason to shoot me if they want to? It's the new commandant. He has to show everyone he is in control."

Tovah pretended to be sleep in her bed across the room, but I could tell by her breathing that she was awake. "Shh," I said by Avrom's ear. "Tovah will hear you. Just be careful."

I eyed him in the dark as he turned away from me, understanding the anger mixed with despair I'd heard in his voice. We thought we'd lived through the worst of it in the ghetto. It would take more resolve than either of us had left to withstand the return of daily terror and death. But we would do what we had to. Fear rose with the sun each morning, and we had to rise with it.

The next day at the factory, I had a headache from lack of sleep. I hadn't even realized I'd stopped working, letting my foot up off the pedal of the sewing machine as I stared off at nothing.

"You think you can take a break?" one of the Ukrainian soldiers asked sharply.

I startled, realizing he was talking to me, and shook my head, quickly getting back to work, but that wasn't good enough. The soldier ordered me to stand. Fighting my rising panic, I slowly pushed to my feet. When he opened his mouth to say something, an SS officer walked over and told him he was needed outside.

With a scowl in my direction, the Ukrainian dismissed me and walked out of the factory with the SS soldier.

I collapsed back onto my chair as the pressure of tears burned my eyes. Breathing hard, I looked around at the others as they worked with their attention purposely turned away from me, as if looking at me would bring a punishment down on them too. Even Liza was afraid to meet my eyes.

As soon as I could gather my wits, my pounding headache was forgotten. I got back to work, making sure to think of nothing but the thread rhythmically moving through the fabric.

When the bell rang, signaling work was done for the day, I feared the Ukrainian would stop me on my way out of the factory, but he didn't. He let me pass and continue on to the roll call. I decided not to tell Avrom what happened, because I didn't want to worry him more than he already was. But I vowed to never let my thoughts wander again while I worked.

"A soldier came in and counted all of us today. He did it twice," Tovah said quietly from her bed that night.

"What do you mean?" Avrom asked, suddenly alert.

Seeing her father's reaction, Tovah hesitated. "We had to stand in a line so the man could count us."

"Did he take anyone away?" I asked.

She shook her head, and we asked no further questions so we wouldn't frighten her. After she fell asleep, Avrom turned to me.

"We shouldn't send her to the children's room tomorrow. She'll stay here."

"She can't. If they're counting the children now too and she misses the roll call, they'll shoot her when they find her."

Avrom's eyes squeezed shut. "Why are they counting the children? They never counted them before."

"The new commandant probably wants a more accurate number. That's all."

"He's ruthless, Meira. You don't know the half of it. I don't want Tovah to leave this room tomorrow."

The fear in his voice made my blood run cold. "What do you mean, I don't know the half of it?"

Avrom's muscles were stiff with tension. I asked the question again, but he wouldn't explain.

"Listen to me," I whispered. "Tovah has to go where she is supposed to tomorrow. It would be more dangerous if they count the children again and she's not there. Please don't worry so much. Did you see? They've started to put more heaters in the barracks in preparation for winter. That's a good sign they intend for us to be here a while, at least through winter. We're going to be all right. After Commandant Glostnik has been here longer, things will settle down again. We just have to stay healthy and do what they want. We've made it this far, haven't we?"

He looked at me as a reluctant half smile lifted his lips. "Yes, we have." Despite his smile, which had only been for my benefit, there was a dullness in his eyes.

The thought that Avrom was losing hope terrified me. He had to stay focused, especially when any small mistake could result in a death sentence. For so long, Avrom's strength of will kept us going. Until he could find it again, my will would have to be enough for both of us.

After roll call one morning, when Avrom and the rest of the men had already left for the fields, rather than send us to our jobs in the factory, the soldiers ordered us each to take a shovel from a pile they'd tossed into the yard and walk toward the woods.

The woods. Liza and I shared a panicked look.

Terrified of what this meant, anticipating the worst, some of the women cried and begged the soldiers not to kill them. But the soldiers ignored their pleas, raised their rifles, and demanded we walk toward the tree line.

Avrom's fears echoed in my head as we moved. What would he think if I didn't return to our room tonight? Would he hear the shots?

Would he understand what they meant? Could he be strong for Tovah on his own?

My trembling hands gripped the heavy metal shovel as I walked with the other women. Once we reached the designated location, a clearing several yards long, one of the Ukrainian men yelled, "Dig!"

Frightened and confused, we hesitated. That was a mistake. A soldier shot the woman standing closest to him as we screamed in terror.

"Dig!" he shouted again.

Gripping the shovel tighter, I began to dig frantically, and so did all the others. Thoughts rioted in my head as I searched for a way to escape.

If I ran, they'd shoot me. If I stayed, they might shoot me anyway. The shovel in my hands was heavy. Could I use it as a weapon? How many could I hurt before they killed me?

All my desperate questions had only one answer.

There was no escape.

With the soldiers looking on, we dug for hours with no breaks, creating a deep ditch in the clearing. When one of the women stopped digging, a soldier came, pulled her out by the hair, walked her into the trees, and shot her. After we witnessed this once, no one else dared to stop.

Sweat poured down my face and into my eyes as I kept digging, ignoring the way my back screamed with pain. I was afraid to even look up from the dirt filling my shovel as the ditch we created deepened.

When the bell rang for lunch, we were finally given a break. The soldiers changed shifts, and the new soldiers brought us bread, but nothing to drink. I didn't eat much, because with no water, the bread got stuck in my parched throat.

After the lunch break, we were ordered back to work.

My body ached from head to toe, but I didn't dare stop or even pause. Instead, I concentrated on the rhythm of the shovel hitting the earth while I pictured one of Tovah's rare smiles, and knew my only goal was to see her smile again.

What was the ditch for? I didn't know, and in that moment, I didn't care. All I cared about was getting back to my family tonight.

where butterflies go

As the air cooled and the sky began to darken, the soldiers finally told us to stop.

Breathing hard, I winced as I peeled my fingers back and let the shovel fall into the dirt. The woman beside me dropped to her knees, and she wasn't the only one. We were dazed, exhausted, and relieved when the soldiers walked us back to camp.

When Avrom came back to our room that night, he found me lying on my bunk with Tovah asleep in my arms. He slipped in behind me and put his arm around my waist.

"I just heard they took you to the forest to dig ditches all day." He said this softly by my ear so he wouldn't wake up Tovah. "Are you all right?"

I nodded, and he moved his hand up to massage my shoulder. "Will they take you to dig again tomorrow?"

"I don't know." I thought of my blistered hands and wondered how I would dig again all day tomorrow.

But the next day, they didn't take us to the woods. Instead, we went back to our jobs at the factory.

Relieved to be sitting at my sewing machine, I glanced out the window as I cut fabric and saw more Ukrainian soldiers march into camp. Liza noticed them too and subtly shook her head.

Why did they need an entire army to guard us?

Avrom's sense of doom was contagious, and nerves skittered down my spine as I watched the soldiers march by the window. Things were changing here, more than just the leadership with the newly installed Commandant Glostnik.

They were preparing for something. But what?

chapter 8

A windstorm the night before brought down all the crimson-colored leaves that once filled the forest. Now they littered the ground and crunched beneath the soles of our shoes as we lined up for roll call.

Many more soldiers than usual were present for roll call that morning. The other prisoners looked around the yard with wide, curious eyes, probably wondering why. I did the same, and stiffened when I saw Commandant Glostnik come out of the main building and walk in our direction. He was rarely present for roll call, and the sight of him there made a nervous buzz ripple through the crowd.

The commandant shouted in German, and the soldiers began to separate us into different groups.

"They're resettling us again," someone whispered.

I panicked because Tovah was still inside. The children weren't required to be at the main roll call, and Tovah often stayed in bed until I came back to wake her for breakfast.

Guns drawn, a few soldiers headed for the barracks where Tovah and the other children were.

With a gasp, I turned to follow them. Avrom grabbed for my arm to keep me beside him, but I tugged free and walked back as quickly as I could. Trying not to draw attention to myself, I braced for the order to halt, but it never came.

Back in our room, I went to the bed and shook Tovah awake. She looked at me with sleepy eyes but remained quiet as I pulled her up and kept her at my side when I walked back out again.

Seconds later, shots rang out inside the barracks. The soldiers were forcing all the children out into the yard. Relief flooded me as I held my daughter close, glad she didn't have to wake up to find a gun in her face.

Once we were in the yard, I saw that Avrom wasn't where I'd left him. Looking around, I spotted him in a line with the other men, his eyes frantic as he stared back at me. It wasn't only Ukrainian soldiers separating people into groups now. SS soldiers from the German army were there too, and frightened whispers traveled through the crowd.

"They're sending us to another work camp."

"No, they're taking us to the woods to shoot us."

Death had been predicted so many times, the rumors no longer filled me with terror, but the thought of being separated from Avrom did. Gripping Tovah tightly, I watched as the group of men Avrom stood with were ordered to walk out of the camp at gunpoint.

The women called out to them, some screaming for their loved ones. One man broke away and started running back. A soldier quickly shot him. There were more screams, and another man broke away.

I took a step in Avrom's direction, but he shook his head at me, his eyes silently pleading for me to stay away. Then a machine gun sounded, cutting through the chaos, and everyone ducked and covered their heads. My heart pushed up into my throat as Tovah flinched in my arms.

When the noise stopped, my gaze went right to Avrom's. He looked back at me with terror in his eyes, but he was still alive. The machine gun had been shot into the air by Commandant Glostnik, who looked around with a completely placid expression on his face.

He is inhuman. A man without a heart or a conscience.

Tovah gripped me, burying her face in the folds of my dress. I bent over her and kept my eyes on Avrom, knowing he thought the same thing I did, that this was the moment we'd dreaded all these years. It took every ounce of my willpower not to run to him. Instead, I held my daughter and tried to be brave for her as tears slid down my cheeks.

Avrom's eyes shone with tears too, and then he broke down completely. His shoulders shook as he stood looking over at us.

The helplessness I felt was overwhelming. Everything inside me screamed across the distance, but I held myself still and bit into my cheek hard enough to flood my mouth with blood.

As we watched each other, Avrom was shoved by a soldier, forced to turn away and slowly walk out of camp with the other men.

I watched his back as he walked away, the same way I'd watched Leah's. I couldn't tear my gaze from him until he'd completely disappeared from sight. Then I collapsed to my knees and steeled myself for what would come next.

Behind me, a soldier yelled at the group Tovah and I stood with, gesturing toward the middle of the yard with his handgun. Tovah's little body shuddered with fear, and she kept her face pushed into my side. If they tried to separate us, that would be the end. I would die to keep her with me. But no one tried to break us apart as they told us to walk toward the forest, in the same direction Avrom's group had gone. As I got to my feet again, I hoped I might see him.

We'd only been walking for a few minutes when shots rang out from within the forest in front of us.

I tripped to a stop, jerking at the sound, and screams rang out from somewhere behind me. Music suddenly blared from the announcement speakers mounted around camp as the gunshots sounded again, one after the other. They were trying to cover up the sound. It was a symphony of death, and there was no question they were shooting prisoners in the woods.

Deep in my heart, I knew one of those shots had been meant for Avrom. My daughter's bullet would soon follow, and mine too.

I tightened my arms around Tovah. At least we were together, leaving this world within moments of each other. Soon we'd see Mama and Papa, and the endless suffering that had been Tovah's life would be over. I should have been out of my wits with fear or fuming with anger, and I was both of those things, but I was also resigned and so very tired of it all.

"Don't be frightened, little one," I said, bending to speak in Tovah's ear. "We'll be someplace better soon. We'll go there together, to a place with no fear and no pain. Just remember how much Papa and I love you."

Frozen in shock, she looked at me with wide eyes. I squeezed her against me as if I could somehow absorb her body into my own and spare her the pain.

If you're going to murder my baby, please do it quickly. Don't make her suffer anymore.

They walked us to the edge of the very same ditch we'd dug only days earlier, and ordered us to get undressed. I looked around but couldn't see any sign of the men they'd shot only moments before.

SS soldiers surrounded us and pointed their guns. Shaking with fear, we all disrobed, a group of forty or fifty women and children, our pale skin making us glow like ghosts in the dim forest.

"Get in and lie facedown!"

This was shouted at us in broken Polish by one of the Ukrainians, and there was no doubt as to what they intended to do. There were too many of us to fit in a single row, so people lay on top of each other, gathering their children close.

When it was our turn to climb down, Tovah asked, "Will you cover my eyes, Mama?"

I looked at her ribs poking through her skin, and nodded as I took her hand. Tovah winced when her foot sank into the cold, rocky dirt, and so I picked her up and cradled her in my arms as I lowered myself into the trench.

"I love you," I said as I lay down in the cold dirt and tried to shield her body beneath mine. Covering her eyes, I kept her pressed against my chest.

"I love you too," she whispered back.

Seconds later, the shooting began.

I squeezed my eyes closed and held my breath. There were so many of us in the ditch that I could feel the jerking of others pressed against me when bullets struck them. Cracks echoed through the forest, punctuating the music that continued to blare from a distance.

A burning pain tore through my arm, and Tovah twitched beneath me. Warm liquid oozed from her head over my hand. A soft breath left her lips, and then she stilled.

I held my own breath, praying for her to draw another, but she never did. I waited, my muscles tense and still, but there was nothing.

Tovah was gone, and an ache, so sweet and acute, bloomed deep inside me. My baby was no longer here, but she wouldn't suffer anymore, and soon I would join her. I would be with her and Avrom and Mama and Papa, and all this suffering would be over. I rested my cheek on Tovah's head and closed my eyes.

Bullets continued to rain down, and I waited for mine. It had been quick for her, thank goodness. The bullet had passed through my arm and into her head. *Would it be quick for me*, I wondered as I waited, listening to the gunshots ring out and the screams that followed. My heart pounded in my ears, and I counted each beat.

One, two, three . . . How far would I get before the end came?

The air was heavy with the sounds of fear and death as more people were ordered into the ditch. Someone lay down on top of me, and the shooting began again. It wasn't long before the body that covered mine twitched and warm blood poured over my skin.

Holding on to Tovah's lifeless body, I waited as the shooting continued. I had no doubt the soldiers were killing everyone in the camp. And still I waited, oddly calm and impatient, wanting it to be over, but my bullet didn't come. Eventually, the gunshots and the music stopped.

The soldiers climbed down into the ditch and walked over the bodies. I could feel the pressure when they stepped on the corpses above me. If there was a sound or a movement, they shot at it.

So I remained still, barely breathing, weighed down by the dead layered over me.

It was dark when the soldiers finally left, their voices fading into the forest. No more cries or moans came from the ditch. It was eerily quiet, except for my own raspy breaths moving in and out of my lungs.

Are they gone? Did they not realize I'm still alive?

I wondered if I was trapped in a new nightmare, or maybe I was dead and didn't know it. But my heart still beat. It had beat thousands of times since my baby's heart stopped. I could feel it pound inside my chest. With all the death that surrounded me, how could my heart still beat so strongly? How could my lungs draw air? I didn't want to be here when Tovah was gone and my husband too. I wanted to be with them. I'd told Tovah I would go with her.

Daring to push past the body that covered me, I lifted my head and looked around, and bile rose in my throat. A sea of bodies surrounded me, unmoving pale skin lying in the moonlight, piled on the dirt. Just above the ditch, in the distance, I could see the rooftops of buildings in the camp. In the other direction was the barbed-wire fence that surrounded the area.

I put my head back down and pressed my cheek into Tovah's hair. Was it over? Were the soldiers coming back? This ditch was Tovah's grave, and it would be mine too. Why had they left?

The bodies that pressed down on mine grew cold as I listened to the wind whistle through the tree branches. A sound broke the silence, and gunshots rang out in the distance. I lifted my head again and saw the glow of fire coming from the direction of the camp. Flames reached toward the sky, and a new terror gripped me.

Were they burning the camp, destroying it all? Would they burn the bodies of the dead? Would I be burned alive if I stayed here?

A sound came from the other side of the ditch, and I heard the crunch of leaves nearby. Looking over, I saw a woman climb out and run into the forest toward the barbed wire fence. Someone else here was alive too. I wasn't the only one missed by the bullets. Pulling on the bottom of the fence, she managed to bend it up enough to lie flat and squeeze through to the other side.

She escaped! My pulse raced as I watched her run away into the trees.

I looked from the fence to Tovah's face, now ashen in the muted light. With a wince, I pulled my arm out from under her head. My skin was covered in blood. A small hole above my wrist oozed more blood each time I moved it. It felt unreal as I watched the blood run down my hand, as though I were looking at it from a great distance.

Even though I could hardly feel my legs and feet from the cold, I knew I could climb out of the ditch if I tried. But I couldn't go. I wouldn't leave Tovah here.

The dead surrounded me, but I wasn't dead. At least, I didn't think so.

Unable to comprehend it, I decided I was having a nightmare. I would wake up and Avrom would be sleeping beside me, his arm thrown over my waist. Tovah would be curled up at my feet at the end of the bed, and this would all disappear with the morning light. Except there was no light, and Tovah was still beneath me, cold and unmoving.

Tovah.

My eyes squeezed shut at the pain.

What if I did climb out of this ditch? Maybe I could take her with me. I thought about pulling her out and burying her in the forest, lying down next to her and staying there with her, but I barely had enough strength to move myself.

Sinking down, I cradled Tovah against me. She was cold and stiff, and I held on tight as silent sobs racked my body.

I can't go. I can't leave her.

I begged for the darkness to take me and swallow me whole, but no matter how much I pleaded, I remained in the ditch, alive and breathing, when I should have been cold and lifeless like the bodies that surrounded me.

My hands held my daughter tighter. Closing my eyes, I rested my forehead in the dirt and heard a quiet voice in my head repeating one word over and over again.

Run! Run! It was Papa's voice.

The soldiers hadn't managed to kill me, and now I was going to just give up? Papa would be ashamed of me, and Avrom too. But which was more cowardly—running, or staying here with my baby like I'd promised I would?

Staying was easier. Dying was easier.

A sound came from deep in the forest, a crunching of leaves. Maybe it was an animal, or maybe it was the soldiers returning.

Tovah was gone. Nothing I did could change that. But I was still here, and it was time to decide if that meant anything.

Run!

I pressed a soft kiss to Tovah's cheek and watched my tears turn the dusting of dirt on her skin into mud. "I love you, little one," I whispered. "I will love you always."

Then, with a muffled cry, I crawled forward, my feet and hands digging into the dirt like a desperate animal. Stiff and clumsy, I climbed up the ragged incline, clutching at tree roots until I was on even ground.

Once on my feet, I stumbled into the woods toward the same part of the fence the other woman had managed to slip under. There I spotted footprints in the dirt where she had approached the fence.

Pushing on the bottom of the metal links in the same place she had, I grunted until it bent up slightly, just enough to push my legs under when I sat in the dirt. Afraid of taking too long and someone finding me, I let the metal scrape my skin as I lay flat in the dirt and forced myself the rest of the way under, gripping the fence and frantically pushing, hardly feeling it when the sharp edges scraped my stomach and breasts. Within moments, I was on the other side.

I scrambled to my feet and ran into the forest, then crouched and leaned against a tree to catch my breath. Rough bark scraped my bare skin as I looked back at the fence and the ditch beyond it. *Tovah.* Swallowing my sobs, I turned away, but I could still feel my daughter in my arms and smell her sweet skin.

My wrist throbbed where the bullet had passed through, and the pain cleared my head enough to focus on a hissing sound that came from behind me. I turned to see the woman who had gone through the fence before me, trying to get my attention.

"The town is a short walk in that direction," she whispered, pointing behind her.

I eyed the blood and dirt that covered her skin and knew I looked the same way. Any sane person would run in the other direction if they saw us.

"We have no clothes," I said softly, fearing people would know we were from the camp and try to send us back.

I eyed her in the darkness, the only other survivor of today's massacre, and we both knew we couldn't stay here. In silent agreement, we stood and met somewhere in the middle.

"What's your name?" I asked.

"Esther." Her voice was a thready whisper as she asked for my name.

"Esther?" I blinked, bringing her face in and out of focus. "Esther was my mother's name."

Was it a sign? I desperately wanted it to be. I told Esther my name, and together we trudged through the dry leaves that carpeted the forest floor.

The sun began to rise as we walked along the road that led into town. Staying to the side, hidden by the trees, we followed the narrow roadway. If we heard the rumble of a truck coming, we pushed deeper into the shadows and hid until it passed by.

It wasn't long before we came across some homes set close to the road. They were quiet; anyone who lived there was still asleep or already off working somewhere for the day. We searched the area, looking for any clothes that might have been set out to dry, but there was nothing.

Esther tapped my shoulder and pointed to a hut set farther back.

Light flickered from an oil lamp on the windowsill. "We should knock on their door. We need clothes and water, and you need a doctor," she said, pointing to my arm. It now hung limply by my side as drops of blood slowly flowed down my fingertips, splattering into the dirt.

Wary of alerting anyone to our presence, I hesitated, but Esther was determined. Without waiting for my answer, she walked to the hut and knocked lightly on the door.

A moment later, it opened, and a gray-haired woman stood there, gaping at us.

"Please," Esther begged, "we need clothes. Anything you can spare."

A man, likely her husband, appeared behind her. "Go! Get away from here." He tried to intimidate us by stepping forward and forcing us to back away from the doorway.

The woman disappeared inside and returned quickly with two blankets. The man scowled, but he grabbed them from her and threw them at us before shutting the door in our faces.

Relieved to finally have something to cover ourselves with, Esther and I wrapped the scratchy wool blankets around our shoulders and walked back into the woods.

Fearing we would have the same welcome if we tried to approach anyone else, we decided to stay farther from the road and walk into town through the forest. Once the sun set, we hoped we could steal some clothes and food, and stay out of sight.

By now my arm was burning, and it felt as if lava ran through my veins. The bullet had entered just above my wrist, and the wound was swollen, crusted in blood, dirt, and pus.

We spent the rest of the day trudging through the forest, cutting our feet on rocks and branches. Neither of us said much, but Esther's wide eyes were windows into the shocked state she was in. I understood because I was steeped in the same numbness. Nothing more than the instinct to survive pushed us forward.

Exhausted, we could see the town in the distance when we came across a small farm. Two cows grazed in a field beside a small structure next to a main house. We didn't expect a warm reception, but we were desperate when we dared to knock on the door.

A young woman answered and gasped at the sight of us. Unlike the couple at the hut, she ushered us inside and offered us water to drink and wash with. Esther and I gulped the water much too fast, coughing up as much as we swallowed. I scooped some into my hands and splashed it onto my face and arms.

"Here," the woman said as she handed us dresses and boots to put on. "You can keep these, but you have to leave before my husband comes home."

We stayed an hour or so and rested by her fire. Feeling stronger, we left and continued to walk on the road toward town.

Because we were now dressed like everyone else, we no longer worried about being seen. But we hadn't realized how small the town was. Two men coming toward us from the other direction immediately knew we were strangers and stopped us.

"Where are you coming from?" one of the men said, looking over our heads in the direction of the camp. "Are you Jews?"

Esther and I both stilled. "We are not Jews," I said, appearing insulted at the very thought.

The men eyed us skeptically. "The town of Kowali is that way. We can escort you there to make sure you arrive safely."

"No, thank you. We're fine," Esther said.

"But we insist."

I glanced at Esther, knowing these men were lying. But if we tried to run, they would catch us, and then who knew what they would do to us?

"This way," one of the men said.

Silently, we followed as my mind spun, thinking of ways to get away from them.

Our chance came when a group of four women came walking down the road from the other direction. As soon as they were close enough, I grabbed Esther and said a polite good-bye to the men, telling them they were mistaken about us. We were here to meet our friends, who were finally here.

I held my breath, wondering if the men would try to stop us from walking away, but instead they watched us go and remained silent while we joined the women. Esther offered the group a friendly hello, and they eyed us curiously but said nothing as they continued on their way with us trailing behind them.

"Those men were going to turn us in once we reached Kowali," Esther whispered. "We can't go into town. There must be soldiers there."

I figured she was right, but the men still watched us from a distance, and the women seemed suspicious now, looking as if they wanted to run away from us.

One of them glanced at my arm. "You are injured."

My arm throbbed painfully, and I knew it was becoming infected. If sepsis set in, I wouldn't get much further.

"You can't follow us into Kowali," the woman who noticed my arm said. "They are checking papers at the gate, and the police will kill anyone who helps a Jew. Everyone knows that."

Esther and I looked at each other, not knowing what to do now.

"You can walk that way to Huti." She pointed. "It's a small village, and they won't ask you for papers. There is a doctor there too."

"How far is it?" I asked.

The woman thought a moment. "Two days walking on this road."

Esther and I exchanged another look as I wondered how we could possibly walk for two more days. Another one of the women took pity on us and handed me her basket.

"Take it. There is bread and fruit inside." Then she turned and motioned for the others to walk away with her.

My arm ached all the way up to my shoulder. My feet were sore and bloody in the boots I wore, and now we had to walk for two days to a place that was as unlikely to help us as this place had been.

Esther's gaze was as weary as mine as we stood side by side and looked down the road.

"At least we have each other," she said. "I don't think I could do this alone."

My teeth clenched together tightly. It was those words that forced me to continue on. If that was her intention, it worked, although the same could be said for me. Without Esther, I would likely have sat down and given up.

With no other option, we walked in the direction of Huti, hoping to find help there. We walked all day and into the night. When we couldn't go a step further, we made a bed out of fallen leaves, ate the contents of the basket, and slept for a few hours before sunrise. Then we rose and walked again.

There was no doubt my arm was infected, and my head hurt too. Esther let me lean on her as we walked, and I slipped in and out of awareness. I tripped and stumbled a few times, but Esther steadied me and urged me on.

I wasn't sure how much time passed. Two nights and two days, Esther told me, but it felt longer when we finally saw the small village the woman told us about. It was late morning, and the streets were quiet when we walked in. There were no guards that we could see, no one checking papers.

We received odd looks from those who passed us, and soon a handful of children began to follow us, drawing unwanted attention. Esther diverted us into a small shop to escape the children, but when the woman inside saw us, she yelled for us to leave. Back out on the street, Esther approached a young woman and asked if she knew where the doctor lived.

The woman looked us over, silently biting her lip while she studied our bedraggled appearance. "Come with me and I will get the doctor for you," she said all in a rush as she glanced over her shoulder nervously.

We probably shouldn't have trusted her, but we had no choice other than to follow her. I couldn't have gone much further.

The woman shooed the children away and brought us to a barn just off the road. After bringing us inside, she left and came back with cups of water.

"I think my sister would be interested in you," she said. "She once tried to help a boy from the camp who escaped, but he was caught, and she was devastated. She would probably help you too. Should I ask her?"

I shook my head, but Esther quickly said, "Yes."

The breathy sound of her voice told me she was as afraid to believe this woman as I was. When the woman left, I told Esther we were being foolish, but she said nothing in return. We had no choice but to wait, and we both knew it.

Soon, she came back with a man who said he was a doctor.

"How did this happen?" he asked me.

My gaze met the woman's. Had she told him we were from the camp?

"A hunter mistook her for a deer," the woman said, answering for me.

I didn't know if the doctor believed her or not, but he cleaned my wound. The antiseptic he used stung, burning all the way through to the bone, but he managed to clear out the infection and stitch up the holes. He gave me some medicine and told me to change the bandage each day. I didn't know how I would do that because we had to keep moving, but I held my tongue.

After the doctor left, the woman's sister arrived and introduced herself as Lila. She was petite with dark hair and warm, sympathetic eyes.

"It's good you got away. They destroyed the camp you were in," she said. "All the prisoners are gone now." There was a halting tone to her voice, as if she was afraid of how we would receive this news.

"We know," Esther said as she took hold of my hand. I squeezed back, holding in the emotions that threatened to spill over.

Lila sat down on a stool in front of us. "I can help you get to Warsaw. You'll be safe there."

"There's nothing for us in Warsaw," I said. My stomach turned at the thought of going back there.

"Most of the Jews are gone. It's true. But there are Poles in Warsaw willing to help Jews who are left. They can hide you until the war is over."

I turned to Esther with a skeptical expression. The Poles had murdered my father and Avrom's.

The woman sensed our distrust. "You will be all right. The Russians have begun to defeat the Germans. Hitler's army is not indestructible."

We didn't know what to make of Lila and her optimism. We knew nothing of the war, other than what we'd experienced ourselves, and we didn't know if she was telling us the truth. She could be our savior, or she could be sending us to our deaths. But at that moment, it hardly mattered, because she was our only hope.

Esther and I slept in the barn that night, and Lila left, promising to return in the morning. As I closed my eyes, all I could see was Tovah, flashes of a chocolate smile and whispers of her sweet voice. I pretended Avrom's arms were wrapped around me as silent tears ran like rivers down my face.

If Lila had deceived us and we woke up to soldiers with guns pointed at us, I wouldn't be scared or angry. I wouldn't feel anything. I had run like the voice urged me to, but I had nothing to run toward. All I had was gone.

part II

chapter 9

Great Neck, New York, 1948

Life has a predictable path for most people. You are born into a family. You go to school and experience your firsts. Your first friend. Your first crush. Your first perfect score on an exam. When you finish school, you meet someone and get married. You have children and grow older, watching your children experience the same firsts you did. You play with your grandchildren, and then you leave this world knowing the family you left behind will continue on. Generations will follow you to remember your family stories and carry on your traditions.

When the war ended, that predictable path was gone. Entire families were eradicated from the face of the earth. Their stories ended abruptly, and the generations meant to follow would never come. It wasn't only the people who were gone—their history was gone too. Heirlooms were stolen. Synagogues were burned down. Traditions were erased.

When I came out of hiding after the war, I inquired about our family home, but the authorities dismissed me as petty and foolish. They would do nothing to help me get back the things I'd lost. I had my life. I should be grateful for that, they said.

The Poles who had taken our home, and murdered both my father and Avrom's when we were forced into the ghetto, were not made to pay for their crimes or give anything back they had stolen. Poland also made it clear that any Polish Jews who survived the war were not welcome home again. Many other countries took the same stance, and the Allies, America and Britain, were forced to create "Displaced Persons

Camps" in places like Germany and Austria. These were fenced-off zones that could be safe places for Jews who had no homes to go back to and no country that wanted them.

Rather than go to another camp, some Jews traveled to Palestine, but that only meant more years of war. After a resolution was passed to create the Jewish state of Israel, the surrounding Arab countries refused to recognize it and vowed to fight to get the land back.

I was done fighting, tired of being unwanted and unwelcome. I wanted to leave Europe and go to America where Zotia was. It seemed as if we should be together. My sister was the only family I had left.

That day in the ghetto, when we were sent to the line on the left and Leah and Heinrich were sent to the line on the right, they were only hours away from their deaths. Everyone in that line went to the gas chamber at a camp called Treblinka. I discovered this just after the war when the Red Cross came to Warsaw with food and medical supplies.

What I learned from them was staggering. The number of Jews the Nazis murdered was beyond comprehension. But somehow, I was still here, although not for any reason I could understand. A Red Cross nurse told me I was lucky. I supposed I was the luckiest unlucky person I knew.

Because of a strict quota system, I couldn't enter the United States until the Displaced Persons Act was passed in 1948 by the American president, Harry Truman. It allowed those of us who no longer had a home in Europe to emigrate to America. If you already had relatives in America, you were given priority. Until then, I'd been living in a displaced persons camp in Germany. Both Esther and I traveled there together from Warsaw after the war. It was still a camp, but nothing like the ones run by the Nazis.

Many were angry to be there, angry that they had lost everything and were all alone. Others were numb, wandering around the camp like ghosts.

I was one of those ghosts, unable to process the horrors of the past few years, unable to think about my life *after*. For me, there was no after. After didn't matter. I woke up each morning and went to sleep each night. Days passed, each one the same as the next, and soon they added up to years, colorless years that passed too slowly. I lived, but I had nothing to live for.

Esther was different. She wanted to put it all behind her and move on. She wanted to find happiness again, and a part of me resented her for that. Being happy diminished what she'd lost and all she'd gone through. How could she move on? Were those who died unimportant? Did their absence from the world make no difference to her? It was petty of me to feel that way, but I couldn't help it.

When she met a man in the DP camp and they decided to go to Palestine together, I congratulated her. Esther deserved happiness. In my heart, I knew that. She'd lost a husband in the war and both her parents. She hadn't lost a child, though, and I wondered if that made the difference. Was that why she was ready to embrace life again, while all I could do was endure it?

The only thing I looked forward to was leaving Europe and seeing Zotia again. The last time we saw each other, she was filled with animosity, but that didn't matter now. Thank goodness she'd left when she did. Otherwise, she might be dead too.

When I finally received my visa to travel to America, a light sparked inside me. It was the only thing that penetrated the numbness. Zotia was a part of Mama and Papa, just like I was. Being with her would be like getting a small piece of my old life back.

When I stepped off the boat in New York that sunny afternoon, I assumed I would stay with Zotia and her family. My eyes filled with tears at the sight of her. She looked much the same, a little older and rounder, maybe, but there was no mistaking her. I ran across the dock and landed in her arms.

Seeing Zotia again shifted something inside me. I'd experienced sunny days since the war, but the warmth of the sun never touched me. I hadn't felt much of anything for years, but that day I did. As we both wept and held each other tightly, I felt everything. I squeezed Zotia so hard, I was sure she couldn't breathe, but I didn't let go for the longest time. She was my connection to a past that hadn't been completely extinguished, because we were both still here.

When I first stood in front of her, the pain in Zotia's eyes was sharp, and I knew she was thinking of Papa, Mama, and Leah. Her pain made mine feel fresh and raw again. I was all that was left, and now that I was here, that fact was all too real to her.

Beside Zotia stood a heavyset man dressed in a dark blue suit. She introduced him as her husband, Eli. Behind him were two tall boys, teenagers with dark blond hair like their mother's, my nephews, Jacob and Isaac.

Zotia might have lost one family, but she had another, and I was relieved to discover I felt only happiness for her, not jealousy or the pettiness I'd felt for Esther. I had my sister now, and two nephews. Papa and Mama would live on in them, and I would make sure they knew who their grandparents were, even though they would never meet them.

Zotia and her family lived in a two-story house an hour away from the seaport in a town called Great Neck. Her house was bigger than ours had been in Poland, and the style was very different and strange to me. The appliances were modern, and came in odd colors like mint green. They had a television in the parlor, big and rectangular shaped. I'd seen televisions in store windows, but it never occurred to me to buy one so I could watch movies shrunk down onto a tiny screen.

From the little I'd seen so far, I could tell that America was different from Europe. It was a happier place, more boisterous, with none of the scars Europe had yet to heal from. In America, the cities and neighborhoods were untouched by bombs, and the people seemed to want to move on rather than dwell on the past.

where butterflies go

As we sat at dinner that night and the conversation began, I came to understand the situation I now found myself in. I couldn't speak much English, but I'd been trying since I'd applied for my visa. When Eli spoke slowly, I was able to understand most of what he said, even though I didn't like it much.

"Your whole family should have left Poland when you had the chance," he said between bites of food. "My family's been here since the nineteen-twenties. They saw the writing on the wall even then. But in the old country, most of you weren't educated enough to see the situation for what it was. You thought you could stay in your own little villages and ignore all the hatred until it finally blew up in your faces."

My fork dropped from my hand, clattering onto my plate. I stared hard at Zotia, but she kept her eyes averted.

"What's that scar on your arm?" my nephew Jacob asked.

I glanced at Zotia and Eli, wondering if it was appropriate to tell him the truth, but Zotia wouldn't meet my eyes. "It is a bullet wound," I said slowly in halting English.

Everyone understood enough to stop eating and look up at me.

"Did you say a bullet wound?" Eli asked.

Zotia's shocked gaze was on me now.

"Yes. I can tell you what happened, but maybe it is better if the boys are not here when I do," I said to Zotia.

"And give us all nightmares? I don't think that will be necessary," Eli said. "It's over now. Better to forget and get on with things, don't you think?"

Forget? I winced at his words as he tucked back into his dinner, and the boys did the same. I didn't like the gleam I saw in my nephew's eyes when I answered his question, as if getting shot was somehow exciting to him.

Every time I glanced at Zotia, she stared down at her plate, avoiding my eyes. She knew as well as I did that her husband was not a man Papa would have approved of, and her boys were more under his influence than hers.

It was then that Eli mentioned the housing he'd arranged for me in Brooklyn through a Jewish organization that helped refugees. I wouldn't be staying here with them, after all, and I wondered if Zotia had ever even considered it. Was I not welcome here? My heart sank as I pushed the rest of my food around on the plate.

"I'm sorry about Avrom and your daughter," Zotia said quietly as she walked me to Eli's car so he could drive me to my new home. Inside the house, Eli was putting on his coat and looking for his misplaced keys.

"Her name was Tovah," I said.

She nodded. "Then I'm sorry about Tovah."

"Do you want to know what happened to her? What happened to Papa and to Mama?"

Zotia blinked back the tears that flooded her eyes. "Eli thinks it's best not to know the details."

"Do you agree?"

"Maybe you can tell me another time," she said.

I couldn't hide my disappointment. As hard as it was to talk about all I'd lost in the war, it kept my memories of my family alive, only no one wanted to hear about it. Not in the DP camp, and not on the ship I took to come here.

But it was different with Zotia. It was important for her and her boys to understand who their family was and what had happened to them. They needed to know who Tovah was, and what the world was missing because she was no longer in it.

"Are you happy with Eli?" I asked.

Zotia seemed surprised by the question. "Were you happy with Avrom?"

"Yes, I was."

Her eyes narrowed slightly. "I'm happy to still have my life, Meira, with my boys and my home. Eli was right. Mama and Papa should have seen what was coming and left while they could."

My spine stiffened. "How could anyone have foreseen what would happen?"

She shook her head. "It doesn't matter. Even if Papa had known, he and Mama wouldn't have left. It's not easy to walk away from everything that's familiar and start somewhere new. You have to be strong to do something like that."

I couldn't believe what I was hearing. "You have no idea how strong Papa was, and Mama too. If you could have seen what they did to survive, you wouldn't say such a thing. Mama died trying to save a girl who was being raped by a soldier. She knew she'd be killed, but she couldn't stay quiet. The street was filled with people, but she was the only one who tried to help that girl."

Zotia blinked, her eyes wide.

"And after the Germans marched into Warsaw, Papa went out each day searching for food, hiding to avoid soldiers with their guns. He was shot at more than once, but he still went out again and again."

She shook her head as tears ran down her cheeks. "I don't want to know this, Meira. Please, I can't."

Eli walked out of the house, and his gaze moved between us when he saw Zotia crying. "What are you saying to my wife? Speak English, not Polish. You're in America now."

We were both speaking Yiddish, not Polish, but I didn't bother to correct him, and neither did Zotia.

"It's nothing," Zotia said. "We were only saying good-bye."

Eli didn't seem to believe her, but he let it go when she pulled me into a quick hug and then turned to go back inside the house.

chapter 10

Brooklyn, New York, 1951

Friday afternoon, the salon was bustling with activity as women came in to have their hair done before their dates that night.

"Meira, we've got another request for you."

I glanced up to see a tall, stylish woman with bleached-blond hair standing by the door. When she caught my eye, she sashayed over, toddling unsteadily in her high heels, which were pink to match the polka dots on her dress. Everything about America was colorful, and that still surprised me. The clothes, the cars, and even the store signs came in every color of the rainbow.

"I hear you give the best bangs haircuts." She blinked hopefully at me. "Could you give me a bangs style?"

I already had Mrs. Bellamy in my chair, and I was nearly finished putting in her curlers.

"Did you make an appointment?" I asked in my accented English. I'd been working hard at smoothing out my accent, but when I forgot to concentrate, like just now, it came through clearly. Sometimes, when customers heard my accent, they didn't want me to do their hair. In their minds, an accent equaled inferior intelligence. I wondered what this woman, who had a sense of entitlement about her, would think of me.

"Make an appointment? Is that what you said?"

I nodded.

"Oh, okay. I could do that. But you are Meira, aren't you?"

When I nodded again, she gave me a bright smile, apparently not bothered by my imperfect English. Perhaps I'd misjudged her.

She went to the front of the salon to make an appointment, I assumed, and I finished rolling Mrs. Bellamy's long dark locks into rollers and placed her under the dryer. When I turned, the blond woman was there again, smiling at me.

"The appointment book says you're free now. How's that for good luck?" She tilted her head and shrugged apologetically.

Yes, how lucky.

With a stiff smile, I led her over to the sink to wash her hair. Only two more hours and I could leave for the day. If the rain held off, I could take my time and walk home through the park.

The blond woman sat in my chair and spoke to my reflection in the mirror on the wall in front of her. "I want those thick bangs like Betty Grable in *My Blue Heaven*, and then I can curl them so they have a little volume in the front. What do you think?"

"I think it is good." I truly hated that look, but it wasn't my business how she wore her hair.

She turned and squinted up at me. "You don't sound too excited about it."

Was this woman serious? What was I supposed to do, jump up and down? "I am very excited for you," I said flatly.

Her eyes widened, and I waited for anger or an insult. Instead, she tipped her head back and laughed. "You think I'm ridiculous, don't you? You have that in common with my husband. Well, your hair is gorgeous, Meira. Why don't you just do what you want with mine. You're the expert, after all."

Hiding my surprise at her reaction, I looked in the mirror because I didn't remember what I'd done with my hair that morning. I saw that I'd worn it simple today, like most days. All I'd done was tease the top a little, and the rest fell around my shoulders. The gray streaks in front blended into the blond, which had lightened in the sun since I spent so many hours sitting outside.

The woman in my chair looked far better than I did with her perfect waves that flipped up at her shoulders. There were diamonds in her ears and on her finger. She was obviously well off, and I wondered why she was here instead of some fancy Fifth Avenue salon.

"How did you get my name?" I asked.

"I asked Blanka who did her hair when she came to clean my house last week. You know Blanka, don't you? She's Polish too."

"Yes, I know her."

Blanka and I shared an apartment in Borough Park. The organization Eli contacted to find me affordable housing helped many Jewish immigrants and owned several apartment buildings in Brooklyn. They paired us together, and we split the rent each month.

Only twenty-four, Blanka was young and attractive, and always willing to let me experiment with different hairstyles before she left to clean the houses of rich Americans on the Upper East Side.

"I complimented Blanka on her hairstyle, and she couldn't stop talking about how great you were with hair." The woman continued to grin at me in the mirror.

I got to work trimming her ends and shaping the line of her hair to her face with some layers. Then I put big rollers at the top and smaller ones at the bottom, and sat her down beneath the dryer.

Mrs. Bellamy's hair was dry by then, so I brushed her out and sprayed each curl into place, breathing a sigh of relief when she left without asking me any more questions. At the beginning of her appointment, she'd been filled with questions about where I was from and why I was here in New York. Then she'd said that too many refugees from Europe had flooded into New York City, and she didn't understand why we couldn't have gone elsewhere.

With my teeth clenched tightly, I'd said nothing. The fact was, the quotas already made it very hard to come to America after the war. If Zotia hadn't vouched for me, I might not have been here at all.

After I turned off the hair dryer, I directed the blond woman back to my chair and began to style her curled locks into a side part that had volume at the top and soft waves cascading downward. I had Rita Hayworth in mind as I sprayed it into place.

"Oh my. Look at that." She turned to glimpse a side view of her head. "I love it."

"No bangs, though. If you did not like it, it would take a long time to grow out."

She stood with her purse in hand. "You are absolutely right. Bangs would have been a mistake. Thank you for saving me from myself." She stuck out her hand. "I'm Karen Green. It's very nice to meet you. I'll see you next time, Meira."

After a brief hesitation, I gave her hand a shake.

With another big smile in my direction, she left a tip on my counter and walked out of the salon. She was what Americans called bubbly, and I wondered what her life must be like to fill her with such easy smiles.

Generally, I didn't interact much with my customers. They were so different from me that I hardly knew what to say. But in the borough where I lived, too many people were like me. We were all the same, shell-shocked and lost, but still breathing and moving around the city. At the synagogue, there was plenty of sympathy and charity, but no one wanted to hear more stories of death and horror from the war. People wanted to turn the page and focus on the future, like Esther, and Zotia's husband, Eli.

That's why I stopped talking about the war, and why I stopped going to synagogue.

Karen Green came into the salon again two weeks later. This time she only wanted me to style her hair, not cut it. She tried to make conversation, and although she seemed very sweet and genuine, I said very little, not being much of a conversationalist.

When she came in again two weeks after that, I nearly laughed. "Do you really need your hair done again?"

She grinned, but Mr. Walek, the salon owner, gave me a pointed look. Clearing my throat, I brought her back to wash her hair. Once Karen was seated in my chair, I came to stand behind her.

"You're not married, are you, Meira?" she asked my reflection in the mirror. "I mean, I don't see a ring, but I didn't want to assume."

I shook my head and concentrated on brushing her hair.

"So, that's a no then?"

With a sigh, I dropped my hands to my sides. "I was married."

"Oh?" She eyed me curiously.

"My husband passed away."

Her expression fell. "Oh, Meira. I'm so sorry."

I nodded and continued brushing her hair again.

"Did he die in the war?" she asked carefully.

I nodded again, but I was thinking that he didn't just die. He was murdered. I couldn't stand it when people worded it that way, *died in the war*, like my husband was a soldier who died in battle, when he was actually executed in cold blood.

Karen was quiet as I finished styling her hair.

"I'm very sorry about your husband," she said as she stood and pulled my tip from her wallet.

"No." I placed my hand on hers to stop her. "You did not need much work this time."

She tilted her head as her expression softened. "I am tipping you, Meira, and that's that. I'll see you next time. No one does my hair like you do."

I felt guilty for how quiet and sullen I'd acted with Karen as I walked home that day. Feeling the need to talk to someone, I stopped by the park.

It was late summer, and the sun was still high in the sky as I sat on my usual bench. Glancing across the street at Diamond Tailors, I caught Mr. Diamond's eye in the window and waved to him. It wasn't long before Chopin filtered out from his store into the street. The music was Prelude in C Minor, and I closed my eyes as the slow progression of chords filled my ears.

Tears slid down my cheeks, but I didn't bother to wipe them away. Even though it hurt, I let myself think about Papa and miss him. This was the one place I could be emotional while I remembered my family. My tears weren't welcome elsewhere because I was supposed to be moving on, not living in the past.

"It may not be my place to say so, but I think your father would not be happy to see you here alone all the time, Meira."

Mr. Diamond lowered himself onto the bench beside me. Even when he wasn't smoking, the smell of his pipe clung to his clothes.

Papa sent this man to me to be my friend. I knew that the same way I knew the sky was blue. I'd already been coming to this park when I first heard the music float out of the tailor shop across the street. Unable to stop myself, I'd walked over and gone inside.

Sandwiched between a jewelry store and a bakery, Diamond Tailors reminded me of Papa's shop with its clothing remnants, boxes of chalk, and measuring tapes hanging on the wall. With his long gray beard and kind eyes, Mr. Diamond reminded me of Papa too. What were the odds of meeting a tailor who listened to Chopin if it wasn't a sign from Papa? According to Mr. Diamond, the odds were very good since the neighborhood was filled with tailor shops run by old men with beards.

"There is nothing wrong with being alone," I said.

Mr. Diamond sat back and folded his hands in his lap. "Of course being alone isn't wrong. I'd just like to look out my window one day and see you sitting with someone else, instead of by yourself."

I smiled at him. "But I am not by myself. I am surrounded by people and memories. See that family over there in the park? If I squint my eyes, I can imagine it is Tovah sitting on that blanket, eating a sandwich and laughing. Or I can listen to your music and pretend it is Papa playing his phonograph while he measures out a coat for a customer. I feel close to them when I sit here in the sun and imagine they are nearby."

Mr. Diamond studied me and smiled sadly. "You're an interesting young lady, Meira."

"I am not interesting or young. I will be forty on my next birthday."

He patted my arm. "Compared to me, you're a youngster." With a grin, he stood. "Enjoy the sun, but then please go and enjoy something else too. Like a movie, or dinner with a friend."

I nodded rather than argue with him, because we both knew I'd do neither of those things.

When I got back to the apartment, Blanka and her American friend Nancy were entertaining two young men.

"This is Frank, and this is Henry," Blanka said, slurring her words as she pointed to each of them.

My eyes narrowed on the young men as I walked over and took the glass from Blanka's hand. A quick sniff of its contents told me all I needed to know.

"Time for you to go, Frank and Henry." I pointed at the door.

They laughed at me. "Is this your mother?" one of them asked Blanka.

"She is not my mother," Blanka said as she swayed on her feet. "My mother is dead."

Crossing my arms, I softened my tone. "This is not going to make the pain stop, Blanka. I think they should go now. Don't you?"

Blanka opened her mouth to argue, but then closed it tight and nodded her head.

"Okay. Party is over. Time to go." I pointed at the door.

One of the men turned to walk out, but the other one decided to challenge me.

"Maybe I'm not ready to go yet." As he stood toe to toe with me, the top of my head only came to his shoulders.

"You are refusing?" I asked.

"Maybe I am." He snickered as he crossed his arms over his chest.

I was tired and had no patience for arrogant American boys. With a quick nod of my head, I stepped around him and went into the kitchen. I heard him laugh as I left, thinking he'd won. His smile disappeared quickly when I returned with a knife in my hand.

"What the hell!" He took a clumsy step back.

"I said you should go. I survived Hitler. You think I am afraid of you?"

"I think you're crazy."

"Yes, probably I am," I said.

"Jeez, immigrants," he muttered as he turned for the door.

Nancy stood and grabbed her purse to follow him out. "Talk to you later, Blanka," she said, pointedly not looking at me before she walked out the door with Frank, or was that one Henry?

"Let's get you some water," I said to Blanka, switching to Yiddish now that it was just the two of us.

She blinked at me and then started to giggle. She kept giggling until there were tears in her eyes. "That was crazy, Meira. Would you have really stabbed him?"

I shrugged. "I don't know. Glad we did not have to find out."

She laughed again, but when her smile faded, she looked tired and defeated. "I was lonely. I just wanted some company and some of that." She pointed at her glass in my hand as I poured it down the sink. "Wouldn't you like a boyfriend? Aren't you lonely sometimes?"

Yes, I was lonely, but the type of loneliness I felt wouldn't go away by filling my life with more people or alcohol or anything else.

"All the boys my age are married or engaged," Blanka said, not waiting for me to answer. "That leaves the younger ones, or the ones who are too old for me."

"You have been through too much for the young ones to handle." I poured her a glass of water and slid it across the counter toward her. "Next time you feel lonely, talk to me. We can go out and do something together."

She eyed me skeptically. "Like what? Go to the library?"

I scoffed. "You think I am that boring?"

"Yes."

I laughed softly. "We could go to the top of the Empire State Building. I hear the view of the city from there is very nice."

She brightened at that suggestion. After she finished the glass of water, I walked her to her bedroom, helped her get changed, and tucked her into bed.

If Tovah had survived the war and I hadn't, I would hope someone would watch out for her. I silently vowed to Blanka's mother that I would do a better job of watching over her daughter from now on.

chapter 11

It's fair to say I was surprised when Karen Green invited me to her apartment for dinner. I told her I was busy, but she kept insisting.

"I'd love for you to meet my husband, and my nephew is learning about the war in school. I thought you could talk a little about it to him, if you don't mind," she said one afternoon as I put curlers in her hair. "My brother gets frustrated because Jonathan, that's my nephew, doesn't take school seriously."

"I do not talk about the war."

"Oh." Her expression fell. "Of course. I should have realized how hard that would be for you. I'm sorry, Meira."

With a sigh, I picked up another curler, feeling guilty again. Karen was so sweet and guileless. It was impossible to refuse her. "I suppose I could talk to him a little about it."

"Really? Are you sure?" she asked hopefully.

"Yes."

"That would be wonderful. You don't have to say anything personal about yourself. Honestly, I don't think those schools are doing a very good job of teaching what really went on over there."

That didn't surprise me. Most of the world didn't want to know what really went on, because then they would have to admit they let it happen. Even America knew about the concentration camps, but they didn't get involved in the war until they had no choice.

"Would Sunday be good?" she asked.

"Sunday?"

"For dinner, Meira."

Right, dinner. I nodded, despite my reluctance to go. For some reason, without much encouragement from me, Karen was determined to be my friend, and I had to admit she was growing on me.

Sunday afternoon, Blanka and I went to the Empire State Building, and then we walked around the city. I didn't put much thought into the dinner at Karen's or what I would wear and whether I should bring something.

That felt like a mistake when I arrived at Karen's apartment on the Upper East Side of Manhattan. I was a bit overwhelmed by how fancy it was with a doorman in the lobby and rich wood paneling on all the walls. Blanka had told me they were well off, and I could tell it was true by the fancy clothes and jewelry Karen wore, but I didn't know quite what that meant or how intimidating it would be.

Dressed in a gray skirt with a blue blouse tucked in, I was sure I stuck out like a *sore thumb*, as the Americans said. But the color of the blouse matched my eyes, and the skirt was simple but clean.

I gave my name to the doorman, and he told me to take the elevator up to the ninth floor. Soon, I was standing in front of the apartment, smoothing my skirt and straightening my blouse. When Karen pulled open the door, I was swept up in a cloud of floral perfume.

"I'm so glad you came, Meira," she said, ushering me inside.

Looking around curiously, I peered into a large living room where heavy gold curtains were tied to either side of a large picture window that looked out onto the park.

"This is my husband, Jerry."

A tall man stood up from the couch and extended his hand in my direction. "A pleasure to meet you, Meira. Karen has told me all about you."

His smile was as wide as his wife's, but as I looked at the two of them standing together, they didn't seem to match. Jerry had thinning black hair brushed back off his forehead, and a stout build that said he enjoyed food. Karen was a little blond pixie compared to him. If he rolled over in bed, he would crush her.

A young boy, about eleven or twelve years old, came running down a short hallway and skidded to a stop in front of Karen. He was skinny with thick, messy hair and wide, curious eyes.

Karen put her arm around his shoulders. "And this little devil is my nephew, Jonathan."

I smiled at Jonathan and pressed a hand to the sudden ache in my chest. Being around children was hard.

The boy made a face. "Not another one, Auntie Karen. Dad isn't going to like it."

Karen's cheeks turned pink. "Jonathan, mind your manners. I asked Meira here tonight so she could tell you about her experiences in Europe during the war."

I smiled at the boy but wondered what her nephew meant about "another one," and why she'd been so embarrassed by it.

"My antisocial brother is around here somewhere. Max!" Karen called. "Come out here and meet a friend of mine."

When no one came, she rolled her eyes and disappeared down the hallway in search of her brother, I assumed.

"Would you like some wine?" Jerry asked.

"Yes. Thank you."

I looked around the apartment, eyeing all the photographs and paintings on the walls. I knew Karen and her family were Jewish, but there was no outward indication of it, not like in my flat back in Warsaw, where my framed *ketubah* had hung on the wall and Shabbat candles sat out on the table. By all appearances, Karen was very American. It made me think of the conversation my parents had with Avrom's parents the night they came to dinner. My father spoke of integration with the Poles to make us less of a target, and everyone disagreed with him. Looking at Karen's family and seeing how thoroughly American they were, seemingly accepted and successful, I wondered if my father had been right.

Karen returned, her easy smile now tight and less genuine. "My brother, Max, will be out in a minute. He's on the telephone, working. He's always working."

"What does he do?" I asked.

"Investment banking, just like Jerry. Don't ask me what that means. I've never had a head for numbers. I'd better go check on dinner."

I sipped my wine slowly, admiring the view of the park and watching Jonathan jump on the furniture as if the living room were his playground. Had Tovah jumped on the furniture? She must have, but I couldn't remember her doing it. She preferred arts and crafts to more physical activities.

"Dinner's ready," Karen soon announced.

We all sat down in the dining room, which had a long table with several chairs. Jerry sat at the head of the table, and Karen sat at the other end. I was alone on one side, and on the other side was Jonathan and an empty place setting beside him.

"Meira lived in Poland when the war broke out," Karen said to Jonathan before passing around a basket of bread.

"Did you see the bombs and tanks?" he asked.

I passed the bread basket on without taking any. I couldn't stomach bread. The thought of it made me gag. The day we were ordered to dig the ditch that would be Tovah's grave, lunch was bread with no water, and the bread had stuck in my throat like a rock. To this day, I couldn't bring myself to eat it.

"There were tanks and bombs," I said. "A bomb destroyed the building I lived in."

Karen glanced up and smiled. "There you are," she said, pushing to her feet. "Max Neuman, this is my friend Meira Sokolow."

Max came around the table and barely looked at me as he pulled out the chair beside Jonathan. He was tall, like Jerry, but that's where their similarities ended. Max was thinner with broader shoulders. His jaw was square, but his hair was his most striking feature. It was thick and wavy, much like his son's, but streaked with gray at the temples.

A scowl turned his lips down, and he seemed perturbed about something. Karen was acting strange too, making me wonder what might have happened before I arrived tonight. I also wondered where Jonathan's mother was, and why she wasn't joining us.

"This lady was in the war. She just said a bomb destroyed her whole building." Jonathan's eyes were wide as he shoved a hunk of bread in his mouth.

"Jonathan, please refer to her as Mrs. Sokolow," Karen said.

Max's eyes met mine across the table, and my stomach jumped at the intensity of his stare. His eyes were green like the sea, and just as stormy.

"Where are you from?" he asked.

I cleared my throat. "Poland."

"Poland? You were lucky to escape."

He wasn't the first person to say those words to me, and as always, I made no comment. I was the luckiest unlucky person I knew.

As I sipped my wine, in my peripheral vision I could see Max unfold his napkin and place it on his lap.

"Are you single, Meira?" he asked.

I glanced up. "Single?"

"Max, please," Karen said in a tight voice.

"There's a lot of opportunity here in America," he said. "Is that why you're here tonight, Meira? Seeking an opportunity?"

My expression must have revealed my confusion, because Karen threw her napkin down on the table and glared at her brother.

"You're unbelievably rude, Max. You're embarrassing me and yourself right now. Meira is the furthest thing from an opportunist. She lost her husband and her whole family in the war. The fact that she survived and is working to make a life for herself here is nothing short of admirable."

My eyes widened at Karen's outburst, and Max seemed a little shocked too.

He looked from me to his sister and back to me again. "I apologize. I didn't—"

"You should apologize. You're terrible sometimes, Max. Just terrible." She dabbed her napkin at eyes that looked perfectly dry to me.

Max released a heavy breath and then turned to me. "My little sister has spent the better part of the past year trying to set me up with women who I could only describe as . . ." He paused, searching for the right words.

"Fortune hunters?" Jerry suggested with an amused smile.

Max grimaced. "I was looking for something a little kinder."

"What is a fortune hunter?" I asked.

"Women who are only interested in Max for his money, because he obviously has nothing else going for him." Jerry grinned, and Max pinned him with a withering look.

"They were not fortune hunters," Karen said.

Jerry and Max exchanged a look that indicated they didn't agree with her.

"My parents are divorced," Jonathan said. "My mom moved out, and Aunt Karen thinks we need another mom to take her place, but Dad and I are fine on our own."

Max's expression filled with what looked like a mix of embarrassment and regret as he turned to his son.

I watched them curiously as I put the pieces together.

I knew what divorce was. A couple who attended our synagogue in Warsaw had a *gett*, a Jewish divorce, but there was shame attached to that situation, and I wondered if it was the same here.

There was an awkward silence after Jonathan's declaration.

"Well," I finally said, "since I am not a fortune hunter and there is no chance I would ever be interested in your brother, Karen, there is nothing for anyone to worry about."

Karen's eyes widened, and then she sputtered out a laugh.

I looked at Jerry, who winked at me, and then I dared look across the table at Max, who wore an amused smile. At that moment, I had to admit he was quite handsome. I wondered why he was divorced. I longed for my husband and child. How had Max willingly given up his family?

During dinner, I let the discussion Max and Jerry were having about business float by me. Jonathan asked me more questions about the war, but they were mainly about the types of guns the German soldiers used and the size of their tanks. Like Zotia's boys, he had silly ideas about war being made up of honor and artillery.

"Were you in a concentration camp?" Jonathan asked as Karen's maid cleared the dishes.

"Yes."

"Can I see the numbers on your arm? My friend Oscar's aunt has one of those tattoos, and it will never come off."

Jerry and Max stopped talking and turned their attention to me.

"I do not have a tattoo. They did not do that in every camp."

Jonathan seemed disappointed, and that didn't sit well with me. His notions were all wrong, and I found myself rolling up my sleeve to disavow him of the idea that war was anything but horrible.

"I have this instead of a tattoo." I held up my forearm so everyone could see the red puckered scar that dented both sides of my forearm. Because it had become infected, the scar was much worse than it otherwise might have been, fanning out from the center of my arm in angry red lines. "This is where I was shot."

"You got shot?" Jonathan sat forward to get a better look. "Who shot you?"

I looked at Max, wondering how much I should say. I didn't want to give the boy nightmares, but Max's expression was blank, giving no indication as to whether I should stop or continue.

"A Nazi soldier. You have heard of the gas chambers?" I asked, and Jonathan nodded. "Not every camp had gas chambers. They had not finished building it in the camp I was in. They had to use bullets instead."

His eyes got bigger. "You're lucky you only got shot in the arm."

Lucky. There was that word again. Rather than respond, I took a sip of water.

"Did it hurt?"

My eyes closed for a moment "Yes." The bullet didn't hurt me, but it ended Tovah's life.

"I think that's enough, Jonathan," Max said.

Jonathan stood. "Can I go to the bathroom?"

Max nodded at his son. I watched Jonathan walk down the hallway and turned back to find Max's gaze on me.

"I'm sorry if his questions bothered you," Max said.

"It is fine."

Feeling all their gazes on me, I looked downward as I folded and refolded the napkin on my lap. I hadn't cried in front of people in a long time, but for some reason, I found myself holding back tears. Maybe it was Jonathan and his curiosity. I hadn't spent much time with children since I arrived in America, and Jonathan was the age Tovah was when I lost her.

Feeling regretful, I rubbed my arm. "Maybe I should not have showed him." I directed my words to Max. "He has a romantic idea about war, like so many other children in this country who see war movies and know nothing about real life. A part of me wants to tell him about each and every horror, and another part hopes he never has to know such things can happen."

Karen reached out and laid her hand on mine. "The world is so ugly sometimes. I'm grateful my grandparents came here before the war, or who knows if any of us would be here now."

I nodded. "When the war was over and I learned the extent of what the Nazis had done, I could not believe it."

"We should have gotten involved sooner. Roosevelt knew what was going on, but he didn't want to get mixed up in it." Max shook his head and tossed his napkin onto the table.

"The German people knew too, even though they pretended not to," I said. "They lived with the camps and crematoriums right in their backyards. Of course they knew."

"I'm so sorry, Meira." Karen put her hand on my arm. "I can't even imagine it." After a long silence, she stood. "I'd better start cleaning up."

Jerry followed, picking up his plate and going into the kitchen.

"Well, I certainly know how to put a damper on a dinner party." I shook my head self-consciously as I stood to help.

Max's expression was sympathetic, but I found it hard to meet his eyes. I spent the rest of the night trying to avoid him, until it was time to go and he offered to walk me out.

chapter 12

"I was what you would call a wet blanket," I said as I watched two puppies chase each other across the grass in the park. "I ruined the dinner for everyone."

Mr. Diamond laughed and patted my knee. "I'm sure you were enchanting, Meira."

"Enchanting? If you call showing everyone at the table my scar and talking about death for half the night enchanting, then you are right. I was very enchanting."

"There isn't a single thing about you that's ugly, including your scar. It has meaning to you. It's part of who you are. If that young man didn't fall in love with you, then he's an idiot."

I narrowed my eyes at Mr. Diamond as the sun set in the distance. "He thought I was a fortune hunter. He says Karen has been setting him up with women who only want him for his money. He did not even want to come to the table to meet me."

"Definitely an idiot."

I smiled at his unwavering support. "That is not all. After dinner, we argued outside on the sidewalk when he tried to drive me home in his big fancy car."

Mr. Diamond raised a bushy gray eyebrow.

"I was perfectly fine on the subway. If he is so afraid of women wanting his money, he should not be so quick to show it off."

"Who won the argument?" he asked.

"There was no winning or losing. I simply walked away and went to the subway stop like I intended to in the first place."

"In the middle of the argument?"

I shrugged. "It was his argument. I had nothing further to say."

Mr. Diamond chuckled and turned to watch the puppies. "I'm glad you got out a little, Meira, even if it didn't go as planned. It's good for you to socialize."

I looked down at my hands folded in my lap. "Karen is nice, and her intentions were good. But last night, I looked at her and her husband, and I missed my family so much. I looked at Max's son, and I missed Tovah so hard, it felt like I could not breathe for a moment. Sometimes I ache so badly for her, it is like physical pain inside me. I do not think that will ever go away."

"Maybe not," he said. "But if you expose yourself to more people instead of keeping yourself apart from the rest of the world, you might learn to tolerate it better."

I smiled sadly, not believing him, but not wanting to disagree and argue.

"You're just marking time, aren't you, Meira? Waiting until you can join them."

Marking time? I hadn't thought of it that way.

"Everyone tells me that I am lucky to be alive, and it is true. Luck is the only reason I am still here. I am not worth more than they were. I am not better in any way. I just got shot in the arm instead of the head. Now every time I wake in the morning, it is a victory. It just does not feel that way. Sometimes the only reason I have to get up in the morning is to spite those who wanted me dead, and that is not a very good reason, is it?"

Mr. Diamond put a gentle hand on my arm. "Think of it this way. If just being alive is enough to spite them, imagine how living a happy life would make them feel?"

I couldn't help but smile at his unrelenting optimism. Looking at him, I thought how much like Papa he was. "You have a knack for bringing conversations around to where you want them."

"I have a knack for telling the truth."

We were quiet after that. Mr. Diamond seemed to know I needed company, not conversation, and he stayed on the bench with me as we watched the sun sink below the horizon.

It had already been a long day at the salon when I looked at the appointment book and saw that Karen Green would arrive soon. Inwardly, I cringed, because there was nothing about the dinner at her apartment that I wanted to rehash. I hoped she was able to keep it light the way she had before the idea of having me to dinner occurred to her.

As I cleaned up my area and waited for Karen, the owner, Mr. Walek, approached me.

"You should be friendlier to the clientele, Meira. They expect to come in here and gossip. You know, girl talk. You're good at hair, but your social graces could use some polishing."

My teeth grated together and then they gnashed even harder when his gaze lingered on my chest before he walked away. It wasn't the first time Mr. Walek had talked to me about my "social graces." I wondered which client of mine might have complained.

A few moments later, the door opened, and in walked Karen, teetering on her typical high heels with her very blond hair teased and pulled up into a swirl at the back of her head.

She looked across the salon to the back, where my chair was, and waved at me. To my surprise, her brother walked in behind her, filling the room with his tall presence, attracting the attention of more than one of the other hairdressers.

Karen grinned. "Max offered to give me a ride today. Wasn't that nice?"

Max smiled and then pushed a hand through his thick hair to keep it off his face. His smile was as jarring as it was surprising. He hadn't smiled much during dinner, and that smile, with all those perfect white teeth, lit up his face, making him seem less imposing.

"As long as he's here, I think he could use a cut too, if you have time," Karen said.

I nearly laughed as I glanced at all the women in the salon. Didn't men usually go to barbers?

"She's right. I could use a haircut," Max said, surprising me again because I assumed he'd dismiss his sister's suggestion.

"Of course she has time," Mr. Walek said immediately. Obviously, he'd been listening. "Men's cuts cost the same as ladies' cuts, in case you were wondering."

"That's fine," Max said.

With a happy smile, Karen plopped herself down into my chair.

"I'll wait outside until you're ready for me." Max turned and walked out of the salon.

Suspicion tickled my spine as I pulled the clip from Karen's hair. "Karen, I hope you are not still thinking that he and I—"

"No, don't worry. I'm done matchmaking. I've officially turned in my resignation. But don't be surprised if he apologizes to you about the other night. He made some silly assumptions, and now he feels really bad about it."

"He does not have to apologize. If that is the only reason he is getting his hair cut, it is not necessary."

"Let him grovel a little. It will be good for him. The truth is, you're the prettiest girl I've ever tried to set him up with. You're also the first woman not to give a lick about him, which I think he finds disconcerting." She bounced restlessly in the chair, obviously enjoying the idea of riling up her brother.

My hands stilled because I didn't like where this was going. "Karen . . ."

"Say no more. If you decide you want to have a man in your life again, I have no doubt that you can find one on your own. Max missed his shot. It would have been nice to have you as my sister-in-law, though." She giggled as I closed my eyes in frustration.

I trimmed her hair and curled it into a poodle style for a change. It was a little old-fashioned, but I'd been wanting to try it and Karen was game.

When I was done, she beamed. "I love it!"

The woman in the chair next to her grinned. "Oh, I'd like that too. Can you do that for me?" she asked Olivia, the hairdresser who worked next to me.

Olivia eyed Karen warily. She and I hadn't exchanged more than two words since I began working here. There were a group of hairdressers who had worked here for years and already formed a tight friendship. They made it clear when I got here that there was no room for me in their circle. They were all Americans, native New Yorkers, and I wasn't.

"I'll go tell Max you're ready for him." Karen left her usual generous tip and went outside.

I took a deep breath and cleaned up my area. Much to my surprise, the thought of cutting Max's hair left me feeling anxious. I would have to talk to him, touch him.

"I understand you're ready for me."

Max had to be well over six feet tall, and I startled a little when he suddenly loomed behind me.

"I could cut your hair if you like," Olivia said. "I doubt Meira has cut men's hair before, and I have lots of experience doing it." She batted her eyelashes, and my own eyes widened.

Max seemed a bit surprised. "I'd prefer Meira, but thank you anyway."

I fought a smile as I led him to the sink to wash his hair.

"She has lots of experience, apparently," Max whispered with amusement as he sat down.

I made a face. "Yes, and I am not surprised."

Max grinned, and my face warmed a little.

Clearing my throat, I turned the water on, waited for it to warm up, and then directed the nozzle at Max's hair. He had hair any woman would envy. Nearly black, save for the gray at his temples, thick and wavy, but not too curly. It was a masterpiece, and I didn't want to ruin it by taking too much off.

I worked the shampoo in and watched with fascination as his eyes closed and he made a low humming noise in his throat. His obvious satisfaction had me putting more pressure against his scalp as I scrubbed and ignored the airy fluttering in my chest. I recognized the feeling, even though it was a sensation I hadn't felt in a long time.

With Max's eyes closed, I took in the dark semicircle of his lashes against his cheeks. His eyebrows were thick dark slashes, and his jaw was strong and square. Once again, I wondered why his wife had left him. I understood that looks weren't everything, but other than his cynicism, I couldn't find anything wrong with him.

After rinsing out the shampoo, I asked him to sit up before I towel dried his hair. When he opened his eyes, they locked on me. A shock ran through my system, and I quickly looked away.

How did he do that? How did he look at me in a way that felt so jarring, like he was really seeing me, including all the parts I kept locked away, instead of seeing through me the way most people in this city did?

"Over here," I said, directing him to my chair.

Purposely not meeting his eyes in the mirror, I combed out his thick locks. "Just a trim," I said to him as much as to myself. "It is too pretty to chop off too much."

"Did you say my hair is pretty?" He arched a dark brow at me in the mirror.

"You know your hair is pretty, and your face is not bad either," I said quietly, thinking of how the other stylists kept sneaking glances at him. "But I think you know that already."

He tilted his head in surprise. "You're pretty, Meira, but you don't seem to know it at all."

My eyes clashed with his in the mirror.

He shifted in the chair and smiled a little shyly. "Sorry, I didn't mean to embarrass you."

"You did not." I concentrated on his hair, trying not to look at him in the mirror again. *He thinks I'm pretty?*

"Meira."

When I didn't respond, he said my name again and waited until I finally looked at him. "I want to apologize for how I behaved at dinner the other night. Between my parents and my sister, I've been thrown into more awkward situations than I care to mention. I was already married once. I don't know that I'll ever want to do that again."

I frowned. *Does he think I want to get married someday? To him? Is that why he's explaining himself to me?* "I suppose some hearts are meant to stay broken. Those around us should try to understand that."

His eyes caught mine in the mirror again, and something passed between us. But it was gone so quickly, I couldn't be sure what it was.

My hands kept moving when I asked the question that was none of my business. "Where is your wife, Max?"

He blinked in the mirror as if he'd been caught off guard. Then his gaze moved around the salon while he decided what he wanted to say. Finally, his eyes connected with mine again.

"She met someone else. She's engaged to him now."

I paused with the scissors in the air. "Oh. I am sorry."

He shook his head. "You don't have to be sorry for me. It's nothing compared to what you went through."

"It is not a contest."

Max pressed his lips together. "I know. But still, it puts things in perspective."

Perspective. Did he mean his life wasn't as bad as he thought it was because mine was so much worse? It might not have been a contest, but I'd won anyway.

Needing to lighten the mood, I glanced at him in the mirror. "Would you like some curlers in your hair? I am very good at the Betty Grable hairstyle."

Max blinked, and when he broke out in a deep laugh, I felt the effects of it all the way down to my toes. He was even more handsome when he wasn't acting so serious.

"Is that a yes?" I held up a pink curler.

"Maybe next time." He smiled, and after I handed him the bill, he surprised me by dropping a chaste kiss on my cheek before he walked outside to meet Karen.

Once he was gone, I stood there frozen for a long moment before I noticed the glares the other hairdressers aimed in my direction.

Clearing my throat, I got to work cleaning the area around my station, but images of Max didn't disappear from my mind so quickly.

chapter 13

The United Service for New Americans was located in a brick building on Sixteenth Street. It was run by a Jewish charitable organization for people who were displaced by the war and needed help rebuilding their lives in a new place. Eli gave me their address when I arrived in America, and they had arranged for my job and housing. Despite their willingness to help, I hadn't been back again, because their opinions didn't match mine about what I should be doing to rebuild my life.

Today, I had no reason to visit the USNA, but Blanka asked me to go with her, and I agreed as long as she would agree to go by subway. She was afraid to take the subway alone, and in my opinion, wasted too much money on taxis.

We walked into the narrow brick building and climbed the stairs to the third floor. Blanka announced herself to the woman at the front desk. Then, after waiting almost twenty minutes, we were shown into an office. It was my understanding that everyone who worked here was a volunteer, and so we didn't complain about the wait.

"I want to make more money," Blanka said to the woman who sat behind a desk cluttered with papers. A plaque said her name was Sylvia Lewis. "Cleaning houses does not give me enough."

Sylvia nodded in understanding and looked down at a list in front of her. "What are your skills?"

Blanka's lips twisted as she tried to think of something.

"She is a fast learner," I said quickly. "Even if she does not know something, she can learn."

Blanka smiled gratefully.

"What is your name?" Sylvia asked me.

I smiled politely. "That makes no difference. I am only here for Blanka."

"Her name is Meira Sokolow. Maybe you have a new job for her too."

"I do not want a new job." I gave Blanka an exasperated look.

Sylvia pulled some files from a drawer and scanned the papers inside. Slipping on a pair of glasses, she read for a few moments and then looked up at me. "Meira Sokolow, it says here that you can sew. You used to be a seamstress in Poland. I can get you a much better paying job than what you currently have. You could work at a department store doing alterations."

"No."

"No?" She eyed me over the top of her glasses. "Why not?"

"Because I do not want to do that."

Blanka stared at me. "It's more money, Meira."

"I do not care."

"Mrs. Sokolow, won't you reconsider?" Sylvia asked in a calm tone that indicated she wasn't done trying to reason with me. This was the same disagreement I had with this place when I first arrived.

"Do you know what I did in the camp?" I asked.

She shook her head.

"I sewed uniforms for the Nazis, and if I did not work fast enough, they would threaten to shoot me. I will not sew again. Not for anyone."

Her eyes widened. Seeming at a loss for words, Sylvia pressed her lips together and looked down at the paper again. It was the reaction I'd expected, but now I felt guilty.

"I am sorry. You could not have known that."

She made a noncommittal sound as she continued to read about me. "It says you were in the Poniatowa camp. I'm not familiar with that one. Have you given your testimony to the Jewish National League?"

"I talked to them in Warsaw after the war." I swallowed and averted my eyes, remembering the hours they made me talk about what happened, leaving out no details, while they wrote it all down.

"I'll have to look for it in the archives. It's important to capture all the testimonies in an official way. Did you know there are plans to sue the German government for reparations? I would think that you should receive something if that goes through."

"Reparations?"

"Money for what they took from you."

"They want to give me money? Can they give me back my family?" Familiar anger made my body go rigid. I couldn't sit here anymore and talk so reasonably with this woman who knew nothing about anything.

Excusing myself, I stood and pulled open the door.

"Please, wait." Sylvia stood. "It also says here that someone was inquiring about you. He left his name, but it doesn't look as if anyone has gotten in touch with you about it yet."

He? My thoughts suddenly raced with possibilities, even though it was foolish to hope it was Avrom or even Heinrich. I'd seen their names on the victims lists, along with Leah's.

"Who?" I breathed out the question more than asked it.

She squinted at a piece of paper. "David Lesner. We couldn't give out your information without your permission, but he left his address and a phone number where we can be reached."

"David?" Images came to me of the skinny boy I last saw in the ghetto. David was alive? "When was he here?"

"About three weeks ago," she said, looking contrite. "I don't know why no one called you."

"Who is he?" Blanka asked.

"A boy I knew in Poland. He was our neighbor, and then he saved our lives in the ghetto by smuggling in food. Last I knew, he stayed in the ghetto, vowing to fight the soldiers who were sent to clear everyone out."

When Sylvia handed me the paper with David's information, all I could do was stare at it, dumbfounded at this piece of the past that I now held in my hand. David was alive and here in New York City. He was one year older than Tovah, which would make him nineteen now.

Blanka sat up straighter, her eyes bright. "Let's go see him."

My stomach jumped at the thought. "No. Not right now."

"Why not?"

My mouth opened to answer, but I had nothing to say. I only knew I wasn't ready to see him yet. "You finish asking about a job. I will wait outside."

With the paper clutched in my hand, I went out into the hallway. Feeling too restless to stay in one place, I walked down the stairs and went outside to pace on the sidewalk.

David. My eyes squeezed closed because every image I had of David also included Tovah. At one time, I thought he and Tovah might make a good match someday. I was pretty sure he loved her.

Did he know Tovah was gone? He must have known. The Nazis were obsessive record keepers, and he probably checked the same victim lists I did when I was looking for Leah and Heinrich. I even looked for Avrom, even though I knew he'd likely been shot only minutes before we were.

I leaned back against the warm brick of the building and tried to catch my breath. It always felt dangerous to linger too long in those memories from the past. But today, I couldn't help myself. *David is alive.* It seemed impossible.

"I'm going to try working in a hospital," Blanka said when she joined me on the sidewalk. "After you walked out looking so upset, I think that lady sympathized with my situation more. I'm going to be a nurse's assistant. She said there's a training program I have to go to first, but the USNA will pay for it."

I heard Blanka, but it felt as if she was speaking from a great distance away.

She gripped my arm. "Meira, did you hear me?"

I blinked her into focus. "Yes, a nurse's assistant. That sounds important."

She studied my expression. "You're upset. You were surprised by that David person looking for you."

"Yes. That is an understatement."

"Were you two close?"

"No. He was close with Tovah, my daughter."

Blanka's eyes rounded. "Meira, you had a daughter?"

I glanced up to find her expression both shocked and hurt. I didn't know why I'd never told her about Tovah. Right after the war, when all I wanted to do was talk about Tovah and Avrom to keep their memories alive, I learned that no one wanted to hear all the tragic details of my life. They wanted to move on.

Blanka was different, though. I should have told her.

"She would have been eighteen now." It was almost impossible to believe that or to imagine what she would have been like. Nearly an adult, but still my baby.

"I'm sorry, Meira. That's why the idea of seeing him is so hard. He reminds you of your daughter." She put an arm around my shoulders. "You'll see him when you're ready."

I nodded, but I didn't know when I would ever be ready.

I felt raw when I went back to work the next day, like my skin had been ripped off and all my nerve endings were exposed. The paper with David's information was folded carefully in my purse, like a precious piece of jewelry or a direct line to another world that I never thought I'd visit again.

It was the wrong day for Mr. Walek to constantly remind me of my shortcomings when it came to chatting with the customers. It was the wrong day for him to leer at my cleavage or my legs every time he turned in my direction. And it was definitely the wrong day for him to squeeze my behind as he walked past.

Karen arrived for her appointment to find me out on the sidewalk, flustered, trying to stuff my collection of hairbrushes and clips into the paper bag I found in a cabinet after Mr. Walek fired me.

"Meira." She grinned, but her smile fell when she saw my expression. "You have to see someone else today. I do not work here anymore."

Her mouth opened in surprise. "What? Why?"

"I slapped my boss, and then he fired me."

Her eyebrows shot up to her hairline. "You did what?"

I glared through the window into the salon. I wasn't even upset so much as outraged by his behavior. "He touched my backside, and so I slapped him."

"You mean he copped a feel?"

"No. He squeezed my rear end with his hand."

"That's what cop a . . . Oh, never mind." Karen's eyes narrowed into slits. "Well, he can't do that, and I'm going to go in there and tell him that. Better yet, I'll send Jerry down to set him straight, or Max. Max won't like this one bit."

"No." I shook my head. "I do not want anyone to do anything."

"I can't believe you slapped him. I don't know if I could have done that. Where will you work now? I'll just follow you to whatever salon you go to next."

I released a heavy breath. Karen didn't understand. "It is not easy to find a new job for an immigrant. Mr. Walek hired me because he did not have to pay me much."

She made a face. "Well, that's not right. You're so talented."

I shrugged and gathered my things in my arms. Frankly, I didn't care about this job, and I was tired of dealing with all the people I saw here each day. I'd do better somewhere that I didn't have to talk to strangers.

"You can come to my apartment and do my hair. I'll tell my friends about you, and you can go to their apartments too. Then you won't have to find a new job and you can work for yourself. Be your own boss."

I pressed my lips together, remembering when I did that exact thing back in Poland, but I no longer had the heart for it. "We will see," I said without much enthusiasm.

"No, we won't see. Let's go over to my place now as long as you have all your things."

Sometimes her unrelenting optimism was too much to take. "Karen, please. I will do your hair whenever you want, but I do not want to be a hairdresser anymore." I pleaded with my eyes for her to understand.

Her expression softened, and the determination of only a second ago dissipated. "Can I at least give you a ride home since you're carrying so much?"

I smiled in relief. "Yes. Thank you."

We were quiet on the ride through the city, and I was grateful that Karen didn't try to fill the silence with more suggestions. When I got home, I was too restless to do much of anything, so I went for a walk to release some of the tension.

I'd only been home again for a few minutes when there was a knock at the door. I pulled it open, expecting to find one of Blanka's young friends, but was surprised to find Max standing there.

"Are you okay?" he asked, his expression tight and his eyes a little wild.

"I am fine." Suspicious of what his presence implied, I crossed my arms in front of me. "Karen told you what happened, after I asked her not to."

He looked sheepish. "She said you didn't want me to know. Can I come in?"

Obviously, she'd told him where I lived too.

Feeling as if I didn't have much choice, I pulled the door open wider and stepped back to let him inside. Dressed in a suit and tie, he walked in and looked around.

The apartment wasn't much. It was in an old building, but it had intricate moldings on the ceiling and a fireplace in the main room. It was cozy, and when I first came here, it was a relief to have a place that I shared with only one person instead of many. But still, it felt strange to have him here in my space.

"Would you like something to drink? Coffee?" I asked as he stood in my living room, looking at me now that his inspection of my apartment was finished.

"Just a glass of water."

I went to the kitchen and returned with his water. When he reached out to take it, I saw that his knuckles were bruised and swollen. "What happened to your hand?"

Max hesitated. "I went over to the salon before I came here."

I was so distracted by his presence in my living room that it took a moment for his words to register. "You went to the salon? And that is why your knuckles are bruised?"

He swallowed and averted his gaze.

"Oh no, Max. What did you do?"

Max pushed his injured hand through his hair. "I did what you think I did."

"You punched Walek?" I was shocked. Completely and utterly stunned.

"If your husband were here, he would have done the same thing."

"My husband?" My lips parted but no more words came out, because I didn't know what to say. Max felt like he had to stand up for me because I had no husband? A burst of anger flared in my belly. "You are not my husband. You had no right to get involved."

"Meira." He said my name calmly, as if my reaction was unreasonable.

"No." I shook my head. "You should not have done that. It is not your business."

Max had the nerve to look hurt at my words. "Meira, please. I didn't mean to overstep. But when Karen told me what happened, I didn't think. I just acted. After everything you've been through, I couldn't stomach the thought of anyone wronging you in any way."

The fact that he would do that for me was hard to believe. A man like him, in his fancy suit, walking into the salon and wiping that smug smile off of Mr. Walek's off his face with his fist? I had to admit, the more I thought about it, the less offended I was.

"Sit down," I said as I turned to get some alcohol and cotton balls. When I returned, Max was still standing there, looking unsure.

"Please, sit," I repeated, holding up the supplies so he'd understand my intentions.

"I came here to make sure *you* were okay." Despite his words, he sat on the couch anyway.

"I am not a delicate flower, Max. He did not cause any permanent damage."

One side of his mouth hitched up. "Karen said you slapped him."

"I did. Perhaps I should have punched him instead."

I lifted Max's hand to inspect his knuckles. His hand was large and tanned compared to my ghostly pallor. I sat a few inches away from him, but he turned when I touched him, and now his knee was pressed against mine. My skin warmed as I patted his knuckles with the alcohol.

When I lived in the displaced persons camp after the war, two kinds of people were there. Those who had lost their loved ones and were desperate to make new connections, and those who had lost their loves and wanted to remain alone. I was in the latter category, and it had been a very long time since anyone had made me feel anything.

Until now.

Max hissed when the alcohol touched the split skin of his knuckles, but I didn't stop until I was finished.

"How long have you been in New York?" he asked as I closed the bottle of rubbing alcohol.

"Almost three years."

He grinned.

"What is funny?"

"You mean *three* years? You pronounced it like *tree* years."

I smiled. "We do not have the *th* sound in Polish. It is hard for me to say."

"It wasn't a criticism. I like your accent."

I narrowed my eyes, wondering if he meant it.

"Why New York?"

"I have a sister here." Sitting back, I put a little more distance between us. His knee was still against mine, and that made it hard to think straight.

My answer seemed to surprise him.

"I didn't know you had family here. I thought you lost . . . I mean, I thought everyone was gone," he said, obviously trying to be delicate.

"My sister came to America before the war. It is only her and her family I have left. She has a husband and two sons."

"Do you see them often?"

I shook my head. "No. We are not close."

Max eyed me curiously, obviously wondering why I wasn't close with the only family I had left.

I sighed. "The truth is, I do not like her husband. That is one reason I do not see them often. Also, she is upset with me for another reason."

His dark brows arched up with curiosity, although he was too polite to ask. For some reason, I found myself telling him anyway.

"There was a misunderstanding over a boy when we were girls in Poland. She thought he was interested in her, but he had gotten our names mixed up, and it was me he liked. Our mother thought he would ask my sister to marry him, and she told everyone that an engagement was imminent. When he did not ask her, my sister was embarrassed. So embarrassed that she came to America to marry someone else."

"That someone else is the husband you don't like?"

"Yes."

"And what happened to the boy who didn't marry her?"

I smiled. "Avrom? He married me."

Max nodded as if that made perfect sense to him.

"It saved her life," I said. "Everything that she thought ruined her life saved it instead."

"But she's still upset about it?"

"I think so. But even before that, we were not close." I sighed, knowing if Papa were here, he would try to be the peacemaker. But the only person Zotia listened to was Eli, and he was the furthest thing from sensible.

"What will you do now that you don't have a job?" Max asked.

I'd been thinking about that, and since Zotia was the only thing keeping me here beside my job, I wasn't sure if I wanted to stay anymore.

"I was thinking of leaving the city and going someplace that is warmer, like California."

"California?" His eyes widened in surprise.

"I do not like the cold. I spent too many winters during the war without heat. I still recall the bone-chilling cold, and shiver for no reason sometimes."

Max scratched the back of his neck. "But you have heat now, and New York has a lot to offer. Have you been to Coney Island or Yankee Stadium? What about the Bronx Zoo or the Met?"

I shook my head.

He acted overly shocked. "Are you kidding? Those are the biggest attractions in the city you now call home, and you've never been to any of them?"

"You are teasing me." I smiled.

"I'm only stating a fact. You can't give up on a city you've hardly experienced. What are you doing this weekend?"

"Nothing. I used to work on Saturdays, but now that is done."

"Let's go to Coney Island. We'll have hot dogs and ride the Ferris wheel. It will be fun. You deserve to have some fun, Meira."

His invitation took me by surprise, and I automatically shook my head.

"Why not? You just said you're not doing anything."

With a sigh, I searched for an excuse. "Max . . . I do not think it is a good idea."

He studied my expression. "It won't be a date, if that's what you're worried about. You already heard my views on that the other night. This is just me showing you around."

My gaze met his again. I could still hardly believe he'd punched Mr. Walek. Why had Max done that? What did he want from me? And why did my chest feel so tight and uncomfortable at the thought of spending more time with him?

Max pushed a hand through his hair like he did so often. It was an endearing habit because it was so useless. His hair always fell back down over his forehead. *Just like Avrom's did.*

Avrom. Before the memory could hurt too much, I banished it from my thoughts. "All right, as long as it is not a date."

"All right?" He seemed more surprised by my agreement than I did.

"Yes, I suppose."

"Now you suppose." He laughed at my lukewarm response as he stood and took his empty glass over to the sink in the small galley kitchen area. "I'll see you Saturday then. Around eleven?"

Despite my reservations, I nodded. "I hope your hand feels better."

He thanked me, and then his gaze dropped to my hand and forearm, and the puckered scar there. Feeling self-conscious, I tugged my sleeve down.

"I'd like to hear your story someday, Meira," he said. "I can only imagine how much courage it must have taken to survive what you went through."

I scoffed. "It is not what you think. I did nothing extraordinary."

A knowing smile turned his lips. "You have no idea what I think."

Then he left, and I had nothing to do but wonder what he'd meant by that.

chapter 14

Music filtered through the air as the sky turned a dark shade of violet. It was Chopin's Ballade No. 1 in G minor, another slow, haunting piece that caused a lump to rise in my throat.

No puppies played in the park tonight, only children walking hand in hand with their mothers and fathers, and babies in strollers being pushed by parents who had to get home to make dinner. At least, that's where I imagined they were going.

Mr. Diamond joined me on the bench. "You look pensive, Meira."

"It is the music you are playing. It puts me in a pensive mood."

"That's all it is?"

I smiled at him and noticed the cookie crumbs caught in his beard again. Mr. Diamond had a sweet tooth, and it was fortunate that his tailor shop was located right next to a bakery.

"I was fired from my job."

He turned toward me. "Why?"

"My boss could not keep his hands to himself."

"What happened?"

I told him the story, and then went on to describe what Max had done in response.

"I like this Max," Mr. Diamond said, folding his hands on his lap and smiling at me.

"It was an odd thing for him to do. To stand in for my husband, or even assume that Avrom would have done something like that."

"Would Avrom have done that?"

I thought for a moment. "No. I do not think so. Avrom was much too calm and reasonable."

Mr. Diamond didn't comment. Instead, he waited patiently, seeming to sense I had more on my mind.

I glanced at him and rubbed my palms over my skirt, wiping off the perspiration. "A boy I knew in Poland was asking after me at the USNA office. I thought he was probably killed, like everyone else, but he is alive. Just hearing his name made my heart hurt."

Mr. Diamond frowned. "Why hurt? This is good news, isn't it?"

"Yes, of course it is."

"But you're upset?"

I turned to him with guilty tears pooling in my eyes. "I have his number and his address, but I have not called him or been to see him yet. I cannot think of him without thinking of Tovah and Avrom. In the ghetto, he tried to convince Avrom to hide in bunkers they had dug below the ghetto streets and fight the Nazis, but we thought it was a suicide mission. It *was* a suicide mission. The ghetto was completely destroyed in the end, and I cannot imagine how he survived. But maybe Avrom and Tovah would have survived too if we had listened to him. But we were afraid. We were always so afraid."

The tears I couldn't hold back any longer spilled down my cheeks.

"Oh, Meira." Mr. Diamond took my hands and held them tightly in his. "You can't blame yourself for everything you did or didn't do."

"I am always so angry. I find myself lashing out at people who do not deserve it. The woman at the USNA office suggested I take a seamstress job to make more money, and I made her feel terrible for even suggesting it." I shook my head. "But she did not do anything wrong. She was only trying to help, and I felt the need to punish her for it."

He squeezed my hands. "*Bubelah*, you're too hard on yourself."

I shook my head, and the tears spilled down onto my sweater. "I feel more distance growing between myself and their memories every day. They had no funerals. There are no graves to visit. I have nothing left of them. It has been years, and everyone thinks I should move on, but I cannot. I do not even want to."

I wept harder, and he gathered me in his arms, putting my head on his shoulder. I let myself sink against him. This wasn't the first time I'd cried on Mr. Diamond's shoulder, and it wouldn't be the last.

Thank goodness I had him. To the rest of the world, I looked as if I were a whole person. But with Mr. Diamond, I didn't have to pretend.

I opened my door on Saturday to find Max standing in the pouring rain with an umbrella and a determined look.

"We're not canceling."

I tried not to laugh at him and the puddle he was standing in. "It is raining."

"What rain? I don't see any rain."

This time, I did laugh. "We can go another day."

"Are you really scared of a little rain, Meira?"

I tilted my head. "I thought there was not any rain?"

"Exactly." He winked.

Shaking my head, I asked him to come inside while I got my raincoat.

Soon, I was seated in the passenger seat of his big yellow Mercury with a black pinstripe down the side, driving from Borough Park to Coney Island. I knew the car was a Mercury because there was a metal sign affixed to the dashboard in front of me that said so.

"There were only black and brown cars back in Poland," I said, amazed by all the flashy buttons and dials. "And horse-drawn carts."

"Did your family have a car?"

I laughed. "No one I knew had a car."

"So you never learned to drive then?"

I shook my head at how ridiculous the thought was. It made me wonder what Mama and Papa would think of New York City, how big everything was and how busy all the streets were all the time. Zotia must have experienced quite a culture shock when she first arrived. Our world and our neighborhood back in Poland, a place we hardly ever left, was so small in comparison, so insulated. Sometimes it was hard to believe it was all gone now. All the people. All the businesses. Gone.

As soon as the roller coaster came into view, the rain tapered off to a light drizzle. The parking lot had very few cars in it, and Max easily found a space by the entrance.

"Have you been to an amusement park before?" Max asked as we walked to the ticket booth with the hoods of our jackets pulled over our heads.

"No." I watched as the roller coaster came around, and the handful of people on the ride screamed out loud, their voices fading as the car zoomed away on the track. My blood started to pump faster.

"I took Jonathan here when his school let out for the summer. It's kind of our tradition." Max turned and saw where my attention was focused. "We don't have to go on every ride. We'll take it easy on you and hit the Ferris wheel first."

I read the letters on the side of the roller coaster. C-Y-C-L-O-N-E. "I would like to go on the roller coaster first."

"Really?"

When I nodded, he gave the ride an uneasy look. "You do not like it?"

He glanced at it again and grinned. "The first time my parents brought me here, it scared the living daylights out of me."

"And now?"

"Not much has changed." He looked chagrined to admit that.

"You do not have to come with me."

"Is that so?" He laughed, seeming to take my offer as a challenge.

With determination, he led us over to the ride, skirting around the puddles along the way. Since the line was so short, the moment the ride ended and the people stepped off, it was our turn.

Anticipation buzzed beneath my skin as I stepped into the small car with Max following behind me. We sat close together as a bar was lowered over our laps, the sides of our legs touching because the car was so narrow. Slowly, with a rhythmic chugging sound, it began to move.

"You're going to want to hold on." He took my hands and placed them on the bar.

There was a long buildup as we slowly inched our way over the track. Anticipation grew in my belly, and I felt Max's gaze on my face, watching to see my reaction. I didn't know what it was about this terrifying ride that attracted me. I'd been frightened enough in my life, and I'd heard far too many screams. But still, I needed to know what this felt like.

We finally reached the top of the incline and then suddenly, we dropped. It was fast and abrupt. My stomach pushed up into my throat as my head whipped back. Then it was yanked in the other direction as we turned and went upward again, my body tossed around like a rag doll. The few other people on the ride screeched with every turn, but Max stayed stoic as the car jerked sharply.

When we dropped again, I let go of the bar and put my arms over my head.

"What are you doing?" Max yelled as he reached for my arm to pull it down.

I laughed. Everyone else had their arms in the air, and I wondered if it was the free-fall sensation that I enjoyed or the feeling of disorientation? I didn't know. All I knew was that I felt alive, and I was too distracted to think about anything else.

"We should go again," I said when the car came to a stop.

He hesitated, appearing slightly pale.

"Max, it is okay. We do not have to."

He rubbed a hand over his face. "I'm good. Let's go again."

Knowing he wasn't good, I decided to have mercy on him. "No. That is all right. We can go to the Ferris wheel now."

His eyes narrowed. "We're going again, Meira."

Bracing himself with his hands on the bar, he faced forward and waited for the ride to start. I pretended not to notice how white his knuckles were. Max was such a good sport that we rode the Cyclone two more times. Then he bought me a hot dog for lunch.

"So, what do you think?" he asked, waiting for me to try it.

I'd forgotten that a hot dog sat in a roll. I eyed it and felt a wave of nausea. I couldn't eat bread, but Max was so excited for me to try one of Nathan's famous hot dogs, that I forced myself to take a bite.

He watched me, waiting for my opinion. "Are you okay?"

I nodded, trying to keep my expression neutral, but I couldn't make myself swallow it. Turning away, I spat it into a napkin.

He smiled good-naturedly. "You *really* don't like it."

"The hot dog part is good." I removed it from the roll. "I cannot eat bread, Max. It is a long story, but I do like the hot dog." I held it in a napkin and took another bite.

Max watched me, a combination of curiosity and concern on his face.

I smiled tightly and averted my gaze, relieved that he didn't ask me any questions.

We ended up going on the Ferris wheel last. The clouds had cleared by then, and the sun heated the wet air, making it thick with humidity. My hair curled around my face, and I had to keep pushing it behind my ears as we rose toward the top and stopped.

The view from the peak of the Ferris wheel was breathtaking. I could see the city on one side and the Atlantic Ocean on the other.

I smiled at Max. His life must have been busy, but today he was here with me, and he acted as if there was nothing else in the world he'd rather be doing. It made me wonder what his weekends were normally like. Did he spend them with his son? Did he still see his ex-wife?

"Does Jonathan like the Cyclone?" I asked.

I turned away from the view and found Max's eyes intent on me as they had been so often today. It was unnerving, the way he looked at me, like I was a puzzle he wanted to solve.

"Jonathan went on the Cyclone once, only once, and that was enough. Sarah wouldn't set foot on it."

"Sarah is your wife's name?"

He corrected me. "Ex-wife."

"That is hard to imagine. Being married to someone and then not being married to them. Did you love her?"

He was quiet for so long, I wondered if he would answer.

"I thought I did," he finally said. "But we were young. I was only twenty-three when we got married, and twenty-five when Jonathan was born. It took a while for us to see how incompatible we were."

Incompatible. That was an interesting word. I thought of Zotia and Eli. They seemed incompatible, but I couldn't imagine Zotia ever leaving Eli.

"How were you incompatible?"

"We had different values and different ideas about how a family should work."

"What do you mean?" I kept waiting for him to say it was none of my business, but he continued talking.

"Sarah didn't want her life to change after Jonathan was born. She wanted to go out every night and be seen around town. She had to have reservations at all the best restaurants and see all the latest shows. When I came home after work, I just wanted to stay home and spend time with her and Jonathan. I tried to play it her way for a while, but I wasn't happy, and we fought a lot."

The life he was describing was so different from anything I'd ever known. Family was a precious thing. At one time, it was the center of my life.

"In the end, she found someone who shared her interests more than I did. Maybe it was for the best, but at the time, I didn't think so. I don't like giving up or failing at anything." Max looked off into the distance. "But I don't know now. Most of the time, I'm too relieved not to be in that house anymore to have regrets."

"I am very sorry."

He acknowledged me with a sad smile. "I worry about Jonathan, though. I'm not sure he really understands what divorce means. I try to spend as much time with him as I can, so he knows I still love him and that nothing that happened was his fault."

"I am sure he knows. You are a good father. If you worry this much about his well-being, you must be."

Max gave me a grateful look, as if my good opinion truly mattered to him, and it stirred something inside me. Feelings of warmth and compassion grew in a place that had been empty for so long, and it felt uncomfortable. I went to turn away, but he took hold of my hand.

"Don't," he said, as if he knew I was about to shut down on him.

I looked at my hand in his and forced myself not to pull away.

"Tell me about your family," he said. "Something good. Something that makes you smile."

My gaze met his again, but the intensity in his eyes was gone. Only curiosity was there, and I wondered if he'd done that on purpose so as not to scare me off.

As I was about to give him a banal, automatic response, I stopped myself, because to my surprise, I wanted to talk. Not about Tovah or Avrom, that would be too difficult, but I could tell him about Papa. No one but Mr. Diamond had made me feel safe enough to do that before.

"I was a daddy's girl," I said. "I always found it easier to talk to my father than my mother or my sister. Papa was my ally and my mentor. He was solid and dependable and always so frustratingly reasonable." I laughed. "I told him everything, even all the things I had done wrong, because I felt too guilty to keep anything from him. I respected him. Everyone in the neighborhood did."

I paused, swallowing past the lump in my throat.

Max squeezed my hand. "I wish I could have met him."

"Me too." I looked out at the view of the city, thinking that Papa would have liked Max.

Max didn't let go of my hand until the Ferris wheel went around again and brought us back to the ground.

"Thank you for bringing me here," I said as we stepped off the ride.

"Have you changed your mind?" He smiled down at me. "Will you stay here, or are you still thinking about California?"

I chuckled. "Coney Island is nice, but it still has winter," I said, and he nodded solemnly, seeming genuinely disappointed that I was thinking of leaving. "To be honest, even though we do not always get along, it will be hard to move so far away from my sister."

"Where does she live?" he asked.

"Great Neck. I take the train every few months to go see her and my nephews. She has two boys."

Max was quiet as we walked across the parking lot. "You could see her more often if you didn't have to rely on the train."

I squinted at him. "You mean take the ferry instead?"

"Not the ferry, Meira. I meant it would be easier if you could drive yourself there."

The idea was so ludicrous, I laughed. "I told you, I do not drive."

"Just because you don't drive now doesn't mean you can't." He continued to walk toward his car in the parking lot.

Why was he persisting with this? "I do not drive, and I do not have a car, Max. I know my English is not the best, but I am sure you can understand me."

He laughed. "Sorry. I just think you might like to drive. It's a useful skill to have. I could help you get your driver's license, and a car too, if you decide you want one."

"You are joking." I'd never thought of myself driving. I didn't even know how I would go about learning, or if I could.

Max stood next to his Mercury now, on the passenger side, waiting for me. "I'm not joking. Let me teach you. After seeing you on that roller coaster, I bet you'd love it. You'd love the freedom it would give you."

"It is not practical. I cannot afford a car, and I do not have to drive to know how hard parking a car in this city is."

His unchanged expression said my excuses weren't going to make a difference. "One lesson. If you don't like it, there doesn't have to be another one. If you had a car, you could go anywhere the road took you. If you got tired of the city, you could drive to the country. You could even drive to California, if you wanted to."

I eyed him skeptically. "Me, drive all the way to California? You are crazy."

"Try it, Meira. What have you got to lose?"

My gaze moved from him to the car window, where I peered inside and examined the dashboard with all its buttons and dials. For a moment, I imagined myself in front of the steering wheel, maneuvering this big machine on the road, and I had to admit, I didn't hate the idea. I also didn't hate the freedom Max mentioned. I would be free to go anywhere at any time. There was a point in my life where I would have given anything for that kind of freedom.

I looked at Max's Mercury again. "Your car is expensive. What if I break it?"

He grinned. "You won't break it."

I squinted up at him. "Why would you want to teach me to drive?"

He lifted a shoulder. "Why not?"

His answer was so easy and casual. Surely, he had better things he could do with his free time.

"Don't overthink it, Meira. Just say yes."

I eyed the car, wondering what Papa would think. Back in Warsaw, he hated cars, with their noisy motors and horns, and the flashy rich people who owned them. But it wasn't only rich people who drove here in America. Everyone did. Maybe Max was right. It wouldn't hurt to learn.

"All right," I said hesitantly.

When I turned back to Max, he seemed far too pleased about my decision. It made me wonder why he wanted me to do this so much. It also made me wonder why I had agreed.

chapter 15

Would I regret my decision? That was the question I asked myself on the way home when Max suggested a time for this weekend's driving lesson.

The truth was that I was looking forward to the lesson, and it had been a long time since I'd looked forward to anything. But the excitement made me uneasy, because it wasn't just about the lesson.

In truth, I wanted to spend more time with Max. I liked how I felt when I was with him. I liked the way he looked at me as if I were the most attractive and interesting person he knew.

It had been a very long time since anyone looked at me that way. It was flattering, but it was frightening too. It made me feel things that reminded me of the girl I used to be. The girl who had a crush on the boy intended for her sister.

That girl's heart beat a little faster when Avrom smiled at her, and her breath stuttered when their eyes met. I was so young then, a naive child with no experience. I was nearly forty now and that naive girl was long gone, but when Max smiled at me, my feelings were so similar to hers.

Maybe it was a good sign that I felt this way. Maybe it signaled some kind of healing. The dark cloud that hung over me those years in hiding and then in the DP camp seemed less heavy lately. It wasn't gone, but it didn't loom as large. It didn't completely block out the sun.

I hadn't known Max long enough to think he was responsible for that, but the tiny spark of energy I felt when I opened my eyes the morning after our day at Coney Island must have been his doing. That spark said I could have a life again, if I wanted one. But did I? Was it disrespectful to move on? When Esther did it, I thought so. Why should it be any different now?

Time. I supposed that was it. More time had passed. The pain wasn't like an angry storm anymore, but more like a constant rain. Although sometimes that raw, familiar pain would sneak up on me and bring me to my knees, those times were fewer now, and that fact in itself hurt.

Later that week, I took the subway to the employment office at the USNA with a mission in mind.

"I would like to apologize for how I acted when you suggested a sewing job," I told Sylvia as I sat down across from her.

She blinked and paged through a file on her desk as if she didn't remember it.

"If it is more money, I think I would like this job now." I was thinking of Max and the possibility of owning a car that could take me anywhere. I needed money for that, and at one time, I enjoyed sewing. It reminded me of Papa.

Sylvia smiled. "Let's see if it's still available." She turned more pages in the file. "There's something at Gimbels. Are you familiar with that store?"

"Yes." It was one of the biggest department stores in the city. Of course I was familiar with it.

She scribbled on a piece of paper and handed it to me. "Take this over there and ask for Bailey Jones. Did I mention you get an employee discount?"

The alterations department at Gimbels was on the fourth floor in a small area behind the men's suits department. I walked through a sea of charcoal, black, and navy as I made my way toward the large archway that was the entrance.

Walking through the archway was like falling into a genie's bottle. Decorated in gold and apricot, the walls sparkled, and a round, cushioned bench in the middle of the room looked like something a sultan would sit on. There were two more doors off the main room, and I heard noises coming from one of them.

"Excuse me?" I called, moving toward the noise. "Hello?" I said after another moment.

"Can I help you?" A man in a dark suit leaned out of the doorway and looked me over.

"I am here for a job."

With barely concealed annoyance, he emerged and came to stand in front of me. His dark hair was neatly combed to the side, and his suit was perfectly pressed. Tall and thin, he cut a severe silhouette as he looked down his nose at me in disdain.

"Sylvia at the USNA office sent me," I said, undeterred. "I am looking for Bailey Jones."

His thin lips pressed together. "I'm Mr. Jones. Do you have any experience?"

"Yes."

He made a skeptical humming sound. "The last one she sent over said that too. She lied."

His appraising eyes moved from my face down to my clothes. I had on a white blouse tucked into a navy skirt. On my feet were comfortable flat loafers. My outfit was plain compared to most of the women in the store with their colorful dresses and high-heeled pumps. I wasn't fancy or ostentatious, but I was neat and presentable.

"You might as well come with me." Turning, he walked back into the room he'd emerged from.

I followed him to find two sewing machines set up on tables in the center of the room. All four walls were completely concealed by racks of clothing. This room had none of the decor of the main room, merely plain beige walls with green tile flooring. A tall dirty window looked out onto an alley in the back.

He pointed to the closest rack. "Everything here has been fitted and pinned. Just follow the measurements and use the matching thread that's attached to each bag. Do you think you can handle that?"

His condescending tone didn't escape me. I looked over at the Singer sewing machines, letting my gaze wander over the spools, and taking in the pedals on the floor. Just seeing them brought a tightness to my chest, and I pressed my hand to the base of my throat.

"Did you hear me? Should I speak slower?"

I narrowed in on Mr. Jones. "I heard you."

He smiled tightly. "Good. Then get started. We work Tuesday through Saturday. You get a twenty-minute lunch break at noon, and the day ends at five."

"My name is Meira Sokolow, by the way," I said when he turned without even asking.

"Last more than a week and then I'll learn your name, honey." He walked out of the room.

Anger tensed my muscles, but I shook it off and laughed softly. Did he really think a bad attitude would deter me? The world was filled with much scarier things than Bailey Jones. *Like sewing machines.* I surveyed the room again, trying not to picture another bigger room I sat in for hours at the camp, terrified to even look out the window.

No, Bailey Jones did not scare me.

I walked toward a sewing machine and let my fingers gently skim over the top. A chill ran through me, and I closed my eyes for a moment.

In Papa's shop, there were old machines with manual pedals. It was the same at the camp, where a single room held more than two dozen machines. Here they were electric with a thick cord that plugged into the wall. I'd always been a fast sewer, and I could only imagine how much faster the power of these machines would make me.

After a moment, I walked over to the racks where men's suits and women's dresses hung side by side. The suits were classic, no different from the ones my father used to tailor in Warsaw. Lapel styles had changed, along with coat buttons and sleeve lengths, but a classic suit was still much the same. The dresses, however, were very different from what I'd worked on before, much fancier and more colorful, not unlike those I saw on the streets of Manhattan each day.

Taking a deep breath, I reached for the dress that drew my eyes first. It was a deep royal blue with a cinched waist and pleats that caused the skirt to flare out. The top had a low neckline with a circular collar that I'd only seen in the movies on actresses like Barbara Stanwyck and Joan Crawford.

As I took it from the rack and noted the chalk marks, indicating where the cuts should be made, I wondered what type of woman had bought this dress. Obviously a wealthy one with a slim figure. The dress was different enough from the uniforms I'd sewn for the Nazis that perhaps past ghosts wouldn't haunt me as I worked.

I brought the dress over to the table and examined it again. Then I got to work.

After fumbling and pricking myself a few times, I got the hang of the modern sewing machine. In less than an hour, I finished the blue dress and moved on to a pink one. That one went much more quickly. Then I worked on the lavender one, and next was another blue one. The rhythm of the machine sped me along as I got lost in the sounds. I worked until there were no more dresses left on the rack, and I had no choice but to move on to the suits.

The suits themselves were lifeless and silent, but the burst of voices that echoed in my mind brought the material to life, filling it with ghosts. The suits reminded me first of Papa, then of Poniatowa. Compared to the dresses, which required me to think and plan, altering the suits should have been like second nature, but something in me resisted.

I bit my lip and forced myself to face them. Pulling one from the rack, my hand trembled. I hated how often I was on the verge of falling to pieces. Every time it happened, I felt defeated.

How many years had to go by before the memories stopped paralyzing me?

I took a few more minutes to pull myself together. Then, with grim determination and unsteady fingers, I began. Pushing away the dark thoughts that tried to creep in, I cut and stitched and cut and stitched in an even cadence, the way my father taught me.

Humming to distract myself, I kept my head down and kept moving without pause. I sewed until my neck was stiff and my fingers ached. When I came to the last suit, the sky outside the window had grown dark.

It was just after seven when I gathered my things and walked back out to the main room. It was eerily quiet, and I realized I was here alone.

Continuing through the archway, I left the store and made my way home.

chapter 16

"Have you called that boy yet?" Blanka asked the next morning.

"What boy?" I asked, even though I knew who she meant.

"The boy who was at the USNA office asking for you."

"I hate telephones. I have his address." I poured my coffee and focused my attention on my mug.

"Let's go there today," she said. "My classes end at three."

I sipped the hot coffee, letting it scald my throat on its way down.

"Meira?"

When I glanced up, she was rifling through my purse and pulled out the paper with David's address on it. I nearly tipped my mug over as I swiped it from her. "What are you doing?"

"Trying to see where he lives so I know how long it will take to get there. It says he's on Exeter Street in Forest Hills. That's in Queens."

Anger had me clenching my jaw as I stared at her. "Mind your own business, why don't you? Going through my purse, Blanka? Really?"

"I'm sorry." She looked hurt. "But I don't understand why you haven't gone to see him yet. If I found out someone I knew from home was looking for me, I'd run to see them."

"Blanka." I shook my head. She sounded so innocent and frivolous sometimes that it bothered me, because I knew what she'd been through. How did she shut out the pain so effectively and focus on the good things?

Before I could say anything else, a knock sounded at the door, and Blanka went to answer it. Happy for the reprieve, I turned back to the kitchen but paused when I heard Karen's voice in the hallway. After refolding the paper, I put it back in my bag and went to see what she was doing here.

"How exciting," she said as she entered the apartment and sought me out. "Meira, Blanka tells me someone you used to know is looking for you."

It was all I could do not to yell at Blanka in front of Karen. She opened the door only seconds ago, and already she was announcing my personal business to our visitor. With her blond hair worn up in a twist and her pumps clattering on our old wood floor, Karen was stylish and attractive enough to have Blanka's obvious admiration.

"Sorry to drop in like this, but you never pick up your telephone, Meira."

"She hates the telephone," Blanka said.

"Actually," I said, giving Blanka a pointed look, "I have not been home. I started a new job yesterday."

Karen beamed at me. "Really? Where?"

"Gimbels department store. I do alterations there now."

Karen tried to maintain her smile, but she couldn't quite manage it. "You're not at a new hair salon then?"

"No. But I will still do your hair whenever you like. Is that why you are here?"

"Never mind about that. Tell me about this person who's looking for you."

I pressed my lips together. "He is a boy I knew in Warsaw."

"That's wonderful news that he's here. But you haven't seen him yet?"

"No. There has been no time."

"Yes, there has," Blanka said.

I crossed my arms. "Blanka, please."

Karen looked between the two of us. Then she glanced curiously at the papers I had spread out on the table. It was the job application Gimbels had given me.

"I never had to fill out a form like this before," I explained. "I have no emergency contact to write down."

"What about me?" Blanka asked.

"You are a child."

Her hands went to her hips. "I'm twenty-four, Meira."

"Exactly."

"You can put me down," Karen said. "In fact, why don't I just fill out that section for you with all my information. Have you got a pen?"

Blanka handed her a pen, made a huffing sound, and then disappeared into her bedroom.

"Blanka and I are not getting along today," I said quietly after Blanka closed her door.

"She is awfully young. It would have been better if they'd placed you with someone you had more in common with. Have you thought about getting your own apartment?"

I shrugged. "It is too expensive."

She nodded and began to read the form. "I hear you and Max had a fun time the other day," she said a little too casually as she wrote on the paper.

"Yes."

"And you're seeing him again this weekend?" She finished and put the pen down.

I wondered if Max was volunteering our plans to Karen, or if she was interrogating him about us. Then I remembered our plans for tomorrow and felt a pang of disappointment.

"I forgot to tell Max. I work on Saturdays now at my new job. Can you please let him know that I cannot have a driving lesson on Saturday?"

Karen stood and gave me an appraising look. "Why don't you call him yourself and tell him? I can give you his number, if you don't have it."

Max had my telephone number but I hadn't taken his. It was cowardly, but I didn't want to call him. I was afraid he'd think I was making up an excuse, which I wasn't. I was also afraid to talk to him in general and to hear his voice in my ear, drawing me into conversation, making me laugh. I wasn't ready.

"Could you please let him know and apologize for me? I have to go to work now. Thank you for putting your name on the form."

I grabbed the paper off the table without glancing at it and stuffed it my purse.

Mr. Jones's steely blue eyes bored into me when I walked through the archway behind the men's suit department and entered the alterations area.

"You sewed every single article of clothing on that rack yesterday," he said. Once again, he stared down his nose at me, trying to intimidate me.

"Yes. Is there a problem?" I asked, not cowering before him the way he obviously expected.

He crossed his arms. "That was an entire week's worth of work. You did it in *one* day."

I arched an eyebrow at him. "That is good. No?"

"Good? No, it's not good. It's fantastic!" He laughed, revealing two rows of small white teeth. "Where on earth did you come from, Meira Sokolow?"

"Poland?" I said, confused. I thought the USNA had already told him that.

Mr. Jones rolled his eyes. "Yes, I know that. I meant where has Sylvia been hiding you?"

That time I didn't answer, because I didn't think he really believed Sylvia had been hiding me.

To my surprise, he put his arm around my shoulders and led me over to an area that had coffee and refreshments for the customers.

"You accomplished so much yesterday that we have time for a coffee break. You understand what a hero you've made me. I told those customers their clothes would be ready in a week, and when I called them this morning to let them know everything was ready now, I suddenly became their favorite person in the world."

"But I did the work."

"Yes, you did, and we'll just keep that between us. All right?"

I agreed, but inside I was rolling my eyes. It was fine that he wanted the credit, as long as I got the paycheck.

Despite how off-putting Mr. Jones's personality was, it felt good to know I'd impressed my new boss. It also made me wonder how incompetent the people who had this job before me were. Perhaps I could stay here for a while, and make enough money to get a new apartment and a new car. I could start to think beyond tomorrow and the day after that.

I got home that night after spending a very different kind of day with Mr. Jones, or Bailey, as he asked me to call him. He chatted with me the entire afternoon, gossiping about people I didn't know. To my surprise, I enjoyed the distraction of his silly conversation about the various customers who came into Gimbels. Bailey knew who was married to whom, and who was cheating on whom. I suspected that most of it was rumor or something he'd made up himself to entertain us both.

To my relief, Blanka wasn't home when I got back to the apartment. After a day filled with conversation, I craved the quiet. Sitting down in our living room, I took the folded paper out of my purse and stared at David's name written there.

I wanted to see him, but I couldn't bring myself to get on the train and go there. That filled me with guilt. He was still a young man, only nineteen, with no family left in the world. What kind of person was I to let him be here alone when he'd gone to the trouble of seeking me out?

Tomorrow was Sunday, and I had the morning to myself. I didn't work again until Tuesday. No matter how hard it was, the right thing to do was to go see David tomorrow. Knowing that was my intention, I spent a long restless night, trying to keep ghosts from the past at bay.

chapter 17

I'd thought going to Queens on a Sunday morning meant it wouldn't take as long to get from Borough Hills to Forest Hills, but I couldn't have been more wrong. There was no direct subway route, and over an hour had passed by the time I got on the train that would take me to the Forest Hills stop.

Max's suggestion of driving myself places by car sounded more appealing every day. But I'd canceled our lesson. Worse yet, I hadn't even called him directly; I had Karen do it.

Was he angry with me? Disappointed? Would he still want to teach me if I called him and asked? I suspected he would. He was too polite to turn me down, no matter how angry or hurt he might be.

It was drizzling by the time I exited the station. It seemed to always rain on the weekends in this city. Zotia had planned Eli's birthday party for today, which was supposed to be later this afternoon in their small yard. At this moment, she was probably making arrangements to move everything inside while he was blaming her for the rain, as if she held some power over the weather. I thought of finding an excuse to not attend the party, but I hadn't seen Zotia since before the summer, and declining wouldn't have been right.

I turned the page of the street map, gripping it tighter when I realized my hands were trembling. Whether it was from nerves or the cold, I didn't know, but both were certainly present that morning. The map was drenched, and I stuffed the disintegrating paper into my pocket as I walked along the sidewalk, my heels clicking out a quick rhythm.

I'd been filled with anxiety all night long, tossing and turning. Blanka hadn't helped when she got up early and asked to go with me.

I had to tell her no several times before she finally accepted my answer. This was something I needed to do by myself, and having her along, chatting the entire way, would have sent me over the edge. Because she had nothing else to do today, I invited her to come along with me to the birthday party this afternoon. I didn't think Zotia would mind one more guest, and I felt bad about how I'd spoken to Blanka yesterday.

Soon, I reached Exeter Street, where David's apartment building was. During the walk here, I'd been cold, but now perspiration rolled down my back as I lowered my umbrella and let the cold drizzle prick my skin.

What would he look like now? He'd been a tall, wiry boy when I last saw him. With his pale skin and shock of black hair, he'd moved quickly through the ghetto streets, dodging soldiers, hiding behind carts and debris, disappearing and reappearing like a ghost. He was always there when we needed him. Tovah's eyes lit up every time he appeared. Although she'd never said anything, I was sure he was her first and only crush.

Blinking away the memory and the pain that came with it, I made my way past the other apartment buildings that lined the street. When I finally reached the address, I stood there and stared.

The door was painted black, and scuffed all along the bottom as if it was kicked open as often as it was pushed. Like me, David probably didn't have much money, and I wondered what he did and how he spent his days. The skills he'd learned in the ghetto probably wouldn't do him much good when it came time to pay the rent in New York City. Unless he'd become a thief.

I rang the buzzer for his apartment number I'd been given. Some buzzers had labels with names typed on them. David's had no name.

After folding my umbrella, I wiped at the drops of water that ran down my hair and face. Even if I wasn't a sopping-wet mess, David would find me much changed.

Sometimes, when I looked in the mirror, I hardly recognized the woman looking back at me with her creased skin and haunted eyes. I wondered how Max could possibly find me attractive. If only he could have seen me before the war. Then the looks he gave me would make more sense.

When there was no response from inside the building, I rang the buzzer again. This was what I'd feared when I left for Queens this morning, that David wouldn't be here. I should have called first, but I couldn't imagine our first words in all this time being spoken over the telephone. I'd hoped that on a Sunday, the odds of him being at home would be higher. Just in case I missed him, in my bag was a piece of paper with my name, telephone number, and address written on it. I also wrote that he could find me at Gimbels during the day.

Carefully, I slid the paper through a narrow gap in the side of his mailbox, but when I turned to leave, I couldn't bring myself to walk away.

What if he'd run to the store and would be back any minute?

Deciding I had time to wait, at least for a little while, I opened my umbrella and walked back out to the stoop. As I stood there, I scrutinized the face of every man who walked past, wondering if it was David. It felt odd to look for a man and not a boy.

As I waited, my thoughts drifted. For once, I didn't try to stop them as I recalled David and Tovah playing in our old apartment. Avrom would come home, find them running up and down the stairwells, and tell Tovah it wasn't appropriate for a young lady to behave that way. The two of them would stop for a minute, and then start right up again once Avrom was gone.

When we lived in the ghetto, David would often return with more than food from his excursions to the other side of the wall. Sometimes he'd bring back puzzles, and once he came home with a chess set. He spent hours teaching Tovah how to play chess. I never learned, but Avrom would play with him sometimes. Mama and I stuck to card games and silly word scrambles to occupy Tovah and the other children.

Once Mama was gone, Tovah wasn't interested in games anymore. She wasn't interested in doing her math and reading lessons. Slowly, the girl I knew disappeared. She stopped talking so freely, and her smiles were few and far between. All the horrible things she saw each day stole the light from her eyes.

There were so many children, too thin and weak to stand up. People were rounded up and shot each day. Soldiers raped girls on the street corner, and then she saw her grandmother killed right before her eyes. She saw horrors no one should see, never mind a young girl. *My girl.* The girl I brought into a world that didn't deserve her.

I squeezed my eyes closed and shivered. My teeth chattered as the rain came down harder. With David's presence looming so large in my mind, even though I knew the dangers, I didn't try to squelch the memories. I let them cascade over me like the rain. I needed to feel close to Tovah, to remember the smell of her hair and the sweet sound of her voice.

"You're drawing butterflies," I said to Tovah.

She nodded. *"I saw one. It landed on my sleeve, and when I tried to touch it, it flew away."*

"What color was it?"

"Yellow with black on the tips of its wings. I thought maybe it was Zayde saying hello. Maybe there are lots of butterflies where Zayde went. If I die, Mama, I'll try to come back and give you a butterfly kiss too."

Tears welled in my eyes. Where was my butterfly kiss? Perhaps Tovah had forgotten. Maybe wherever she was, she was so happy, there was no need to come back for butterfly kisses. I hoped so. Her little spirit deserved so much better than this life gave her.

"Remove your clothing and lay down in the ditch." The soldier punctuated his order with the barrel of his gun.

Tovah and I took off our clothes, trembling from fear more than from the autumn chill in the air. I climbed down first and turned to bring Tovah with me.

"Cover my eyes, Mama," she whispered.

Standing on the stoop, I covered my own eyes and pressed my fists into them to make the images disappear. But they wouldn't stop. There was no filtering out the nightmare and leaving only the good moments. Once the train left the station, there was no calling it back. I heard the echo of gunshots, smelled the metallic scent of blood in the air, heard the moans of the dying rise up from the ditch.

No. No. No.

Something pressed on my shoulder, and my blood ran cold.

It felt like a hand, and I whirled around to knock it away. The shadow that touched me took a step back and said my name.

Struggling to focus, I blinked against the rain, and a pair of worried green eyes came into view. They were eyes I recognized, eyes that weren't from the past. I wasn't back in Poland with Tovah. I was in New York City, and Max was here, soaking wet, with his clothes plastered to his body.

When I didn't say anything because I hadn't found my voice yet, his face took on a desperate look, like he wanted to help but didn't know how. The next thing I knew, he'd pulled me into his arms and said that it was going to be okay. His hand moved over my back, up and down, as he repeated reassurances into my ear. It was so easy to lean into the warmth of his body and take comfort in the strength of his arms.

"Did something happen? Did you see your friend?" he asked.

Comforted by the way his voice rumbled in his chest, I let myself lean on him for another moment before I took a step back. "What are you doing here?"

Rather than answer, Max scanned my face. "You're shivering, Meira. My car is right over there. Can we talk inside?"

I must have been quite a sight. My teeth were chattering and my clothes were soaked through, but his were too. How long had I been standing there? How long had he tried to get my attention when I was too lost in my own head to notice?

Max took my arm and walked me toward his car parked by the curb. After getting me settled inside, he took something out of the trunk before he slid in on the driver's side and handed me a blanket.

"Thank you," I said quietly, and used it to wipe the rain from my face before handing it back for him to use.

"Put it around yourself. You're shivering."

"You are cold too." I handed it back again, feeling bad that he was cold and wet because of me.

"Meira. For God's sake," he muttered through clenched teeth. Taking the blanket from me, he reached behind me and pulled it around my shoulders, then deposited the ends in my lap.

My cheeks heated with embarrassment as he huffed from his side of the car and pushed his hand through the wet hair that hung in his face.

"How did you know I was here?" I asked.

"I went by your apartment and spoke to Blanka. She was worried when you didn't come home in time to get ready to go to some party. She told me I might find you here. She knew the street, but she didn't remember the exact address. So I've been driving up and down Exeter for the past twenty minutes looking for you."

I shrank down further into the blanket. "I am sorry. You did not have to come."

"You don't have to apologize."

"You are angry, and I—"

He turned to face me. "You think I'm angry with you? I'm not, Meira. I'm worried. What would have happened if I hadn't found you? How long would you have stood there like that? My God, your eyes were so haunted. It was like you didn't even know where you were."

Haunted. He was right.

"Why didn't you tell me about your plan to come here when we were at Coney Island? We spent the whole afternoon together, and you never said a word. I would have driven you if I'd known. I could have been here for you. Helped you through this." The way he spoke, it was as if he thought we were a couple.

"I am fine, Max. I have been fine on my own for a very long time. Please do not take it personally. I told no one. I talk to no one, not about anything. Blanka only knows because she was there with me when I found out about David."

Max looked at me for a long moment. He seemed to want to say something, but changed his mind as his shoulders sank and whatever he was feeling drained away. I couldn't tell if he was angry anymore when he sighed and turned to face forward, away from me.

"Tell me about this David," he said. "Blanka said he was someone you knew in Poland. Someone you didn't even realize was alive until he tried to get in touch with you."

"Yes. That is right."

Max waited for me to say more, but I didn't even know where to start. How could I make him understand who David was and what he represented?

When I didn't answer right away, he looked hurt. "If you missed David today, you can come back another time. If you won't ask me to drive you, at least go when the weather is better."

His defeated tone tugged at my heart. "Please understand, Max. It is hard for me to talk. After the war, all I wanted to do was talk, but no one cared, and that made it so much worse. Now, after being silent about it for so long, it is hard to talk. When I do, it all comes back like it was yesterday. If I am going to wake up each morning and get out of bed, it cannot feel like it happened yesterday. Do you understand? I do not want to hurt you or disappoint you. You have only been kind to me. But if you expect more from me than I can give you, I am afraid I will always disappoint you."

He blinked, and sadness seeped into his eyes. "I could never understand or even imagine what you went through, but you will never disappoint me, Meira. Surprise me? Yes. Impress me? Definitely. But disappointing me is one thing you don't have to worry about."

His smile was hesitant when it came, but I was relieved to see it.

Max started the motor and looked over his shoulder to check for traffic as I tried to think of a way to make things right with him. He was so kind and caring. Hurting him was the last thing I wanted. If it pleased him to drive me places so I didn't have to take the train, perhaps I could ask him to drive me to Zotia's house today. As much as I disliked asking anyone for help, with Max it was different.

"The party I have to go to this afternoon is for my brother-in-law's birthday. They live on Long Island," I said.

He glanced at me. "Great Neck. You mentioned that."

"Right. Like you said, it is a long way on the train."

"It is," he said after a moment, and one side of his mouth turned up slightly.

I cleared my throat. "Maybe, if you are free, you could drive me? If you do not mind."

He glanced at me again. "I'd be happy to drive you to Great Neck, Meira."

I smiled gratefully. A part of me wondered if he'd say no or hold a grudge, but I should have known better. That wasn't who Max was. "Blanka too, if you do not mind that either. I invited her to come along."

"I don't mind at all."

"Thank you."

The tension between us lifted, and I pulled the blanket tighter around my shoulders.

Max feeling hurt because of me was the worst feeling I'd had in a long time. As much as I didn't want to hurt him again, I couldn't promise him or myself that I wouldn't.

chapter 18

When Max came back to our apartment after going home to change his clothes, Blanka was so flustered by him that she gawked awkwardly and could hardly string two words together. Tall and lean, dressed casually in a fitted button-down shirt that accentuated his broad shoulders, Max cut a handsome figure.

"Are you sure this is all right? You do not have Jonathan today?"

"He's with Karen and Jerry. I have plenty of time."

"Well, thank you again," I said as I grabbed the present I'd wrapped for Eli and smoothed down my dress.

"You look very nice, Meira. And so do you," he said to Blanka, which caused her face to turn the color of a tomato.

Max's gaze returned to me and lingered long enough to make my cheeks feel a little flushed too.

"You will come in and meet my family?" I asked Max, knowing it was the polite thing to do, even though I was torn as to whether I wanted Max to stay or not. Eli could be embarrassing. He was practically a different species from Max. Where Max was well-spoken, well-mannered, and oozed class, Eli was none of those things. But it was rude not to invite Max to stay after driving us so far.

"I'd love to meet your family," he said. "But I have a few things I could do in the area while I'm there, so I don't have to stay."

"Oh." Did that mean he didn't want to stay? If so, why was I disappointed? Turning away to hide my expression, I retrieved my coat and purse, and then we all filed outside.

In Max's car on the way to Great Neck, we chatted about my new job and Blanka's nurse training. Max mostly kept the conversation going by asking us questions. I had to admit, he was easy to talk to, and he said nothing about this morning, which I appreciated.

When we pulled up to Eli and Zotia's brick townhouse, there were balloons tied to the railing next to the front steps.

"How old is your brother-in-law?" Max asked.

"Fifty today."

"That old?" Blanka said from the back, and Max and I exchanged amused looks.

"What did you get him?" she asked, handing me the wrapped present from the back seat.

"A shirt from Gimbels. I get a discount."

Her eyes widened. "You didn't tell me that. Can I use your discount?"

"I am not sure. I can find out." I hadn't mentioned the discount to her because I didn't want to get into trouble for abusing it. Despite Blanka's lack of money, she loved to shop.

Max got out and came around to open the door for Blanka and me. We were late, and cars were already lined up on the street. Even though the roads were still wet, the rain had finally stopped about a half hour into the ride.

"Your brother-in-law was born here in the States?" Max asked.

"Yes. His family has been here for generations, as he would happily tell you."

Blanka chuckled and wrinkled her nose. "Meira doesn't like him. She doesn't think he likes her very much either."

"Blanka, shush. We are standing outside his house."

Max gave me a long look. "Maybe I'll stay for a little while, if you don't think they'll mind."

I bit back a smile, a little too pleased. "I can promise the food will be good. My sister learned to cook from my mother. I spent more time at the tailor shop with my father."

Zotia must have seen us on the walkway. Before we reached the door, she pulled it open, and the noise from inside spilled out.

"Meira, thank goodness. I could use some help. Eli invited every one of his customers and only told me this morning." She looked past me and noticed I wasn't alone.

She'd greeted me in Yiddish, but I made the introductions in English so she would know to use that. "You have met Blanka before, and this is Max."

Zotia smiled politely at them both, but curiosity lit her eyes when she turned to Max.

"Nice to meet you." Max smiled and nodded at her.

"You could have warned me you were bringing people so I would have enough food," Zotia said in Yiddish.

I shot Blanka an embarrassed look. She understood Yiddish, and Zotia knew that. "I am sorry. It was all very last minute."

"Never mind. It is fine. Eli is in a good mood today. Someone brought him a forty-year-old bottle of Scotch. Forty years old, but I bet it will not last the day."

Blanka raised her eyebrows at me as we all walked inside.

"Everything okay?" Max asked.

"Of course." I gave him a tight smile.

The noise level increased as we entered the living room, filled with their friends. It always surprised me that Eli had so many acquaintances and customers. I supposed he could be jovial and fun when he wanted to be. He certainly liked to talk a lot and tell jokes. Other Americans seemed to like that.

As I looked around, I saw some familiar faces I'd seen at Zotia and Eli's summer barbecues in years past, and some new faces I didn't recognize. Every time I came to Zotia's house for a gathering, I couldn't help but think about who was missing. *Our family.* They should have been here to celebrate each occasion. I tried to picture them standing in Zotia's living room, chatting and laughing, but this house was so modern and Americans dressed so colorfully, it was nearly impossible to picture them here. They wouldn't have fit in, just like I didn't quite fit in either.

"Where are Jacob and Isaac?" I asked Zotia, referring to my nephews. It was hard to believe Isaac would be heading to college soon.

"Off with their friends somewhere."

Eli broke away from his friends to welcome me with a kiss on the cheek, and I introduced Blanka and Max to him. I should have anticipated an embarrassing comment when Eli turned wide eyes in my direction as he shook Max's hand.

"Have you finally got yourself a boyfriend, Meira?" he asked, and then he spoke to Max. "How did you manage that? This one's a tough nut to crack."

I knew better than to let Eli's comments affect me anymore, but having Max hear them made my cheeks redden.

Max narrowed his gaze on Eli, but before he could say something, I redirected the conversation to Eli's gifts and asked what his favorite was so far. That launched him into an enthusiastic speech about receiving season tickets to Yankee Stadium from one of his customers.

When he was finished, I escaped into the kitchen where Zotia was putting together sandwiches at the counter. I moved beside her to offer my help.

"So . . . Max," she said, and waited for me to explain him.

"He is a friend."

"Just a friend?"

"Yes."

Zotia eyed me for a moment before making another sandwich. "You know, it would be okay if he were more. Avrom has been gone a long time."

My hands paused, and I turned to her with raised eyebrows.

"What? You do not think I want you to be happy?"

I chose my words carefully. "I would hope so. I want you to be happy."

She made a huffing sound. "You do not believe I am happy?"

Zotia got defensive so easily because she knew I wasn't a fan of Eli. "If you tell me you are happy, I will believe you. But you have never told me that."

She put the container of mustard on the counter and turned to face me. "How can I tell you that? How callous would that be? Happiness would be having Mama and Papa here, and Leah too. My happiness is like this cheese." She held up a slice of swiss. "Filled with holes. I will never be completely happy, and that is why I do not go around saying how happy I am. Can you understand that?"

I nodded and swallowed the emotions her words evoked. "I understand too well. In that way, we are alike."

Zotia turned back to the sandwiches. "Our happiness will never be complete. But we can still find some. I hope you find yours, Meira. I really do."

Before I could respond, she picked up a tray of sandwiches and went back out into the living room.

Closing my eyes, I leaned against the counter and ran her words through my head. Zotia surprised me sometimes. *Happiness that was filled with holes.* That sounded like something Papa would say if he were here.

I blinked away the tears that threatened to fall and arranged another tray of sandwiches. Then I walked back out into the commotion of the living room.

It was easy to spot Max. He towered over most of the men here, and all of the women. He was talking to one of Eli's friends and said something that caused Eli to join the conversation.

I took the opportunity to watch Max without him knowing. My gaze took in the square cut of his jaw with its dark shadow of stubble. His hair was perfect, thick and soft, and always a little mussed. I knew how soft it was because I'd run my fingers through it when I cut it for him. I also knew how muscular his arms and chest were, because he held me against him when he found me in the rain.

Did Max want more than the help he so readily offered? He claimed he didn't want to date, but the way he looked at me and how hurt he'd been when I didn't share the details of my life said something different.

What if he did want more? Did I? Other than admiring his looks, which any woman with a pulse would do, was I developing a genuine affection for Max?

Yes. The answer came quickly. Too quickly.

But was I ready for anything more? I didn't know. I told Max I would disappoint him, and I was afraid it was true.

Releasing a frustrated breath, I watched Max smile and chat. He turned and caught me staring. My face flushed, and his eyes immediately warmed as he watched me from across the room.

"Meira!" Eli called, beckoning me over to them. "You didn't mention that your friend Max works for Goldman Sachs."

"What is that?" I asked, coming to stand with them, and Eli laughed at me.

"It's the firm I'm at," Max said. "It's fairly well-known."

"Fairly?" Eli laughed again and turned his full attention on Max. "I've had this idea of franchising my stores for years. Let me put a proposal together and send it over to you."

Max scratched his cheek. "We don't generally invest in small businesses."

"There's nothing small about our business. Come down and take a look. This could be good for you too. We've got a perfect location right on Cedar Drive. Plenty of traffic around there. People on foot and in cars."

Max looked so uncomfortable, I felt the need to rescue him.

"Eli," I said. "You should enjoy your birthday party. There will be plenty of time for business again on Monday."

"Shut up, Meira. You have no idea what you're talking about."

I pressed my lips together, mortified to be spoken to that way in front of Max.

"Excuse me? What did you say to her?" Max asked.

When I looked at him, I was surprised at the thunder in Max's expression.

Despite his lack of sensitivity, Eli seemed to realize his error.

"I only meant that she doesn't know anything about business. She's a woman, and fresh off the boat too." He laughed to lighten the sting of his words.

"I have yet to find anything that Meira doesn't understand. For example, she's especially perceptive about people." Max excused both of us from the conversation and used the pressure of his hand on my lower back to maneuver me away.

"I am so sorry," I said under my breath, still embarrassed, even though I was silently cheering at the way Max defended me. I only hoped I wouldn't get an earful from Zotia later.

"You don't have to be sorry for him. If that's how he speaks to you, I can see why you don't like him."

Looking up at Max, I smiled, thinking of how he also stood up for me with Mr. Walek at the salon. It seemed Max was determined to save me from all wrongs the world might inflict. If only he could.

"What are you two doing over here in the corner?" Blanka asked. She held one of the brisket sandwiches I'd made. "You were right about the food. It's delicious."

I tore my gaze from Max and fell into a conversation with Blanka. We stayed at the party a little longer, and despite my fears. Eli didn't approach Max again. He stayed huddled with his friends, drinking his Scotch.

Soon, we offered our farewells to Zotia, and she insisted on sending Blanka back to the city with some leftovers after she raved about the food.

Back in the car, Blanka filled the air with talk about the different people she'd met, what they did, and where they lived.

When Max stopped in front of our building, he said, "Stay a minute, Meira."

Blanka raised her eyebrows at me and slid out of the back seat to go inside.

When she was gone, Max turned to face me with a surprisingly somber expression. "Are you going to be all right?"

"You mean because of what Eli said? Yes, of course. I do not let him bother me."

"No," he said quietly. "I'm thinking of what happened earlier today. I can't seem to stop thinking about it. The look on your face when I found you on that stoop, it scared me."

"Oh." I turned away from the concern in his eyes.

"Who is David?"

I released a shaky breath. "He was a boy I used to know."

"Yes, you said as much. That's all? A boy you knew upset you that much?" He sounded skeptical.

"No. That is not all, Max. That is not even close to being all. But . . ." I shook my head. "What you are asking for is a very hard conversation. Someday I will tell you, but not today. Not sitting here in your car when I am about to go inside and go to sleep. If I tell you now, there will be no sleep for me, not for a long time."

Max's expression fell. His eyes tightened and familiar frustration darkened his expression. "All right, Meira. I won't ask you to explain if it upsets you. Just promise you'll call me to take you when you go back to see him?"

"I will. I promise." Based on the disappointment in Max's voice, I didn't think it was all right. He wanted me to trust him enough to tell him everything when he asked, but it wasn't that simple. Despite his saying that I couldn't disappoint him, that was how it felt.

When I walked into the apartment, I found Blanka sitting on the couch, already digging into the food Zotia had packed for her.

"Did you enjoy the party?" I asked her.

She grinned. "I did. And I really like Max."

I smiled. It was obvious how much she liked him.

"He really likes you, Meira. When you weren't with him, he kept looking around the room for you. Then when he saw you, his whole face lit up. It was so romantic."

Butterflies fluttered in my stomach at the thought of that being true.

"Do you like him the way he likes you?" she asked.

Perhaps I can. Perhaps I already do. "I am glad you had fun at the party, but I am tired. I am going to bed now."

"Because if you don't like Max, you won't mind if I go on a date with him."

My steps faltered. "Wh-what?"

She smiled and took a bite of a cookie. "Would you mind if I dated Max?"

My lips pressed together. "He is too old for you."

"You said I would do well with an older man."

"Blanka." I pressed my fingers to the pounding that had begun in my temples.

She laughed. "I'm teasing, Meira. I just want you to admit you like him."

With a scowl, I sat down on the couch beside her and took a cookie from the container. "It is complicated."

She grinned. "Then you do like him."

"I did not say that. I said it is complicated."

"That's because liking him is complicated. Not liking him would be easy."

I couldn't help but laugh because she was right. It would be so much easier if I didn't like Max.

Settling into the cushions, I tried to imagine Max and me together, but I couldn't. With Avrom, we were so similar that we fit together easily. We were friends, and we loved each other, but we didn't consume each other.

With Max, it would be different. Everything about Max was *more*, somehow. He was more charismatic, more intimidating, and more direct. He had a possessiveness about him in the way he wanted to protect me and defend me. He was kind and patient, but he was also determined. If I were with Max, he would demand everything from me—body, mind, and soul, but I wasn't ready for that. I didn't know if I would ever be ready for a man like Max.

"Are you too tired to play gin rummy?" Blanka asked.

"Go get the cards," I said, happy for something to take my mind off my thoughts.

With a little cheer, Blanka leaped off the couch. I smiled as she rifled through a drawer in the kitchen, looking for the deck of cards.

In a different universe, would Tovah have grown up to be like Blanka, happy and frivolous, so easily pleased by the smallest things? If so, I wouldn't have minded, because Blanka was definitely growing on me.

chapter 19

There was a chill in the air. Fall was approaching. I dreaded fall, not only for the cold that it brought, but because I lost Tovah and Avrom in the fall.

"Here again, *bubelah*?"

Mr. Diamond lowered himself onto the bench beside me. It seemed that he moved slower and more carefully than usual.

"Is your arthritis acting up again?"

He shrugged. "If it isn't one thing, it's another."

The musical tones of Chopin drifted from his shop, and I smiled at his thoughtfulness. "I'm going to synagogue to say a *kaddish* for my husband and daughter. Would you like to come along?"

"Don't you have someone else you could ask to go with you?" he asked.

"I thought you might want to pray for the family you lost too."

He shook his head. "I don't need to go somewhere to pray for my family, Meira."

Looking out at the children playing in the park, I understood how he felt. "I go this time of year because it's when they died, and I want to honor our traditions. Papa would want me to do that, but I don't know that anyone hears me. I don't know that I believe in anything anymore."

Mr. Diamond patted my hand. "If going to synagogue to say *kaddish* helps you feel closer to those you lost, then maybe that's enough, whether they hear you or not."

It wasn't enough, but maybe that's all there was. "Did I ever tell you about the butterfly Tovah saw?" I asked.

"The butterfly?"

I smiled at the memory. "After my father died, Tovah saw a yellow butterfly in the ghetto. She said it landed on her, and then it flew away. Everything was so bleak that seeing one yellow butterfly felt magical. She thought it might be her grandfather's spirit coming to say hello, giving her a butterfly kiss. Tovah said if she died, she'd come back as a yellow butterfly to give me a kiss."

He smiled kindly. "And have you seen any yellow butterflies?"

"No. I haven't seen a single one."

His large weathered hand encircled my smaller one. "The butterflies are there. Even when you don't see them."

I looked at the city around me, hoping that was true. "When I first came to New York, I promised myself I'd tell my nephews about the family they lost to keep their memories alive. Then I met my brother-in-law, and I let the notion go, but I was wrong. No matter what Eli thinks, his children should know who their grandparents were and what they were like. They should know they had a cousin, a beautiful little girl, and a kind uncle. They should know their family, even though they will never meet them."

"You should talk about them more. I think it would be good for you."

Biting my lip, I nodded, even though I wasn't sure that was true.

"And what of the boy from the ghetto?"

A red ball came bouncing in our direction. I bent to pick it up and tossed it back to a girl who waited with outstretched arms.

"I tried to see him," I said as I kept my gaze on the girl and her ball. "He wasn't home. Something happened when I was there."

"What do you mean?" Mr. Diamond shifted on the bench, resting his arm along the back of it as he waited for me to continue.

"I thought about the past and lost track of time. I stood there shivering in the rain for I don't know how long before Max found me."

"Max again." Mr. Diamond gave me a small smile that lifted the white hairs of his mustache and beard. "Your eyes shine a little brighter when you say his name."

I smiled wistfully, knowing it was probably true.

He squeezed my hand and released it. "If he's who your heart wants, your head will eventually warm to the idea. Give it time."

Time again. It was already dulling the edges of my memory. When I pictured Max's kind green eyes and the way they softened when he looked at me, it felt like he could help heal the parts of me that were still broken.

But did I want him to? Could I let him? Who would I be without the sharp pain of all I'd lost? I simply didn't know.

Bailey Jones came striding into the tiny sewing room with a tape measure draped around his neck. "Have you ever made a custom suit, Meira Sokolow?"

I'd been at Gimbels a full month now, and he always called me by my first and last name. Because I did good work, and I did it quickly, Bailey didn't dislike me, but I didn't think he actually liked me either.

"A custom suit?"

He huffed impatiently. "Yes. Have you ever taken measurements on a man, cut the fabric, and sewn it together according to those measurements?"

"No."

He arched one dark brow. "No to which parts?"

"I have never taken measurements myself. I have been given measurements and then made the suit."

"Well, get ready to learn. Come with me."

Slightly annoyed at the way he spoke to me, I followed Bailey out into the customer waiting area. I'd met several customers by now when they came for fittings, and Bailey seemed to like having me nearby to do the more menial tasks, like taking notes or getting coffee.

"This is Mr. Berger," he said.

I nodded and smiled at the customer.

Mr. Berger, a large man with a barrel chest, smiled back at me. There was something familiar about him, but I wasn't sure what it was. He looked austere and important with silver hair greased back from his prominent forehead. A khaki raincoat was folded neatly over his arm, not quite covering what looked like a fancy gold watch.

"Take this and write down everything I tell you." Bailey handed me a notebook and pencil before he took the tape measure from around his neck and stretched it wide. Then he instructed Mr. Berger to put down his raincoat and take off the suit jacket he had on.

Next thing I knew, Bailey was wielding that tape measure the way an artist wields a paintbrush, calling out measurements while I scribbled everything down as fast as I could. Mr. Berger stood in front of a full-length mirror, occasionally smiling at my reflection behind him.

"That's it," Bailey said a few moments later and gave me a pointed look. "Did you write all that down, Meira Sokolow?"

"Yes, I have it all."

Mr. Berger eyed me with more interest than before. "That accent. Where are you from?"

He had an accent too, although it wasn't as obvious as mine. "Poland."

His gaze traveled over me, from the top of my head down to my toes, making me more than a little uncomfortable.

"She's an excellent worker. Those Eastern European women are a sturdy bunch," Bailey said with a laugh.

I tried not to frown. *Sturdy?*

"We can have your suit ready in a week."

Mr. Berger nodded and filled out a contact sheet that Bailey handed him. After retrieving his suit jacket and raincoat, Mr. Berger turned to me.

"*Arbeit macht frei,*" he said with a grin, and then he walked out through the archway.

Bailey said something after that, but I couldn't hear a word of it because of the loud buzzing sound in my head. My hands trembled as

I grabbed for the form that Mr. Berger had filled out, and looked to see what he'd written down, but there was only a phone number scrawled beside his name, Henry Berger.

That isn't his name.

Adrenaline crashed through my veins, and my ears rang painfully as I ran out of the alterations area with Bailey calling my name. I rushed down the stairs to the first floor. The store was crowded, but I caught sight of the man's silver hair as he moved toward the exit.

I didn't know what I would do when I caught up to him, but he had no gun and no soldiers to back him up here. It was just him and me, and I wouldn't let him say those words with a smile and walk away.

Pushing through the people who loitered near the door, I called out to him. "I know who you are! Commandant Amon Glostnik!"

He ignored me and kept walking.

"How many did you kill," I yelled at his back, "besides my husband and my daughter? Was it hundreds? Was it thousands that you murdered?"

He continued toward the main door without turning, but his shoulders tensed. He knew I was talking to him. He wanted me to know who he was so he could lord it over me and smile victoriously. I didn't know how he'd escaped the Allies and come all the way to America, but he wouldn't get away with taunting me like that.

"Guard!" I yelled to the security guard at the store entrance. "This man stole something. He is a thief!"

Commandant Amon Glostnik finally turned to look at me, his mouth flattened in annoyance. The security guard approached and spoke to him.

"I stole nothing. She's crazy." Glostnik stood there as the guard began to pat him down.

While the security guard had Glostnik's attention, I moved closer and took his wallet from the back pocket of his pants.

"Stop!" He reached for me, but only managed to brush my arm before I moved away.

Now the security guard looked at me too, but I ignored them both and pulled Glostnik's identification out of his wallet before tossing it back to him. Then I rushed out of the store.

I was out of breath, having jogged nearly all the way to the USNA building, when I threw open the door to Sylvia's office.

Startled, she bolted from her chair. It took a minute to find my voice, and in that time, she came around her desk to stand in front of me.

"Meira? Are you all right?"

"This man came into Gimbels today for a suit." I held out his identification card to her, and she took it, shooting me a curious look.

"When I spoke to him and he heard my accent, he asked me where I was from. I said Poland, and he looked at me for a long time. He knew I was Jewish. Then he said *'arbeit macht frei'* with an arrogant smile on his face. You know what that means? *'Arbeit macht frei'*?"

Her expression turned solemn. "'Work will make you free.' It was written on the entrance to Auschwitz."

"Not only Auschwitz. It was written at Poniatowa too."

Her face was pinched as she went around to sit in her chair again with the stolen identification in her hand.

"I think he is Commandant Amon Glostnik. He was the man in charge at Poniatowa. He ordered the deaths of everyone in that camp, including my husband and my daughter. How can he be here in America instead of dead or in prison?"

"Are you sure it was him?"

"He is much changed, but I think so. I am sure he is a Nazi. He wanted me to know. He was smug about it, the way he spoke to me."

Sylvia eyed me over the rims of her glasses. "Sit down, Meira. Please."

Out of breath, I lowered myself into a chair, my whole body trembling.

"The ratlines could be why he's here. He may have used them to escape."

"Ratlines?"

She looked up from the stolen ID card. "That's what they call the escape routes formed after the war. They were organized by sympathizers who helped Nazi soldiers travel from Germany to Spain or Italy, Switzerland too, and then to South America, although some came here to North America."

"Who would help those murderers to escape?" My stomach churned at the thought of Nazi officers escaping and not paying for their crimes, although I suspected more than a few of them disappeared back into their lives in Germany.

"The Catholic church helped, and so did the Red Cross. Although the Red Cross says it was inadvertently done because there were Nazis passing themselves off as refugees. With the Catholic church, it wasn't so inadvertent. In any case, it's all been documented by the State Department."

I swallowed the bile rising in my throat. No matter how many times I heard of how others helped the Nazis, the thought of it still made me sick. It made me feel as if the whole world was against us. The same way it felt during the war.

I pointed to the ID. "His address is there. We know where he lives. So, what do we do about it?"

Sylvia sighed. "We can call the State Department. If he's in this country illegally with forged documents, they can deport him back to Germany. But it's unlikely the Germans will do anything about him."

"But they have trials there. They had the Nuremberg trials."

"Yes. They're still trying war criminals. But if there are no witnesses, most of those on trial end up being acquitted."

"Because they killed all the witnesses. Was that not smart of them?"

Her expression turned sympathetic. "I'll make some calls. At the very least, we can tell Immigration about him and make his life a lot less comfortable."

"I can make his life less comfortable myself."

"Meira, no. You should stay away from him. By the way, do I even want to know how you got his identification card?"

I swallowed and pressed my lips together. As she frowned at me, the phone on her desk rang and she picked it up.

"Mr. Jones. How are you?" she asked as she glanced at me.

From where I sat, I could hear Bailey Jones giving Sylvia an earful. It appeared as though I was out of a job again.

chapter 20

"He is not pressing charges because he is a Nazi war criminal," I said a short time later, frustrated to have all these people in my apartment when I only wanted to be alone. "There must be someone who can do something. Does President Truman know there are Nazis hiding in his country?"

"You want to call the president now? You do realize that Gimbels is threating to sue you for damages," Max said as he paced my living room.

"They already fired me. Without a paycheck, how could I possibly pay them anything?" I asked, not at all bothered about losing my job compared to the other monumental event that happened today.

Blanka stared at me wide-eyed from the end of the couch, where she'd been planted since Sylvia brought me home from the police station and told Blanka what happened. She was terrified at the thought of Nazis in the city, and I felt guilty for frightening her.

Max, Karen, and Jerry were all here in my small living room, along with Sylvia and Blanka.

Gimbels' security guard had called my emergency contact after I left the store. Apparently that was Max, not Karen, which was why he was here. Then Bailey Jones had called Sylvia to tell her I was fired, and Max apparently told Karen what happened. Now they were all here. The fact that Karen had put Max down as my emergency contact when she'd told me she was listing her own information was an argument for another day.

When Sylvia told the police my story, including my history, they let me leave the station. They were actually very kind, and even offered to look into Henry Berger's papers to see if he was a war criminal in this country under false pretenses.

"Since she knows his address, I'm afraid Meira is going to take matters into her own hands," Sylvia told everyone, talking about me as if I weren't in the room.

Max's gaze zeroed in on me. "Meira knows better," he said, making it sound like a warning.

I rubbed the heels of my hands against my eyes, hoping to relieve the pressure building inside my head. Then I looked around, and my heart felt full as I took in the scene before me. All these people were here for me. How I had accumulated so many good friends in this city, I didn't know.

"Thank you for coming," I said. "I am very grateful that you would all drop everything and come here so quickly, but it has been a long day and I am very tired."

"Meira." Max took a step toward me, but I shook my head and walked away to my bedroom.

Closing the door behind me, I stood there in the dark and took a shaky breath. My nerves were raw and I knew I would never sleep, but I needed quiet. I wanted to be alone. The noise in my own head was so loud, I couldn't stand the sounds of others anymore. I didn't want to listen to everyone talking around me.

After slipping off my shoes, I lay down on the bed and stared at the ceiling, struggling to keep the tears at bay. How I had any more tears left after all these years, I didn't know. I supposed my supply was endless.

As I lay on my bed, listening to the muffled sounds from the other room, my door opened quietly. Light sliced into the darkness as someone slipped inside. Without looking, I knew it was Max, and a part of me was glad he hadn't listened and came to my room anyway.

The mattress sank as he sat down beside me, and I turned to look at him. When I met his worried eyes, I felt the pooling of tears in my own.

What was it about this man? Why did his presence seem to bring out all the emotions I tried to keep bottled inside? And why did I want to be with him more than I wanted to be alone?

Wiping at my damp cheeks, I sat up. At the same time, Max leaned in closer. It was the most natural thing in the world when he wrapped his arms around me and pulled me close. His hand moved through my hair and over my back in slow, soothing motions.

I couldn't deny the relief I felt at having him hold me this way. In Max's arms, I felt safe, as if he could keep all the monsters away.

I knew better, though. No one could do that, no matter how much they wanted to.

"I had a daughter," I said softly. "Her name was Tovah."

Max loosened his hold to look down at me. "I know."

My lips parted but no words came out. Had I told him about her?

He saw my confusion. "Karen was asking after you the last time Blanka came to clean the apartment, and she told Karen about your daughter. I wanted to say something, but I was waiting until you were ready to tell me yourself. I'm so very sorry, Meira."

I rolled up my sleeve to reveal the only visible scar I had. The rest were hidden inside. "She died when the Nazis liquidated the camp we were in. The soldiers had us lay facedown in a ditch that they had ordered us to dig ourselves. I covered Tovah's eyes because she asked me to. Then the soldiers stood around the edges and fired down at us. The bullet that killed Tovah passed through my arm and went into the back of her head. She was only ten years old."

Max's eyes were wet when he lifted my arm to his lips and gently kissed the scar there.

I swallowed against the tightness in my throat. "She resembled me. She was starting to be like me too, a little outspoken, a little precocious. Then the Nazis came, and our lives turned into a nightmare."

"Meira." Max still held me as he pressed another kiss to my forearm.

Tears flowed down my cheeks in a steady stream as I told him everything, from the moment the Nazis marched into Warsaw until I climbed out of the ditch, joined Esther in the woods, and searched for help in nearby towns.

When I finished, Max wiped at his own eyes.

"We've all read about what happened in the papers," he said, "but to hear you tell it is . . . I don't know. There are no words for how it feels to hear you describe what you went through. All I know is that I'm angry at the whole damn world."

His eyes met mine, and his expression was so heartbroken, I got the feeling if he could have lived it instead of me, he would have.

"I am angry too, but being so angry has gotten me nowhere. Mr. Diamond said that I am only marking time, waiting to join my family."

"Who's Mr. Diamond?"

"A friend. A nice old man I met in the park."

Max pushed a lock of hair behind my ear. He hadn't stopped touching me since he walked into my room. "You don't give yourself enough credit, Meira. There's no road map for surviving what you did. No timeline. You're alive, and you still have time to figure the rest out."

Figure what out? My life? That seemed like too large a task. All I knew right then was that it felt so good to have Max here, to hold me and to talk to.

Reaching up, I touched his rough cheek the same way he had touched my face. "Thank you. You have all been so kind, but especially you."

His gaze held mine as he smiled, but it didn't quite reach his eyes.

The sadness I saw there reminded me of Zotia and what she'd said about her happiness having holes in it. Now that Max knew my story, he saw the holes too.

As we sat in the dark, his hands cupped my cheeks, and he looked into my eyes before he pressed a light kiss to my forehead. It wasn't too much or too little. It was exactly what I needed to keep me from falling into those holes.

I was up early the next morning. Emotionally spent after yesterday, I'd expected to have a restless night. Instead, I'd managed a few hours of sleep, enough to have a clear head and a new determination as I got dressed for the day.

When I stepped out onto the sidewalk, I was surprised by a familiar face.

"Where are you going, Meira?"

Max. What is he doing here?

After a moment, it dawned on me, and my eyes narrowed in his direction. Dressed in a navy suit with a crimson tie, Max looked very dapper as he innocently stood on the sidewalk outside my apartment building.

I folded my arms and angled a look at him. "You thought I would go to that man's apartment, and you came here to stop me. If you must know, that is where I was going. Not to do anything rash, only to see if he is still there and make sure he did not run off."

"Not smart." Max's words were clipped, all signs of good humor gone.

"I do not have a job, but you do. Should you not be at your office?"

He waited for some pedestrians to pass before he approached me. "It's early. I'll get to the office on time."

The fact that he knew I would want to go to Mr. Berger's apartment today and he came to stop me wasn't sitting well. "What if they do nothing about him?"

Max bent to put us at eye level and make sure I listened. "I've already made calls, and so has Sylvia. Something will be done about him. No need for you to intervene."

"What? What will be done?"

"At the very least, the INS will pay him a visit. They handle these things." Max cleared his throat and tried to turn me back toward the door, but I could see something was wrong.

"What? Is there something you are not saying?"

He looked around. "Can we go inside for a minute?"

"Why can we not talk here?"

With a sigh, he took my arm and moved me closer to the building. "I learned something today, a possible reason why he's here in the first place."

His stiff posture caused a knot to form in my stomach.

"The government helped some high-ranking Nazis come to the US after the war so they could get information from them, political information about Russia and other Axis countries. They made deals with them."

"Your government helped them?"

A tight, angry nod was his answer. "If that man yesterday received that kind of help, there might not be much anyone can do. But he shouldn't have taunted you that way. He won't get away with that."

I laughed at the irony. "I am very glad he can kill millions, but taunting me is out of line."

"Meira." He touched my arm, but I shrugged him off.

"Go to work, Max. I am fine."

His jaw muscles tensed. "I struggled with whether to tell you, but I don't want to lie. You deserve better than that. It was wrong to make deals with those killers. Of course you should be upset, but don't let it drive you to do something stupid or self-destructive."

My spine stiffened. "Stupid?"

He grimaced. "I didn't mean you're stupid. You know I don't think that."

My lips pressed together tightly as I looked everywhere but at him. I hated this combination of anger and helplessness. It made me feel like a balloon filling with air and no way to release the pressure.

"Meira." His voice softened as he took a step closer. "Sylvia said you should come by her office today to see about another job. Let me drive you there on my way to work?"

When I didn't answer right away, he said my name again to get my attention. He didn't trust me not to go after the Nazi myself. That's why he wanted to drive me to Sylvia's office.

What would you do? I wanted to ask him. I wanted to ask Max what he would do if it were his son who was murdered, and he knew the address of one of the accomplices. But I wouldn't give voice to that thought because I would never wish that on him, or even want to make him think about it.

"All right," I said, hearing the defeat in my voice.

"All right?" Max seemed surprised by my easy agreement.

"Yes. For now."

I was already wondering about my options, like going to the Justice Department and reporting him myself. I could always follow him around and taunt him the way he taunted me. Let all his neighbors know that a Nazi lived among them.

This was New York City, not Warsaw. Here, he could have me charged with harassment. At the worst, he could decide to finish the job and kill me, but then he would go to jail.

That might be worth it.

chapter 21

When I arrived at the USNA building, someone else was already in Sylvia's office. Her door was closed, and I could hear voices inside.

Deciding to wait, I leaned against the wall across from her office and let my thoughts wander. The anger I'd felt since I saw Commandant Glostnik yesterday still burned hot inside me.

What would I do if nothing was done about him? How far would I go to see he was punished? Not everyone got what they deserved, and I didn't know if I could live with that.

The door to Sylvia's office opened, and I looked up to see a man fill the open doorway. As I began to nod a greeting to the stranger, I froze, because he wasn't a stranger.

Flashes of images tumbled through my mind, memories of a young, courageous boy who always seemed to be there when we needed him. Gone now was the skinny boy I remembered, and in his place was a tall man with carved cheeks that were shadowed by dark stubble. A shock of nearly black hair hung over his forehead, and familiar brown eyes widened at the sight of me before he smiled.

"David?"

"Hello, Meira," he said in a deep voice I didn't recognize. He was an adult now, just like Tovah should have been.

I must have been sliding slowly down the wall, because the next thing I knew, he'd caught me in his arms and pulled me against him in a hug.

"It's so good to see you," he said in Yiddish.

I squeezed him tightly, afraid if I let go, he'd disappear.

where butterflies go

I didn't know how long we stood there that way, but when we finally broke apart, I took a step back to get a better look at him. I could hardly believe this tall, lanky man was the same boy I once knew.

"You survived. You got out, and now here you are. We should have listened to you, David. We should have stayed in the ghetto and fought."

"No." He shook his head. "Most didn't survive. I got lucky."

Lucky. "That's what everyone said to me, that I was lucky, but I hate that word because I never felt lucky. I never wanted to be lucky in this way."

"I understand. I never felt very lucky either."

"Come back in the office, both of you," Sylvia said with tears in her eyes as she ushered us both inside.

David and I kept looking at each other, not breaking eye contact for more than a second at a time as we settled side by side into chairs across from Sylvia's desk. Again, I wondered why I'd put off seeing David. I should have rushed to find him the moment I heard he was alive.

"I was so happy to see your name on the survivors list," David said. "Most of the people in the ghetto were sent to the gas chamber at Treblinka."

I nodded. "Yes, that's where Leah and Heinrich went. Tovah, Avrom, and I were sent to Poniatowa."

David nodded. "I know. I read the account you gave to the Jewish National League. I still think about Tovah."

Tears pressed at my eyes again. I was so tired of tears.

"I loved her, you know," he said softly.

I nodded. "She loved you too."

He reached across the short distance to grip my hand, and I squeezed my eyes shut as the pressure in my chest grew. I was glad David thought of Tovah. She deserved to be remembered by more than just her mother.

"Tell me what happened after we left the ghetto," I said. "How did you survive?"

David took a breath and gripped his hands together in his lap. "We all assumed we would die, but we wanted to take as many of the Nazi soldiers with us as we could. It was the first night of Passover when they came to kill everyone who refused to volunteer for deportation. They had tanks and bombs. We surprised them, emerging from bunkers in the ground they didn't know existed, using guns they didn't know we had. After that first day, they retreated, and it felt like a big victory. It invigorated us. But then they came back with reinforcements. We fought them off for another month before they decided to raze every building and burn the ghetto to the ground. Some stayed and fought until their last breath. The rest of us escaped to the Aryan side through the sewers. The Nazis tried to flood the sewers, but we'd made contact with the Polish resistance and managed to blow up the main line to stop the water and escape to the other side of the wall."

My pulse raced faster as I listened to his story. "My God, David. I cannot believe you did all that. You were only a boy."

He brushed aside my amazement. "I hid in the woods for the rest of the war, along with some others. Sometimes we fought with the Polish resistance, other times they couldn't be trusted not to give us up to the Nazis. Some starved to death. I stole like I always had and managed to survive, but I wouldn't have wanted that for Tovah. She couldn't have survived it. Don't regret not staying to fight. The end would not have changed for her."

Sylvia handed me a tissue, but all I could do was clutch it in my hand.

We all had our tragic stories, our regrets and sadness, but David's courage was unlike anything else I'd heard. I was in awe of him.

Sylvia cleared her throat softly. "I'm so glad you two have been reunited."

We'd been speaking Yiddish, but Sylvia never interrupted, even though she couldn't understand us. I was certain she must have heard David's story already.

"Now you live here in New York too?" I asked David in English.

He looked at Sylvia and shifted in his chair. "I'm here occasionally, but I mainly live in Israel now. That's why I haven't been to see you yet. Yesterday, Sylvia called and told me about the man you saw. He goes by Henry Berger?"

I looked at the two of them, wondering why Sylvia had called David. "Yes, but I think his name is Amon Glostnik."

"He's not Amon Glostnik," David said. "Glostnik escaped to Italy after the war and died of a heart attack in a hospital there. We think the man you saw was Gerhard Halder, one of the commanding SS officers who ordered the death marches out of Auschwitz."

"Wait." I blinked at David, trying to understand. "Commandant Glostnik is dead? How do you know this?"

"I just do, Meira. Glostnik died in Italy, but Halder and Glostnik looked similar to each other. I can see how you would make that mistake."

"Glostnik never went to jail? He was never punished?"

"No. I'm sorry."

I was stunned and so filled with anger that my hands fisted in my lap.

"You're not the first to make this kind of mistake," David said. "That's why it's so hard to prosecute soldiers for war crimes. You were traumatized every day, and your brain can play tricks on you. But the man who spoke to you is just as guilty as Glostnik was. You still found a war criminal in the city, and now that you have, he can be brought to justice. Do you know about the death marches, Meira?"

I nodded. I'd heard about them from the survivors in the DP camp. The death marches were the Nazis' attempt to cover up what they had done as the Allied troops were entering Germany. The weak, nearly starved prisoners were marched out of the camps and across the countryside in freezing-cold temperatures without food or adequate clothing. Those who tried to escape were shot. Those who died of exhaustion were left on the road.

"Even though Gerhard lives here now, the Americans can't put him on trial, and they probably wouldn't if they could. But the Israelis can." David leaned in toward me. "I intend to take him to Israel, where he will be arrested and charged with war crimes."

"Take him?" I asked. "He will not agree to go with you."

"No, probably not. Not willingly." David sat back, and his expression hardened. "But he will get there one way or another. I can promise you that."

What did he mean? Was he going to kidnap Gerhard and take him by force? I nearly asked as much before I registered the determined look on David's face. He'd meant every word he said. As that possibility sank in, my gaze moved over him, from the top of his head down to his boot-clad toes.

"Who are you now?"

His expression didn't change. "I'm your friend. I always have been."

"Are you an Israeli soldier? You are only nineteen."

"I am an Israeli. That's true. I fought in the Arab–Israeli War and earned my homeland. I'll do anything to serve it. My age is irrelevant."

For David, the war didn't end in 1945. He was still fighting. While I was simply marking time, David was fighting for what he believed in. He was doing something important with his life, and a part of me felt ashamed that I was doing nothing.

"I am so proud of you, David. I was proud of the boy you were, and now I am in awe of the man you have become. I wish I could do something to help you."

"You have helped. You delivered Gerhard Halder. The families of his victims will be grateful."

"I happened to run into him. That is all."

I couldn't stop looking at David and thinking of all he'd done. He was always so strong, but as I sat next to him now, it was hard to believe he was the same boy who sat in the stairwell with us in Warsaw, his eyes wide as the first bombs fell. It seemed like a lifetime ago.

David reached into his jacket. "When I first learned you were in New York, I wanted to find you to give you this."

He held something out to me, a worn photograph, creased at the edges. When I looked closer, I saw it was a picture of Avrom, Tovah, and me. We'd sat for it when Tovah was five years old. My hand trembled as I held it in front of me.

"How do you have this?" I asked. I had nothing from my life before. No possessions. No photographs. Nothing.

"I took it from your apartment before we were forced to leave. Then I hid it behind a loose stone in the ghetto wall. I should have given it to you then, but I wanted to keep it safe for Tovah. I thought if anything happened to you or Avrom, she'd want a photograph to remember you by. I never imagined that she would be the one who was gone."

I stared at it as I traced my finger over Tovah's forehead and down along the delicate line of her neck to where her lace collar began. I remembered the dress she was wearing. Papa had made it for her. I took in the warm smile on Avrom's face and drank in each of their features, one by one, pausing at Avrom's brown eyes and Tovah's clear blue ones.

These eyes weren't the ones I remembered, dulled by starvation and too many nightmares. They were creased at the edges by their smiles, and filled with humor because the photographer had said something to make us all laugh. Even my own eyes in the photograph were unfamiliar to me. They weren't the wounded ones I saw in the mirror each morning.

When I was about to look away, I noticed the gold rose pin on my blouse in the photograph, and it felt like someone had wrapped their hand around my heart and squeezed. It was the pin Avrom made for me when we first began dating. He'd melted down cuff links and crafted it himself. I could so clearly recall the feel of it in my hand and the way I'd rub the edges of the delicate petals with my thumb.

Where was that pin now? Lost in the rubble, most likely, or bulldozed away when rebuilding began. Maybe it was stolen with so many of our other things, and was now worn by someone who didn't know the history behind it and didn't care.

Avrom gave me that pin a lifetime ago. The happy family smiling at me from this photograph had no idea what was going to happen. If only I could go back and warn them.

I looked at David. "I am glad to know there are people like you, still fighting, still trying to right the wrongs that were done."

He looked wistfully at the photograph he'd carried with him for so long.

"Please tell me how I can help," I said. "With Gerhard Halder, what can I do?"

David shook his head before I even finished asking. "Nothing."

"But I want to help. I *need* to do something."

"I have an idea for you, Meira," Sylvia said. "For your next job. If you truly want to help, I know a way."

I eyed her skeptically. Another hair salon or a department store?

Sylvia rested her elbows on her desk and clasped her hands together. "The organization I work for has ties all over the world. In addition to helping refugees, they've taken on another mission to spread awareness of the atrocities that took place during the war and the dangers of anti-Semitism. They're putting together lecture tours and are looking for volunteers who are willing to tell their stories. Survivors like you, Meira."

I looked from Sylvia to David. "Lecture tours? Who would want to hear me talk?"

David straightened in his chair. "Did you know that there are those who deny the fact that six million Jews were murdered by the Nazis? They think it's an exaggeration, or that the Nazis' *Final Solution* was fiction and none of it ever happened. These are dangerous lies. They can't be allowed to take hold. Telling your story is the best way you can help, even more important than catching criminals like Gerhard Halder. The world needs to know the harm that hate can lead to. Talk about what happened to Tovah and the rest of your family, Meira. Tell as many people as you can. Tell them again and again."

Tell my story again and again? Talk about how I lost everyone I loved to a roomful of strangers? *What if no one cares? What if no one believes me?* I already knew from experience that people wanted to forget and move on.

I was about to tell David that until I realized this was exactly what he'd meant. Forgetting was dangerous. Not believing it ever happened or could happen in the future was also dangerous.

"Think about it," Sylvia said.

I looked from Sylvia to David, feeling the pressure of their expectations. Did I want to put myself through that? Was I strong enough?

"Do it for Tovah and all the other children who can no longer speak for themselves," David said, repeating my own words back to me.

For Tovah. I would do anything for her, and he knew that.

"I will think about it," I said.

chapter 22

My family was now merely a faded photograph I kept inside the pocket of my coat. Maybe I should have left it in my apartment to keep it safe, but I wanted it with me. I took it out to show Mr. Diamond.

"She looks like you," he said, a flash of white teeth showing beneath his mustache as he studied the picture. "And that's Avrom. The two of you were a handsome couple."

I smiled, thinking the photograph didn't do Avrom or Tovah justice. It didn't capture the twinkle in Avrom's eyes when he teased me, or how the tip of Tovah's tongue touched her top lip when she was lost in thought. Those images would always exist only in my memory.

He handed the photograph back to me, and I slipped it into my pocket. "Have you seen Max again?"

Mr. Diamond watched to see if my expression would change, and I smiled, giving him the response he wanted.

"Yes, I have seen him."

"And?"

"And what?"

"Don't be coy, Meira." His tone was firm, but there was humor in his eyes.

I sighed and looked out over the playground where a handful of children were climbing the structures. "I like him. Probably more than I should."

"No, *bubelah*. You like him just as you should. And I suspect he likes you the same way."

I recalled the way Max spoke to me the other night, and how he touched me. "It scares me."

Mr. Diamond's hand lightly touched my arm. "What scares you?"

I shrugged. "The thought of loving someone again."

"Love is a gift. One that you generally keep." He grinned and patted my arm.

"Who do you love?"

He ran a hand over his salt-and-pepper beard. "I've loved many people in my life, but they're all gone now, and I miss them."

"Do you ever wish you hadn't loved them so you wouldn't have to miss them? Maybe your life would be easier that way."

"No," he said without hesitation. "Do you wish you hadn't loved Avrom?"

"No, not Avrom, but sometimes I wish I hadn't had Tovah, and then I hate myself for thinking that. She only had six good years in this world, and then four years of hell before it was all over." My gaze flicked from him to the children on the playground who laughed and played. "It was not fair. If I could go back, I would not have children. It is such a selfish thing to want a child, someone to carry on your legacy when you are gone. It is the most self-indulgent act there is."

"If that's what you think, why did you have her?"

Feeling something hitch painfully inside my chest, I shook my head. "Because Avrom and I loved each other, and that is what you do."

"And it brought you no joy to bring a baby into the world?"

I scowled at him. "Of course it did. But I had no idea what kind of world I was bringing her into. I had no business having her if I could not protect her."

He sighed and turned to face the playground. "You know better than that. You couldn't see the future, and you were unfortunate to live in the place you did at the time you did. I won't say things happen for a reason, because I don't believe they do, and there can be no reason why your little girl should have died that way."

Glancing at me, he said, "What I will say is that you have to move on. No matter what you do or how you feel, you can't change the past, but you can build a future. I never met your family, but I know with certainty that they would want you to be happy. Deep down, I think you know that too."

My hands twisted in my lap. What he said made sense, but moving on wasn't so simple.

Mr. Diamond turned to face me again and made sure to meet my eyes before he spoke. "They say you should look before you leap, but I think you should close your eyes and leap, Meira. Enough time has passed. It's time to grab hold of the happiness that could be yours, if only you'd accept it."

His gaze was so intense, I knew he believed every word. Why was it so hard for me to believe it?

"What if I leap and I fall down?"

He smiled. "Then you'll get back up again, my girl. Like you always do."

You have to move on. That was easier said than done.

Avrom and Tovah had been gone for eight years. *Eight years.* Sometimes it felt like a lifetime ago, and other times, it felt like I climbed out of that ditch in Poniatowa only yesterday.

I often thought of how quickly Esther had moved on, finding a new husband in the DP camp, and how thoroughly I'd disapproved. When was the appropriate time to move on? Was it wrong of me to want to?

Maybe it was the words "move on" that I had trouble with. In my mind, they meant leaving something behind in favor of something else. I could never leave Tovah behind, or Avrom or the rest of my family. They were a part of me, and what happened to all of us was also a part of me.

But lately I'd felt a strange kind of shift, a sort of restlessness I couldn't define. It wasn't moving on; that was something I couldn't do. Instead, maybe I could break free. In my mind, that meant no longer using loneliness as a punishment and anger as a shield. It meant making peace with the pain that still held me hostage.

I didn't think Avrom or Tovah would hold that against me. I shouldn't have held it against Esther. The path of grief was different for everyone. I was still on that path, but maybe it was okay to have hope for the future and not feel guilty about wanting to be happy.

But was I brave enough to do it? The fact that I was having these thoughts seemed like a good sign. I wouldn't have dared to think such things even a year ago.

Picturing Max, I smiled to myself.

Close your eyes and leap.

chapter 23

It was just after dusk, and there weren't many children in the park tonight. The sidewalks were another story, packed with people leaving their offices for the day, all in a hurry to get to their destinations. I scanned the crowds, looking for Max's familiar walk.

When I'd called him out of the blue, he'd thought something must have been wrong, because coming to my rescue was practically his second job. When I told him nothing was wrong, he sounded so pleased that I'd initiated contact between us for the first time, I couldn't help but shake my head. Max was *good*, right down to his core. If my calling him made him so happy, I should have done it sooner.

I caught sight of the top of his head in the distance, moving in my direction. That thick, shiny dark hair of his was unmistakable. He was also taller than almost everyone else around him. He was so handsome, I practically melted into a puddle when I saw him.

I recalled meeting him for the first time at Karen's house, how standoffish he'd been and completely closed off. It was hard to believe that man was the same one smiling at me now. But that man was still in there somewhere. Max carried his own disappointments in life.

Now that I knew the kind of person he was, I suspected that separating from his wife couldn't have been easy, but he never said a word against her or hinted at his own heartache. He was always more worried about me. But I didn't want to make him worry anymore. I only wanted to make him smile.

"This is a nice surprise," he said, freeing the bottom button of his suit jacket before he sat down on the bench beside me. Leaning over, he kissed my cheek, his gaze quickly sweeping over me before returning to mine.

My cheeks heated and I smiled a little shyly, feeling more like eighteen than nearly forty.

"Lenore hearts Charlie," Max said.

Confused, I frowned at him. "What?"

He pointed to the wooden back of the bench. Carved into the green paint, revealing the raw wood beneath, was the name Lenore followed by a heart and then the name Charlie.

I reached over and traced my finger along the heart. That wasn't there before, was it? If so, I'd never noticed it in all the times I'd sat here. Seeing it now, something about it made me feel optimistic, like if Lenore and Charlie could find love, maybe there was hope for the rest of us.

Max seemed amused at the way I stared at the words. Did he know I was stalling?

After a slow exhale, I faced him. "I have something I want to show you. I finally saw David. He got in touch because he wanted to give me something that he took from our apartment in Warsaw."

"When did you see him?" Max asked, seeming shocked by my news.

"He was at Sylvia's office when you dropped me off the other morning. I could hardly believe he had held on to it for so long and kept it safe." I took the photograph from my pocket and held it up for Max to see. I'd already looked at it hundreds of times.

Max took the photograph from my hand. At first, he seemed stunned, his gaze moving from it to me. Then he stared at it for the longest time. "Look at you, Meira," he finally said. "Always a beauty."

I bit back a smile. "That is my husband, Avrom, and my daughter, Tovah. She was five there. My father made that dress for her."

"She was beautiful too." He reached out and lightly touched a fingertip to Tovah's face.

"She was. Inside and out."

"And that's your husband." He held the picture a little closer. "I can't imagine how it felt for him to watch his family suffer that way. I think about that sometimes. If it were Jonathan and Sarah, how I would have handled it. What I would have done."

"No, Max. Do not think about that. Be thankful you were not there. I will tell you that Avrom had more strength and courage than I knew. He kept us alive for years in the ghetto, doing anything he had to, things he would not even tell me about. But it tortured him to see how Tovah suffered, and me too. In the end, his spirit was broken. It was all too much."

"But they never broke your spirit."

"Yes, they did. It just took me longer to realize it."

"Meira—"

I shook my head. "I do not want to cry every time I talk about them or look at this photograph. I only wanted to show you my family and to share them with you."

He studied the picture a moment more before passing it back. "Thank you for sharing this with me."

I smiled wistfully. "I have something else to tell you, but you cannot tell anyone else. At least, not until after it happens."

He arched an eyebrow curiously.

"The man who spoke to me at Gimbels was not Commandant Glostnik. I found out that Glostnik is dead. He escaped after the war and died a free man in Italy. The man I saw is Gerhard Halder. He was SS at Auschwitz, and no less guilty than Glostnik, but he will not be a free man for long. The Israelis are taking him to Israel, where he will stand trial for his crimes."

Max sat a little straighter. "How do you know this?"

"I cannot say, but since your government is unlikely to take action, the Israelis are going to see that justice is done."

"Did Sylvia tell you this?"

I shook my head and pressed my lips together. "It was hard to hear that Glostnik was never punished, but at least Gerhard Halder will not be able to live his life as if he did nothing wrong."

Max touched my arm. "I'm sorry about Glostnik. But this other man, it sounds like you're saying the Israelis are hunting down Nazis."

"Yes. It seems they are."

Max looked as astonished as I'd felt when David told me.

"Knowing that there are people out there seeking justice for what happened gives me a sense of peace I was missing before. I would like to visit Israel someday. If the world were to go crazy again, there is at least one place that would welcome me."

He smiled. "Yes. I would like to go there someday too."

Maybe we could go together. "Max, there's something else I wanted to talk about."

He laid his arm across the back of the bench and shifted to face me.

Close your eyes and leap. My palms began to sweat as I tried to decide where to start. "That first night when we met at your sister's apartment and you did not want to be introduced to me or anyone else—"

He shook his head. "Meira—"

"It is all right. I understood. I did not want to meet anyone either, but now I think I have changed my mind."

"You changed your mind?" His gaze sharpened on mine.

I nodded, and my heart sped up to a gallop.

"Why have you changed your mind? Have you met someone?" he asked.

"Yes."

Max looked stricken. Was this not good news to him? Did he misunderstand my meaning?

"It is you, Max. You changed my mind."

At first, he had no reaction, and I worried that I'd read the situation wrong. Did he not feel the same way I did? Was I making a fool of myself?

Then it all changed. His gaze warmed, and he leaned in closer. "You want to date me, Meira?"

Nerves jumped beneath my skin as I nodded, still unsure of his feelings. His smile was so subtle, I might have missed it if I hadn't been watching him so closely.

"I changed my mind too," he said. "I changed it that very first night, but by then I'd already been unforgivably rude to you. So I've spent all this time trying to show you that I'm not the man you met that night."

He'd changed his mind the first night he met me? I watched him, wondering if he was serious.

Max's hand came up and cupped my cheek, and he looked into my eyes as if searching for something. "I'm glad you changed your mind, Meira."

"It has been a long time, Max. I am still a shadow of the person I used to be, and so afraid of disappointing you."

He shook his head. "Not possible."

Then, ever so slowly, giving me time to turn away or say no, he leaned in and touched his lips to mine. Cupping my face in his hands, he pressed in closer.

The subtle scent of his aftershave surrounded me as I got caught up in the sensation of Max's breath mingling with mine. I kissed him too, my hand wrapping around the back of his neck to keep him close. The blood pounded in my ears. It was frightening to feel so strongly about someone again, but it was also exhilarating.

When the kiss ended, Max still held on to me as his chest rose and fell like he'd just run a race. "Do you think Lenore and Charlie had their first kiss on this bench?"

I pressed my forehead to his and smiled at the thought.

"Maybe we should commemorate ours." Max reached inside his jacket pocket. "Where's a Swiss Army knife when you need one?"

I suspected he was purposely trying to make me laugh because he was worried. "I am all right," I said, noticing the creases in his forehead.

"Are you sure?" he asked, and I knew I was right.

"Yes, Max." I pressed a hand to his cheek and smiled. "I am sure."

His eyes locked with mine, filled with so much emotion, it was as if his gaze held me just as tightly as his arms could. I got the feeling that he was afraid to look away, because then I might disappear.

"Have you had dinner?" he asked.

I shook my head.

"Would you have dinner with me?"

"Are you going to buy me a hot dog again?"

He grinned. "I was thinking of something a little nicer."

"Nicer than a hot dog and a Ferris wheel ride?"

"Yes, nicer than that, and quieter and—" He abruptly stopped and looked at his watch. "But I have Jonathan. I'm sorry."

I tried to hide my disappointment, but I couldn't begrudge him time with his son. "That is all right. Another time."

He raked a hand through his hair. "Would you really be okay with something as simple as a hot dog?"

I hesitated, not sure why he was asking.

"If so, I have an idea, but it's not Coney Island."

"What is it?"

"I'm not going to tell you and risk your saying no. But Jonathan will have to join us, if that's all right."

He wanted me to join him and his son? "Are you sure? I do not want to interrupt time with your son."

"You're not an interruption, Meira. You'll come then?"

I frowned. "But I do not know what I am agreeing to."

Max chuckled. "Do you trust me?"

"Yes."

"Then trust me." With a grin, he stood, held out his hand to me, and I took it.

Nerves rioted in my belly. When Max asked me if a simple dinner was okay, I wasn't expecting this.

"You're eating slowly to avoid the inevitable," Max said with a knowing smile.

"This is a very large portion. How fast do you think I can eat?"

"I've already had three egg rolls and all the lo mein," Jonathan said, bragging from the back seat.

Max turned to face him. "And did any of that spicy mustard make it into your mouth, or are you saving it all for later on your shirt?"

"Ha-ha." Jonathan uselessly dabbed a napkin to one of the stains.

"Don't worry about it, kiddo." Max winked.

We all sat in Max's Mercury eating Chinese food from cartons. I'd eaten Chinese food many times before, but somehow it tasted better eating it with Max and his son in a dark, deserted parking lot in Queens.

"Maybe it would be better to do this during the day," I said.

"I can't believe you've never driven a car before." Jonathan chuckled. "And I really can't believe my dad is letting you drive his car. What if you wreck it?"

My eyes widened at that thought.

Max gave Jonathan a quelling look before turning back to me. "You're not going to wreck it, Meira. Don't you want to learn?"

Did I? Of course. The thought of driving this big machine still excited me. "Yes."

"Good thing you got the Merc-O-Matic Drive, Dad. Imagine her trying to figure out the clutch."

"What is a clutch?" I asked, looking over the complicated dashboard.

"That's a third pedal on the floor you press to shift gears. This car doesn't have that," Max said.

"Only girls drive automatics. This was supposed to be my mom's car when Dad ordered it."

Max turned to the back seat. "Automatics aren't just for girls, and that's enough from the peanut gallery." Then he looked back at me. "It's easier to learn to drive an automatic car. So, really, there's nothing to be nervous about. Ready to switch places?"

Without waiting for my answer, Max got out of the car and came around to the passenger side where I sat.

Before I got out, I turned to look at Jonathan. "Do you really think I can do this?"

My question seemed to catch him off guard, as if he were surprised I'd ask his opinion. He took a moment to think.

"Dad said you went through a lot of really bad stuff before we met you. If you could do that, you can probably do this too."

My chest tightened with emotion. "I think so too."

"And since we're only in a parking lot, you can't get into that much trouble."

Max chuckled behind me.

I got out of the car and exchanged a smile with him as I passed. "What is a peanut gallery?"

"Just a saying from a kids' TV show. Good going with the encouragement, champ." Max reached in and mussed his son's hair.

When Max first asked me to join them tonight, I wasn't sure how I would feel about the three of us being together, wondering if it would bring back too many memories of my own family. But I shouldn't have worried. Jonathan was very different from Tovah. The way he related to his father, the teasing and joking, was as unique to them as it was heartwarming to see.

Max moved the driver's seat in closer for my shorter legs. When I slid behind the wheel and wrapped my fingers around it, I felt a zing of excitement. To be in control of this large vehicle gave me a feeling of power I hadn't expected, and we hadn't even moved yet.

"Now you're in park," Max said. "When you want to move forward, step on the brake and push this to *DR* for drive."

Max explained all the switches and dials, and when I felt ready, I did as he said. I stepped on the brake and moved the lever to *DR*.

"You've got plenty of running room," Max said. "Move your foot to the gas pedal now."

"Oh!" I squealed as the car lurched forward.

"Step on the brake, Meira." Max leaned over and pointed to the other pedal on the floor.

I pressed the brake and the car jerked to a stop.

Jonathan laughed from the back seat.

"It's okay," Max said. "Try again, but this time press lighter on the gas pedal."

Gripping the wheel tightly, I took my foot off the brake more slowly this time and barely touched the gas as the car rolled forward.

"Good." Max smiled with encouragement. "Press down a little more to go faster."

I clenched my teeth as I pushed down more on the gas.

"I'm doing it." I beamed at Max.

"A snail could beat you in a race," Jonathan said and rolled around on the seat, holding his tummy as he laughed.

I turned to glance at him, and Max grabbed the wheel. "Eyes straight ahead. Always keep your eyes on the road, or in this case, the parking lot."

"Right. Sorry." I looked out the windshield and flexed my fingers on the wheel.

Next, Max showed me how much to turn the wheel and how to gradually come to a stop. Even as my heart raced, I grinned the entire time as I circled the parking lot, enjoying the way the car responded to each action I took.

"This is fun," I said after circling for the third time.

"Just wait until he lets you go over ten miles an hour," Jonathan said, joking.

"One thing at a time." Max said.

"I think I can drive us home," I said, heading for the exit.

"No way!" Jonathan yelled as Max's eyes widened.

"Now I am joking." I chuckled.

Max shook his head and smirked. "It was a great first lesson, but how about you park it over there?"

I turned the wheel and maneuvered into the parking spot he'd indicated.

"You're a natural," Max said when we switched places and he came back to the driver's side.

As Max drove home, I watched what his hands and feet did, now that I understood what it all meant. When we got to my apartment,

Jonathan stayed in the car while Max walked me to the door. It was a fun night, the most fun I'd had since coming to this country.

"Thanks for being such a good sport," Max said. "Sorry if Jonathan picked on you too much. He thinks he's a comedian."

"He is very spirited. No need to apologize." I smiled as I thought of the silly jokes the boy had made, mainly at my expense.

Max's grin faded as he slowly backed me into the doorway, out of view of the street. "I like it when you smile, Meira." He ran the back of his fingers over my cheek. "I like when you smile at me even more."

It was my smile that he kissed. His lips moved against mine until the smile was lost among our kisses. After dismissing this part of myself for so long, I was relieved that I could feel this much after trying so hard not to feel anything.

After Max left, I walked into the apartment in a daze. Blanka's bedroom door was closed, leaving me both relieved and disappointed.

On the one hand, I wasn't ready to share my news about Max. I wanted to keep it to myself for a little while, savor it like a sweet secret. But on the other hand, I would have enjoyed reliving it again with Blanka, knowing I couldn't find a more enthusiastic audience.

As I got ready for bed, my thoughts were full of Max—how he smelled, how he moved, the deep tone of his voice, and the way he looked at me. I think I liked the way he looked at me the most.

I didn't want to compare Max to Avrom, but I couldn't help wondering if Avrom ever looked at me that way. He looked at me with affection, but not like he couldn't bear to look away. The first kiss I shared with Avrom didn't curl my toes the same way Max's kiss did. His touch didn't set me on fire.

But I was so young when I first met Avrom. Every look we shared seemed so meaningful. I made him the star of my girlish romantic dreams. After what happened with Zotia, I didn't want to let those dreams die. I sought Avrom out while he stood back and waited. He was quiet, more reserved than Max, and he never talked about his feelings, but neither did I. We just *were*.

Then the war broke out, and survival was all we could think about.

What would Avrom and I have become if the war had never happened? Would our love have grown deeper over time as we watched Tovah grow? It wasn't hard to imagine what life with Avrom would have been like. I could picture it so easily, much more easily than I could picture a life with Max.

I looked out my window into the dimly lit courtyard behind the building and thought that ten years ago, I couldn't have pictured this life either. Just me, alone in New York. But here I was.

If there was one thing I'd learned, it was that the future could not be predicted.

chapter 24

Some mornings my eyes would open at first light, and it would all come rushing back at me—everything I'd lost, like a freight train barreling into me head on. Other mornings, I would awaken quietly, sluggishly moving through my day in a dark cloud of anger and denial.

But this morning, my eyes opened, and the light pouring through my window looked brighter than it had before. I had new things to think about, possibilities I hadn't considered before.

I'd spent a week thinking about the new job Sylvia had proposed, and the more I thought about it, the more I came to understand that I couldn't say no. It didn't matter how I felt about it or how much it scared me, I owed it to my family to talk about what happened to them. I owed it to my heritage, and to the generations of families that would never be.

And I owed it to myself. It was time to stop hiding in my apartment, to go out and do something meaningful, like David was doing.

Then there was Max. Thoughts of him were never far from my mind. He had woken up a part of me that refused to go back to sleep again.

Max had come to my apartment twice since I had my driving lesson last week. The first time, Blanka was here too, and we all had dinner together while she ogled him and laughed at his jokes. The next time he came over, it was just us, and I melted each time he touched me.

This weekend, Max was going to give me another driving lesson, and this time he wanted me to come to his apartment afterward. There was no Blanka at his apartment, and Jonathan was with his mother. We could be alone there.

It had been a long time since I'd felt close to someone or let someone get close to me. I was no expert at relationships or how they worked here in America, but the last time I saw Max, it seemed as though something was off. He was distracted, not quite himself. Afraid I had done something wrong, I asked him if he was all right, and he alluded to an argument he'd had with his ex-wife, but wouldn't elaborate.

I got the feeling she bothered him more than he let on, but Max didn't like to burden people with his problems. He was too busy helping everyone else. I let him know he could talk to me if he wanted to. I hoped he'd want to. He'd done so much for me. He deserved to have someone to take care of him sometimes.

The telephone rang as I was on my way out to buy groceries, and I answered it for a change. Since Max now telephoned regularly, I regularly picked up. This time it was his sister, Karen.

"Did Max tell you it's his birthday on Saturday?" she asked.

My jaw dropped at that news. "No, he said nothing."

"I'm not surprised. He hates when people make a big deal over him. But that's too bad, because I'm throwing him a surprise birthday party on Friday night at my apartment. Can you come, Meira?"

I hesitated. *A big party that he wouldn't want?* "Are you sure you should have a party?"

"Max is having a birthday party whether he likes it or not." She laughed.

"Can I ask how old he is turning?"

"Thirty-seven. Sometimes I can't believe he's the same kid who used to throw frogs at me when we went to the park."

I laughed, thinking if he was turning thirty-seven, that meant there were only two and a half years between us. I was afraid it was more.

"Max seems very happy these days. I understand things are going well between the two of you."

"Yes. Things are good." I was pleased to know Max seemed happy.

"I knew you two would hit it off. Took a while, because my brother can be really thickheaded sometimes, but he isn't stupid. He knew a good thing when he saw it."

Embarrassed, I chuckled. "He is the good thing."

Karen was quiet for a moment. "You're both good for each other. Now don't forget. Friday night at seven o'clock sharp, and don't say a word. It's a surprise."

After I hung up the telephone, I racked my brain for the perfect gift to give Max. I thought of clothing or a gadget of some kind, but those seemed so impersonal.

Then it hit me, the perfect gift. It would be personal and meaningful to both of us.

There was no ignoring the anxious flutter in my stomach as I rang the bell to Karen's apartment on Friday night. I'd curled my hair so it flipped up at the ends, and I wore a blue dress that matched my eyes, instead of the usual browns and grays I generally preferred.

This night would be different from the first time I came here. Tonight I was dining with people who had become my friends. Karen had invited Blanka too. She was coming by later after her date. One of the waiters at the diner down the street from our apartment had asked her out. She'd been brimming with excitement when she left for her big date.

"Meira!" Karen opened the door and pulled me into an embrace. "How are you?"

I smiled at her enthusiastic greeting. "I am fine. Thank you."

"You didn't spill the beans, did you?" My confusion must have shown, because Karen chuckled. "That means slip up and tell Max about his party."

"No, I did not."

I actually hadn't spoken to Max much since Karen called about the party, and I assumed he was busy with work and Jonathan. Even though

I now knew his birthday was coming up, I couldn't say anything, because then he would know how I knew. I kept hoping he'd mention it, but he never did.

"Come on in," Karen said. "I want to introduce you to my parents. They've already heard so much about you."

My eyes widened in surprise. I was going to meet Max's parents? I hadn't anticipated that, and wanted to make a good impression.

I smoothed my now-damp palms over my dress and smiled politely as Karen led me into the living room. The television was on, and Jonathan sat with some others on the couch watching a show. They kept erupting in laughter.

"Have you seen this?" Karen asked. "It's called *I Love Lucy*. It's about this redhead named Lucy, and she always gets herself into trouble with this neighbor of hers. Then her husband, who's a handsome Cuban nightclub singer, finds out and blows a gasket every time."

My eyebrows inched upward. "This is a good show?"

"It's hysterical."

Karen led me past the television and into another room, where coworkers of Max's and their wives were standing around talking. She made the introductions and then took me out into a hallway.

"When does Max get here?" I asked, wondering if we were supposed to hide and yell "surprise" at him, which I was certain he wouldn't like.

Her smile faded. "He's supposed to be here at eight."

"What? Do you think he will not come?"

"He'll come. I just hope he gets here on time . . . and alone." She muttered the last two words, but I'd heard them. Who would he bring?

"Karen—"

"Come on, Meira. There's more people for you to meet."

Without explaining, Karen brought me over to a tall, distinguished-looking man. He had dark hair, except for some prominent gray streaks at his temples. Beside him was a petite blond woman, dressed all in red with diamonds sparkling at her ears and throat. They

where butterflies go

looked like one of those couples I'd sometimes see coming out of the theater on my way home from work.

"Meira Sokolow, these are my parents, Charles and Nina Neuman."

My stomach did a cartwheel as I smiled. "Nice to meet you."

"It's very nice to meet you, Meira." Max's father shook my hand and bent to kiss my cheek.

His mother held a delicate hand out to me, and I shook it as her perfume enveloped me in a floral cloud.

"We've heard a great deal about you," Mrs. Neuman said, but her stiff smile gave me pause. Had she not liked what she heard?

"What you went through was just horrible," Mr. Neuman said. "Did you know many Jewish groups here in the States lobbied Roosevelt to get into the war sooner? If he'd listened, maybe we could have stopped Hitler and saved some lives."

My forced smile faded. "Yes, I had heard that."

"Not an appropriate subject for a party, Charles," Max's mother said.

Just then, Jonathan came in and walked over to his grandparents. "Hi, Meira." He grinned and rubbed his eyes, looking tired, and I wondered if it was past his bedtime.

"How are you doing, champ?" Mr. Neuman asked the boy as he ruffled his hair. Champ was what Max called Jonathan too.

"Did you tell her the news?" Jonathan asked Karen with a smile that stretched from ear to ear.

I eyed Karen curiously, and she bit her lip as she shook her head at Jonathan, who was oblivious to her gesture.

"My parents are getting back together," he said, grinning widely.

Karen put a hand on my arm. "You don't know that, Jonathan."

"My mom said so. Can I have some more cookies?"

Karen nodded, and Jonathan walked past us into the kitchen.

Karen's lips turned down once he was gone. "Sarah gives me such heartburn sometimes. She and her fiancé broke up. She called Max in tears the other day, saying that divorcing him was the biggest mistake of her life and she wants him back. Then today, she had a crisis of some kind and begged him to come over. He's there now, making sure she's okay. Of course she has to do this on the night of his birthday party when I have thirty people here."

A knot twisted in my stomach as I listened to Karen. I'd known something was going on with Max, but he hadn't mentioned any of this, just like he hadn't mentioned his birthday either.

"I hope Max makes things right with Sarah. Divorce really is a terrible thing," Mrs. Neuman said.

"But she was awful to him, Mother," Karen said.

Max's mother shrugged. "Every couple goes through a rough period. You saw how excited Jonathan was."

Karen shook her head. "Sarah never should have said that to him. Max is not getting back together with her."

"You don't know that," her mother said, frowning. "A family should be together. Don't you think so, Meira?"

My spine stiffened. Did she know Max and I were romantically involved? The unfriendly look in her eyes told me that she did know, and she didn't approve.

Beside me, Karen's cheeks turned pink with embarrassment as she glared at the woman. "Mother." Then she looked at me. "Can I talk to you, Meira?"

Without waiting for my answer, Karen steered me away from them, back into the hallway.

"I'm so sorry," she said once we were alone.

"Max and his wife back together again. Is that a possibility?" I asked.

She shook her head vehemently. "Max doesn't want Sarah. He wants you."

"He told you that?"

"I know what he wants, and it's not Sarah."

Karen wanted me for Max, that much was clear, but I couldn't blame his parents or Jonathan for wanting Max and Sarah back together again. Was that why Max hadn't called as much lately or mentioned anything about Sarah's breakup or his birthday? Was he pulling away? Was he afraid to tell me he wanted his wife back?

I looked over my shoulder at Max's parents, and his mother's cool gaze found mine again. There was no mistaking her dislike.

What if he came tonight with Sarah? He had no idea I was here, or that a party waited for him. I couldn't imagine how awkward that would be, to walk in with Sarah and find me here. I didn't want to do that to Max or Jonathan.

I handed Karen the gift-wrapped present I had in my purse. "Please give this to Max and tell him I said happy birthday."

"Meira, no. Don't leave."

"I do not want to embarrass Max if he comes with Sarah tonight. That is who you meant when you said you hope he comes alone. You meant without Sarah."

She pressed her lips together and nodded. "I wouldn't put it past her to find some excuse to tag along with him."

I pulled in a shallow breath and tried to ignore the sharp pain in my chest. "Family is important. If there is one thing I know, it is that. Max knows where I am if he wants to talk."

"Oh, Meira." She pulled me into a hug, but I broke away first because I didn't want her to know I was on the verge of tears.

Rather than take the subway, I walked home quickly, as if I could run away from the heartache that would inevitably find me once I was alone with nothing but my thoughts for company. But no matter how fast I moved, there was one truth I couldn't run from.

My family was gone, but Max's was here and they wanted him back. How could I stand in the way of that?

chapter 25

"First you go to Washington, DC. Then Ohio and Los Angeles," Sylvia said to me as I sat in the chair that faced her desk.

"Who is paying for me to go to all these places?"

"The American Jewish League. They've been around forever, but their charter changed after the war to promoting awareness. They're more than happy to fund the program."

My hands trembled ever so slightly as I turned the pages of the document she'd handed me, detailing an itinerary that would take me away from the city for over a month.

"But this says I need to be in Washington next week," I said. "I do not have anything prepared. I have no speech written and no experience doing this. How many people will come to hear me in each place? How do you know they want to hear anything I have to say?" I rambled, my nerves running away with me.

Sylvia laid her hands flat on her desk and leaned in my direction. "Meira, look at me. All you have to do is talk about your life. Describe your childhood in Poland. Talk about meeting your husband and having your daughter, and then tell the people what happened to your family. Why they're gone. Say as much as you want or as little. But it's better if you can paint a picture for the audience and speak from your heart. Believe me, there's nothing to be nervous about. Before you even step up to the lectern, you'll have the respect of the entire room."

I gripped the folder in my hand. *Paint a picture.*

When I closed my eyes, I saw so many pictures flashing through my mind, of Mama and Papa, of Leah and Heinrich, of Zotia leaving us to sail to America. And, as always, Avrom and Tovah. All of them gone. I also saw the soldiers from the ghetto with their guns pointed at our heads and their loud voices barking orders, and the ones from Poniatowa. The ones who ended it all.

Except me. They didn't end me.

I swallowed past the lump in my throat. "All right," I said as I closed the folder and eyed Sylvia steadily, even though I was more nervous than ever.

She smiled with encouragement. "Can you be in DC by next week? I can push it back a week, but that's it. Do you have any loose ends that can't be tied up in time?"

Loose ends? Was that what Max was now? A loose end?

"I can be there by next week," I said. "But what about the apartment? With no real job, I cannot pay my half of the rent. Should Blanka find a new roommate?"

"Don't worry about that. I'll hold your apartment for you until we see how things go. If you want to continue and you won't be in the city as much, we could make other arrangements for you and find another roommate for Blanka."

I would miss Blanka, but we would stay in touch.

With the folder in hand, I walked the five blocks home. The air was always frosty now since fall was well underway. Pulling my coat tighter around me, I watched the people who rushed by. Everyone was always rushing as if they were late to wherever they were going.

When I first arrived here, I envied them with their busy lives, full of people and conversations. My life was empty then. All the hours in the day were my own, laid before me like blank pieces of paper I had no incentive to fill. But now, it felt like I was finally writing words on that paper, slowly filling those pages with new experiences, new purposes, new joys, and new heartaches.

When I got home, a part of me was surprised to see Max seated on the stoop in front of my apartment building, but another part knew he'd come. It wasn't his style to avoid an issue or to merely call to discuss something important.

My pulse raced faster as I wondered what this visit meant. Was I going to be let down easily? Would he deliver the bad news in that calm, reasonable tone of his? Images of Zotia standing in our kitchen in Poland, learning about Avrom and me, popped into my head. I had a feeling I was about to gain a better understanding of how my sister felt that day.

Max had been staring down at his hands folded in his lap until he heard my heels clicking on the sidewalk. Glancing up, he spotted me and pushed to his feet.

"Meira." He smiled my name as much as said it, and reached for me like nothing had changed.

Instinctively, I took a step back, already steeling myself for bad news. I hadn't planned to, and when his face fell, I rushed to make it all right.

"Happy birthday," I said in an overly bright voice. "You did not tell me your birthday was coming up."

His eyes searched mine as if he were trying to read my thoughts. Then he opened his hand, and I recognized the Swiss Army knife resting in his palm. "Thank you for my present. I wish you'd stayed and given it to me yourself."

A lump rose in my throat. "Were you surprised?"

"Yes, I was," he said in a quiet voice that made it sound like it wasn't a good surprise. His lips pressed together as he looked down at the pocketknife. "Lenore and Charlie. You remembered."

"Of course I did." I tried to smile, but my bottom lip trembled. My feelings about Max had been so hopeful when I'd bought the gift.

"Can we go inside and talk?" he asked.

Dread filled me, but I nodded anyway. His hand rested on the curve of my back as we entered my apartment, and I leaned into his touch because I couldn't help myself. I craved the pressure of his hand. I needed him more than I wanted to.

"Would you like a glass of water?" I asked as I put the folder Sylvia had given me on the counter.

"No, thank you."

I kept my back to him and slowly sipped the water I'd gotten for myself. It was a delay tactic, and he knew it. A moment later, his hands were on my shoulders, turning me around. He took the glass from me and placed it on the counter.

"Karen told me what Jonathan said and what my mother said to you, and I'm sorry for all of it. If I had any idea you'd be meeting my parents, I would have warned you, and I definitely would have wanted to be there with you."

"They were only being honest, Max."

"That's probably true in Jonathan's case. He's just a kid, but my mother knew exactly what she was doing."

"Even if that is so, I wish you had told me what was happening in your life. You did not mention that your wife wants to be with you again, and that she keeps giving you reasons to go there and see her. You did not tell me that your son thinks you are getting back with his mother, and that he hopes for it so much. I know those things have been weighing on you."

"They're my problems, not yours. You have enough on your mind."

I was afraid he would say something like that. "Then we are not equal. You take on my problems, but you do not believe I am strong enough to help you with yours. You do not even talk about them to me."

"Meira." Frustrated, he raked his fingers through his hair. "You are the strongest person I know. I've told you that. Don't let what my mother said get to you. She doesn't care what I want. All she cares about is how things look to other people."

I smiled sadly and looked up into his eyes. "I think she does care about you and her grandson. I think they all want you to give Sarah another chance. What if Sarah could change? What if she knew she made a mistake and wanted to make up for it? Would you feel differently then?"

His eyes closed as he searched for patience. "She's not going to change."

"But what if she could? If you had not met me, would you consider giving her a chance?"

"What are you doing?"

"What do you mean?"

"It feels like you're trying to get me to admit something that will give you an excuse to walk away."

"I am not looking for excuses. I am trying not to be the excuse for a ruined family and a brokenhearted boy."

Before I knew his intentions, Max pulled me to him and kissed me. When his lips covered mine, I wanted to resist him, but I couldn't. I wrapped my arms around his shoulders and kissed him back. I pressed my body against his and felt the way he shuddered in relief. When he held me this way, so close and so tight, I could almost forget all my doubts. *Almost.*

Max leaned back and looked down at me. "You're not my excuse for anything, Meira. What can I say to make you believe that?"

I did believe it, but the hesitation tugging at my heart wouldn't go away.

Reluctantly, I stepped out of his arms and picked up the folder on the table. "Sylvia offered me a new job. It will take me away from the city for a while."

He glanced at the folder. "What job?"

I explained about the lecture tour. "It feels right. I need to do *more* and be *more*, and I think this is my opportunity. It is going to be difficult talking about the past, but people need to know what happened. It is important they understand."

"It is important, and you're the perfect person to do it."

Even though he wanted to, Max couldn't object. The cause was too good, but disappointment and uncertainty lingered behind his eyes.

"When do you leave?" he asked.

"Next week."

"So soon?"

"I know it is quick. I wish I had more time to prepare, but it is already arranged." I hesitated before saying the next part. "I think the timing is good, Max. I need to be on my own for a little while."

He watched me as frustration came off him in waves. "You've been alone for a long time, Meira."

"Yes, I have been alone. I have been lonely and sad. I have done nothing but wait to join my family. But this will be different. I will not only be marking time, but I will be making the time count. I know you say I am strong because of what I survived, but deep down, I do not feel strong. I need to feel that way for myself. I need to believe it. Until I can, it will always be me leaning on you. I want you to feel like you can lean on me too. If you are honest, you will admit that you do not feel that way."

I could tell by the way his eyes stopped making contact with mine that I was right. He didn't feel like he could lean on me, but he also didn't think it was a problem. He released a heavy breath, and the fight seemed to drain from his body.

"When do you get back?" he asked.

"November twentieth."

He nodded and looked at me with a hurt expression.

"This is not good-bye, Max. I would not be able to do this if it was not for you. You woke up a part of me that I thought died long ago. You are the one who made me want more again. Thank you for that."

"I don't want you to thank me, Meira. I want you to love me."

My lips parted, but no sound came out. His words felt like a punch to the stomach.

Max swallowed hard, his deep green eyes stormy and vulnerable. "I want you to love me because I love you. It's not fair to tell you that now when you're leaving. The truth is, I've loved you for a long time, but I understand that you need to do this. I'm proud of you for doing it."

He loves me. His words sank in and tried to wrap around my heart, but I resisted.

Max watched me closely, looking for my reaction, probably hoping to hear me say the same words back to him. But I'd been full of anger and sadness for so long, I didn't know if I was capable of love anymore. Did I even remember how to love?

I was desperate not to hurt Max. He had to understand that I'd lost almost everyone I'd ever loved. If I let myself fall in love with Max and I lost him, I couldn't survive it again. I wouldn't survive it.

"Meira, stop. I can see the thoughts racing around in your head." He took my hand. "I only wanted you to know how I feel. I didn't want to upset you."

Tears pressed at my eyes. This amazing man was consoling me when I was the one who had hurt him.

"I wish you all the best with your new job," he said. "I hope it helps you believe what everyone around you already knows."

He is saying good-bye. I blinked, and tears spilled onto my cheeks.

"The day after you get back, if you want to see me, I'll be at Lenore and Charlie's bench in the park at dusk. If you don't come, you don't have to feel bad. I'll never regret loving you, Meira Sokolow."

He pulled me into the warmest, tightest hug, and we stayed that way for a long time before he let go and walked out of the apartment.

Once he was gone, I sank to the floor and stared at the closed door. I cried harder and harder, until I couldn't catch my breath.

That was how Blanka found me, on my knees, tears running down my face, afraid I'd made a terrible mistake.

chapter 26

Aaron placed the steaming cup of tea down beside me. "That should help."

My throat was sore, and my heart was pounding so hard, I was sure it would pop out of my chest in the middle of my speech. That would certainly wake up anyone in the audience who was in danger of falling asleep from boredom.

I smiled politely at Aaron and sipped the hot tea.

"Relax, you'll be fine." He grinned and patted my shoulder.

The American Jewish League had assigned him to be my liaison and general caretaker throughout the lecture tour. He handled reservations and spoke with the organizers at each venue. He also arranged dinners with local synagogue leaders, which meant I wasn't only talking all day about my life, I had to retell it again each night at dinner.

This was only the second stop on the tour. The first lecture in DC had very little turnout; fewer than a dozen people came, and even fewer than that attended the second night.

Perhaps it was a good thing. My first time speaking in public was an awkward, humiliating experience, but at least there weren't many people there. For some reason, because I was so nervous, my accent got thicker. At one point that first night, I slipped into Yiddish, and Aaron had to come out and remind me to speak English. I turned bright red as I stood at the lectern and resisted the urge to run off the stage.

The second night, I did slightly better. I spoke English the entire time, and I knew better what to expect. I was able to put my thoughts together more coherently, having learned from my mistakes the first night.

Tonight we were in Cleveland, Ohio, which had a very large Jewish population. I could already hear the low hum of the crowd gathering in the auditorium. We were at one of the universities in the city, and Aaron hinted that they had nearly sold out all the tickets, but he wouldn't tell me how many people were out there because he didn't want to scare me.

Too late.

I missed Max terribly and wished he were here. I could have used his encouragement and his solid presence to lean on. But I was also glad he wasn't here in case I made a fool of myself.

"Ten more minutes."

Aaron buzzed with energy and that only made me more nervous. With his pale, almost translucent freckled skin, his every emotion brought a flush to his face. He wasn't married. He'd mentioned that enough times for me to believe he was telling me for a reason, although I pretended not to understand.

Finishing my tea, I took some deep breaths and felt as ready as I was going to feel by the time Aaron returned to escort me to the lectern.

No one in this auditorium knew me, but they all clapped when I walked out onto the stage. This was the worst part. Getting acclimated to the crowd and trying not to squint at the lights all pointed at my face.

As my eyes adjusted, I could see the shadows of heads in almost every seat. There must have been hundreds of people out there. Who were they? Why would they come just to see me? I didn't know the answer. I only knew that I had to paint them a picture, like Sylvia said. A picture of my life, and the colors had to be bright enough that they could see and feel everything I described.

That night in Cleveland, I spoke for two hours. I cried and laughed as the people I'd loved and lost became flesh and blood again. The audience came to know them by the stories I told. They laughed with me when I spoke of how badly Mama wanted to impress Avrom's parents at dinner. They cried when I described the bullet that tore through my arm and pierced my daughter's head. I had them in the palm of my hand the whole time, and their reactions made me feel less alone as I lived it all over again.

At the end, when the stage lights dimmed and the auditorium lights came up during the audience question-and-answer session, I spotted a tall, familiar figure slip out the doors at the back. *Max?*

I missed the first question as I debated running out those doors to see if it was him. Had I imagined him here? Had I conjured him up because I missed him so much?

"Meira?"

Aaron repeated the audience member's question for me, and I shook off my thoughts, deciding I must have imagined seeing Max.

Thirty minutes later, Aaron greeted me backstage. "You did great, Meira. I have so many people here who want to meet you. Are you up for that? I can tell them you're too tired, but I think you should talk to them."

I truly was exhausted, completely spent after talking for two hours straight, but how could I say no to someone who wanted to speak to me? "I will stay until everyone who wants to meet me has done so."

"Atta girl." Aaron winked, and I shook my head. He was so eager and attentive, I couldn't help but smile.

Mostly it was Americans who had only read about the war from a safe distance who wanted to talk to me. Some hugged me, even though they were total strangers. Their eyes brimmed with tears as they expressed their condolences.

I didn't know what to think about that. Total strangers crying and embracing me? Some said they were crying for Tovah, and hearing her name spoken by so many people who never met her pulled at my heartstrings. Their tears meant they understood, or at least they understood as much as they could. Tovah would be remembered. All those who suffered would be remembered by the people here tonight.

Despite how I watched the door as Aaron ushered people inside, none of them were Max. I couldn't help but look for him. By the end of the night, I decided that it must not have been him I saw leaving through the back. He wouldn't come without saying hello. Would he?

"This is Raizel," Aaron said, bringing the last person over to me. "She's also from Poland and wanted to meet you."

"I was in the Lodz ghetto," Raizel said in Yiddish.

My eyes widened at the sound of my native language spoken in the familiar accent I knew so well. I took her hand when she offered it to me, and estimated her to be close to my age despite her bent posture. In the DP camps after the war, many people looked like Raizel, their bones brittle from years of malnutrition.

"I lost my family," she said as she squeezed my hand. "Everyone is gone."

"I am so sorry, Raizel."

"But they did not win, because I am here and you are here, and we won't stop telling the world what they did."

"No. We will not," I said as tears pooled in my eyes.

"This is my husband and my son." She gestured toward a short, stout man and a boy who looked to be about nine or ten. "I met him here in Cleveland after the war."

I smiled in their direction. "Nice to meet you."

"Finding him and having my son was a blessing. I thought my life was over, but now I have another chance. So they truly did not win." She smiled sadly, her throat working as she held back tears.

"No, they did not." I thought of Max, and worked hard not to fall apart in front of her.

By the time everyone was gone and Aaron came back in, I had pulled myself together. Every time I went out there and told my story, it felt like I was breaking apart and then coming back together again piece by piece, but Raizel made that task more challenging. She made me feel like a phony tonight. She was brave enough to live her life to the fullest despite all she'd lost, and I wasn't. It should be her giving these lectures, not me.

Aaron said it was time to head to the restaurant, and so I gathered my thoughts, tucked them away, and prepared myself for another night of nonstop talk.

Next, we were scheduled to move on to Chicago.

When I first looked at the itinerary Sylvia provided, I scanned it for November third, the anniversary of Tovah and Avrom's deaths. I usually spent that day alone, wandering the city, using the noise to distract me from my thoughts. It was a dark day, filled with pain and memories.

As Chicago and November third approached, I wondered how I would get through my lecture that night. I knew I couldn't repeat the same things I'd said before. This night was different. I had to do more than just talk about my life. I had to pay tribute to my family.

As I walked out onstage that night with the audience silently waiting for my first words, my hands trembled. I stared out at the people who sat so still in their seats as I moistened my dry lips.

How could I make them feel what I felt on this day every year? How could I reach into their hearts and make them understand the bitter injustice? How could I move them to spread this understanding to others so that everyone could know the terrible consequences of hatred? Lastly, how could I recount it all without feeling hatred in my own heart?

I wasn't sure I could. All I knew was that I had to speak now, and it had to come from the very bottom of my aching soul.

After clearing my throat, I leaned toward the microphone. "My daughter's name was Tovah. She was strong and brave and precocious and silly. She had blond curls that bounced around her face when she ran. She had pie-in-the-sky little-girl dreams, and a terrible sweet tooth. When she smiled, it seemed as if the whole room lit up. Today, November third, is the day I lost her forever. I lost my husband too, only minutes before. I often wonder how those Nazi soldiers did not hesitate when they murdered my baby. They terrified and starved her first. They did that for years. Then in cold blood, with blank expressions on their faces, they shot her and countless other children."

Scanning the audience, I said, "It is hard to believe they were only men who did this. Flesh-and-blood humans who hid behind their uniforms and somehow justified their actions to themselves. When the

Nazi soldiers who were on trial at Nuremberg were asked why they killed so many innocents, they said they were just following orders. That they had no choice, or they would have been killed for disobeying their superiors. Do you know how many Nazi soldiers were killed for disobeying orders?"

I paused and looked around the room. "None. There is no record of even one, and as we know, the Nazis were scrupulous record keepers."

The audience reacted as I expected. It was a shocking statement that still made me feel sick inside, but it was the truth. When the various aid organizations came to speak with us in the DP camp, I learned that the war was so much worse than even I knew.

"Hitler's *Final Solution*, as it was called, was the Nazis' long-term plan to wipe the Jewish race from the face of the earth, and it almost succeeded. It came frighteningly close to its goal. Now, it is up to us to learn as much as we can from what happened, because if we turn away from it or try to forget it, it could happen again."

I pulled in a deep breath and looked around the auditorium. "For a long time after the war, I was angry and lost, and filled with hatred. I still feel all of those things sometimes, but I have learned that focusing on them is not a good use of my energy. Carrying on the toxic hatred that fueled the Nazis' actions would be another tragedy in itself. So I choose not to hate. It is not easy to make this choice, and I only came to it gradually after a very long time. But we all can choose, and if we choose not to hate, I have hope that this will never happen again."

Stepping back, I looked around. The people were so quiet, I didn't know what to think.

But then someone applauded, and soon, the entire room joined in.

The oddest feeling flowed through me then, like a cool breeze traveling over my skin. An image of Tovah smiling up at me popped into my head. *She is proud of me.* I sensed that as strongly as I felt the goodwill of the people who clapped.

Overwhelmed, I nodded gratefully at the crowd and walked to the side of the stage where a smiling Aaron waited. He patted my shoulder and told me this had been my best night yet. *My best night on the worst day of the year.* I supposed it was fitting.

Something made me turn and look out at the auditorium again. In the back was a familiar silhouette. *Max.* He seemed to be looking straight at me before he turned and walked out the door. Now I was sure I was seeing things, conjuring up Max from thin air.

He loves me. Those three words repeated in my head.

Max loved me, and all he wanted was for me to love him back. Why was that so hard to do?

When I thought I saw Max again in Denver, I wondered about my own sanity. Why would he come to each lecture and never say hello? Why would he travel around the country just to walk out at the end?

As the tour continued, I grew more confident with each lecture. The words came easier, and I learned not to hold back my tears because they punctuated the story. They were honest and true. As I spoke, there were times you could have heard a pin drop, because the audience hung on my every word.

They were with me in Warsaw when the bombs began to fall. They were by my side in the ghetto when Mama was shot, and they were with me in the ditch when I lost Tovah. Their reactions of anger and grief on my behalf made me feel less alone. They made me feel like I had an army of allies ready to come to my defense.

What surprised me the most was that people had heard some of what happened during the war, but most didn't know the full extent of it. Those who had heard about the camps and gas chambers were sure the stories had been exaggerated. I told them that wasn't the case.

As the tour came to an end, Sylvia called me at my hotel and said the American Jewish League wanted to expand the tour to more cities. Was I interested?

My first thought was, *what about Max?* "Can I let you know?"

"Don't wait too long. Plans need to be made."

I hung up, knowing I would agree to more dates. It felt like my story was making a difference to the people who came. There were so many more people I could reach, but what about Max?

Would he be waiting at the park bench when I arrived home, or had he changed his mind and given up on me? More importantly, would I be there?

Only if I loved him. I couldn't go unless I knew that I loved him. Anything less wouldn't be fair to Max.

My flight from Los Angeles was delayed, and then the connecting flight was late. I'd only flown in an airplane once before the lecture tour began, right after the war on an army transport plane. After being on almost a dozen flights in the last month, I had probably been in more airplanes than cars.

I finally arrived back in New York City late on the morning of the twenty-first. That still gave me plenty of time to shower, nap, and make myself presentable if I was going to meet Max in the park at dusk. Nerves bounced around in my belly.

What if I go and he isn't there?

I'd already decided that I would go, no matter what. I missed him too much not to see him. Besides, if I was going to love anyone again, it would be Max. I knew I didn't want to lose him. Losing him would be like losing the best part of myself. If he was willing to give me time, I thought I could love him. Was it fair to ask that of him?

I didn't have any answers. All I knew was that I could hardly wait to see him and hold him again. New York City never really felt like home, but Max did.

As I wearily entered the apartment I shared with Blanka, I felt different from the woman who left here a month ago. I could feel the change within myself. My gaze was steady and straight instead of tending to turn downward, and my smiles were more frequent. I was in the moment more, completely present, not lost in the past. Yes, I still had bad days. I always would, but I was stronger. I believed in the one thing I'd told Max I needed to believe in. *Myself.*

"Meira! You're back!" Blanka came running from the kitchen, and I barely had enough time to put down my bags before she pulled me into a hug. "How was it?"

"Long and tiring," I said with a laugh.

She made a face. "Poor Meira, jet-setting around the country."

"I am hardly a jet-setter."

"That's good, because you really don't look like one." She eyed me from head to toe and wrinkled her nose.

"I have hardly slept in two days. Flying is not as glamorous as the ads make it seem. I need a shower and a nap."

Blanka picked up one of my suitcases and helped me carry my things to my bedroom. "Have you talked to Max?"

Of course she would mention Max first.

I sat down heavily on the bed. "No, I have not. What about you? Are you still dating the waiter from the diner?"

Blanka's cheeks turned pink. "Yes. He's perfect, Meira. He's even taking classes at night to be a plumber. He's got . . . what's the word?"

"Dreams, prospects, ambition."

"Ambition! That's the one."

I smiled at her enthusiasm. "He sounds perfect. I would like to meet him sometime." I reached out and squeezed her hand, and she made a face.

"Maybe when you're cleaner. I would shower first and then nap."

I chuckled. "Are you going anywhere today?"

"I only have classes in the morning, and then I'll be back."

"Could you wake me up by four if I am still asleep?"

"What's at four?"

"I am meeting someone."

She tilted her head and waited for more, but I didn't tell her. There was too much to explain, and if Max wasn't there, I definitely didn't want to talk about it with her when I got home.

Blanka rolled her eyes at me, but she wasn't upset. Her smile was so bright, I wondered what she'd been up to on her own in the city for a month with her new soon-to-be-a-plumber boyfriend. I would have to make it a point to meet this young man soon.

chapter 27

When my eyes fluttered open, I was confused at first. I'd slept in so many hotels and woken up in so many strange beds. I blinked at my surroundings, trying to make sense of them. Then I remembered and sat straight up.

What time is it?

Grabbing the clock by my bed, I saw it was almost six thirty, and the sky was already dark. Did I miss dusk? When was dusk, anyway, and why didn't Blanka wake me up at four?

Panicked, I kicked off the covers and ran for my closet. A quick glance in the mirror reminded me that I'd gone to bed with wet hair. One side was matted flat against my head, and the other was a tangled mess. I'd wanted to take my time dressing and getting myself prepared to see Max. But now all I could do was drag a brush through my hair and pull on one of the only dresses that wasn't a wrinkled mess in my unpacked suitcases.

"Blanka!" I called out as I slipped into my loafers. There was only silence, and I clenched my teeth. I was certainly more dependable than this when I was her age.

Rushing around my bedroom, I pondered dusk again. Was it just before full dark? If so, I'd missed it by almost two hours. Did Max think I wasn't coming? Had he already left? Was there any point in going down there now? Maybe I could call him instead and explain that I'd planned to be there.

No. I couldn't call. That bench symbolized something, and the two of us meeting in that spot meant something.

Grabbing my keys, I rushed out the door without a coat or purse.

I had no money for the subway or a cab, but it didn't matter because I could get there faster on foot. As I dashed past strangers on the sidewalk, looking frenzied, they eyed me strangely, but they had no idea how important this was. For a month, I'd thought of this moment, and now I was afraid I'd missed it and ruined everything.

After five long blocks, the park came into view. It was a glorious place this time of year. As much as I dreaded the month of November, I couldn't deny its beauty. The ground was littered with leaves, a colorful carpet of red, yellow, and orange beneath the children's feet. Those who were out on this cold night were bundled in coats, and the bench, which I could now see clearly, was empty.

My stomach dropped as I scanned the area and saw no one familiar. Not even Mr. Diamond was here with a shoulder for me to cry on.

Breathing hard, I stopped beside the bench and pressed a hand to my chest. Was I really too late, or had Max not come at all? I looked at every face in the playground and every face that passed on the sidewalk. No face was the one I longed to see.

Slumping down onto the bench, I dropped my head in my hands. How long had he sat here before giving up and walking away? I pictured his anxious expression as he glanced at his watch and began to realize that I wasn't coming. I imagined the hurt in his eyes. Hurt that I had put there. *Again.*

As the thought that I might have lost him sank in, my chest squeezed tight with regret. I'd been such a fool, trying to protect myself by not admitting to my feelings. The truth was, I finally knew what those feelings were. I finally understood how deep they ran.

I loved Max. Only love could hurt this much.

My teeth chattered as the chilled night air seeped through the thin material of my dress. It was too cold to be out here without a coat, but I didn't want to leave. Not yet. I couldn't bring myself to walk away.

After a moment, the soft sound of music came from the distance. It was Prelude in C Minor again, that moody piece by Chopin that had followed me throughout my life and evoked so many emotions. My throat tightened at the sound of each deep, slow note. I could always count on Mr. Diamond. He must have been working late tonight. Turning around, I glanced toward his store, but the window was dark.

The rough wood of the bench rubbed against the back of my dress, and I remembered the *Lenore hearts Charlie* carving. Turning to look at it, I smiled sadly. I envied Lenore, and wondered if she and Charlie were still in love.

Beneath the familiar carving was a new carving that hadn't been there before. The raw wood showed clearly beneath the green paint. Leaning closer, I squinted at the words.

Max hearts Meira

I blinked and read it again, wondering if I'd imagined it there. Reaching out, I touched the tip of my finger to the heart.

"You like it?"

Startled, I jumped at the sound of Max's voice behind me. I turned to find him standing only a few feet away, his hands pushed into his pockets, his eyes sparkling under the streetlamps.

Emotion swept through me, clogging my throat and filling my eyes. *Max is here!* I could hardly believe it, afraid if I blinked, he might disappear. He looked so handsome, still in his suit and tie from work.

I stood to face him. "I thought I had missed you."

He shook his head. "I thought you weren't coming."

Oh, Max. "I am sorry. I was late, but I was never not coming."

His gaze wandered over my face like he was drinking in the sight of me, but he seemed unsure, afraid to approach me.

"I missed you, Max." I took a step closer to him.

He pulled in a quick breath. "I missed you too."

I could feel my heart knocking against my ribs. "Are you here because you still feel the same way about me?"

He made a sound of surprise at my question. "You mean do I still love you? Yes. I do." He pointed to the carving in the bench. "And now everyone who sits on this bench will know it."

My bottom lip quivered as I smiled. I hadn't lost him. He was the same Max I remembered, kind and steady, and full of surprising gestures that took my breath away. My gaze met his, and I knew I had to tell him everything I was feeling. I had to make him understand, because I couldn't lose him.

"I did not want to love you, Max. I did not want to love anyone again, but you are not just anyone. You are the voice I hear in my head when I need advice. You are the person who is there to pick me up when I fall down. You are my safe place, my protector, but you never make me feel like I am less than you. You are everything I never knew I needed, and I do need you. Somehow, you slipped inside my heart, and then you helped to heal it. I love you, Max."

His eyes flared as his hands came up to cradle my face. He looked at me hard and whispered my name before he pressed his lips to mine.

I wrapped my arms around him and pulled him closer. I couldn't get close enough as I kissed him with everything I had. It was like a dam broke inside me, and all the emotions I'd tried not to feel for so long came pouring out. The thought of losing him terrified me, but not enough to miss out on the opportunity to love him.

We kissed for a long time before I finally leaned back to look at him. His cheeks were flushed and his eyes were shiny.

"I'll make you happy, Meira. I promise."

"You already do. I am sorry it took me so long to tell you how I feel. I thought about you every day. I missed you so much that I imagined you were there with me. I kept thinking I saw you in the back of the audience."

He swallowed. "I was there."

"You were?" I stared up at him, trying to remember how many times I thought I'd caught a glimpse of him. "Why did you not come talk to me?"

He took my hand and sat on the bench, tugging me down beside him. "I wanted to hear your whole story. You think you told me everything, but it felt like you were trying to protect me from the worst parts. I wanted to hear those parts too. As hard as it was, I needed to know it all. But you wanted time away from us, and I wanted to respect that too. So I didn't tell you I was there."

I thought back to all the things he must have heard, and a part of me was glad he knew everything now. He knew *me* now. All the broken pieces. Everything I'd lost.

Max took my hand. "You spoke so well, Meira. You moved every single person in that room in every city you went to. I thought I would just come to one, but then I found myself in the next city too and the one after that. You were so emotional, but so strong at the same time. I wanted to be there for you, even if you didn't know I was there. This is what you're meant to do, and I'm so damn proud of you."

My chest swelled with pride and with the love I felt for Max. He took me in his arms and kissed me again. Then his hands were rubbing up and down my arms.

"You're shivering, Meira. Where's your coat?"

He began to take off his own coat to give it to me when I heard familiar music coming from the tailor shop. *Mr. Diamond.*

"Shh. Do you hear that?" I asked as he draped his coat over my shoulders. "Before we go, I would like to introduce you to my friend, Mr. Diamond, the one I told you about. His tailor shop is just over there. I told him about you too. That is his music playing. He always plays Chopin while he works, just like my papa did."

Max's brows knit together. "I don't hear any music."

"Listen. It is soft, but it is there."

He shook his head. "I'm sorry. I don't hear it."

I smiled, remembering the music he listened to in his car before my driving lesson. "If it was Elvis, I bet you could hear it."

He grinned.

"Let us go visit. His store is right next to the bakery. Mr. Diamond says he does not like sweets, but there are always a few telltale cookie crumbs hiding in his beard."

I laughed, giddy with elation and this newfound feeling of closeness to Max. Just holding his hand had me smiling as I took him past the jewelry store and then past a dry cleaner. Next thing I knew, we were standing in front of the bakery.

"Wait one minute." Going back the other way, I brought Max with me as I made another pass, but I saw only the jewelry store and the dry cleaner again. No tailor shop.

"Where is it?" he asked.

"Here. It was right here."

Max looked around. "Are you sure it's on this block?"

"Yes, I am very sure. And I know he is working because I can hear—" I strained my ears, but now I only heard traffic, no music. My pulse picked up speed as I scanned the entire block. "I do not understand."

"Meira?" Max sounded concerned, and I wondered how silly I must seem. Why wasn't the tailor shop here?

"The bakery," I blurted out. "They must know him there."

I rushed over and went inside, hearing a bell ring when the door opened. A woman with white hair pulled back into a bun stood behind the counter.

"Excuse me? Do you know Mr. Diamond? He owns Diamond's Tailors next door. He comes in here to buy your cookies, a heavyset man with a salt-and-pepper beard."

She narrowed her eyes. "There's no tailor shop next door."

"Of course there is. Right next to your bakery. He has been there for decades. How could you not know that?"

The woman's gaze moved to Max, who stood beside me.

His hand put light pressure on my back. "You must be mistaken, Meira."

"I am not mistaken." Shaking my head, I walked out of the bakery and stared in through the window of the dry cleaner. "This is where it should be. Right here."

Max was watching me closely with concern, and my face flushed with embarrassment.

What is going on? Feeling strange and dizzy, like the ground had shifted beneath my feet, I reached out and pressed my hand to the window of the dry cleaner.

"Mr. Diamond should be right here. He was my first friend in New York. He reminded me of Papa because he was a tailor and he played the same Chopin music while he worked. Even his shop smelled like Papa's. Sometimes I thought Papa had sent him to me so I would have a friend to talk to. Every time I was here, he would come out of his shop to sit with me. He was there for me when there was no one else." I turned to Max, a desperate feeling welling inside me. "He was here. Wasn't he?"

Max looked lost for an answer. "He sounds a lot like your father. Maybe too much like him."

"You think I missed Papa so much that I imagined Mr. Diamond?"

"Maybe it helped you deal with his loss." Max's voice was hesitant because he didn't want to upset me, but his thoughts were clear enough in the sympathetic way he looked at me.

Had I made up Mr. Diamond? I looked up and down the block and then back over at the bench as I thought of all the conversations we'd had.

"I am not crazy," I whispered.

Max put his arms around me. "Of course not. You were alone for a long time, and you missed your father."

They say you should look before you leap, but I think you should close your eyes and leap, Meira. Enough time has passed. If you have a chance at happiness, you should grab it.

Was that me telling myself to take a chance with Max? Was it all me? Talking to myself?

"Come on," Max said, putting an arm around my shoulders. "Even with my coat on, you're still shivering. We can come back tomorrow and look for Mr. Diamond."

But he didn't really believe Mr. Diamond would be here tomorrow, or the day after that either.

"He seemed so real. Why are you not more alarmed? I sound like a crazy person."

Max smiled down at me. "I'm not alarmed because you're not crazy. You're coping, and if this man helped you, does it matter if he was real or not? Sounds to me like everything he said were things you needed to hear or already knew yourself. It sounds like you found a unique and productive way to deal with everything you were feeling."

He sounded almost impressed. Was he right? Did it matter if Mr. Diamond was real or not?

I thought back to all our conversations, all the times I'd cried on his shoulder, all the advice he'd given me. He was so much like Papa. Papa was the one person I always went to for advice, the person I trusted most in the world before Max came along.

Did I recreate Papa here in New York City? Was it silly to think that I was going to miss Mr. Diamond if I never got to speak to him again?

When we left the park, I didn't want Max to take me to my apartment. I wanted to go to his. I wanted to see where he lived, and I wanted to be alone with him. We wouldn't be alone at my place.

Max lived in a building with a doorman and an elevator. Based on the dark wood paneling and chandelier in the lobby, the apartments here had to be grand.

We took an elevator up to the tenth floor, standing close together, holding hands. It felt like Max wanted to keep me near him. Even though we knew each other, this physical freedom was new. Giving in to the need to touch each other was addictive. Neither of us wanted to stop.

When he took me inside his apartment, he didn't turn on the lights, and I got the impression of an empty cavernous space. Floor-to-ceiling windows were covered by sheer curtains that muted the moonlight. We took off our coats and looked at each other in the darkness.

"Would you like something to drink?" he asked.

I shook my head as I noted how empty and cold his apartment felt. So unlike him.

"I haven't done much with it yet," he said, reading my expression.

He hadn't made it a home. He didn't have his son with him all the time. There was no wife or family around anymore.

Picturing him sitting by himself in this empty place, I wanted to wrap my arms around him and never let go. He needed me, and I needed him. Instead of fighting it or pretending it wasn't there, I let it wash over me, until that was all there was. My need for Max and my wish to give all of myself to him.

With my eyes on his, I began to unbutton my dress, starting at my collar and moving downward.

Max stepped in close and stilled my hand. "Are you sure?"

I nodded as I reached for the buttons on his shirt, but he took my hand and lifted my wrist to his lips before he kissed the jagged scars that snaked down my forearm. I nearly cried at the tender gesture. He was sharing my pain but healing it at the same time.

He continued to undress me so slowly, his hands pushing away the fabric and then his lips trailing kisses over the exposed skin. It was agonizingly slow, and when I reached for his shirt and impatiently tugged at the buttons, he laughed softly and undid them himself.

When our clothes were in piles on the carpet, he lifted me and carried me to his bed.

There were no nerves or second thoughts. Looking into Max's eyes, as deep and green as the sea, I welcomed him inside me. I let myself love him without reservation. If it all ended tomorrow and this night was all we had, I wouldn't have wanted to miss this moment for fear of losing all the moments to come.

chapter 28

One month later . . .

Max had no inhibitions when it came to his naked body. I would wrap myself in a blanket when I slipped out of bed or quickly pull on a shirt. Not Max. He walked around the bedroom without a stitch of clothing on while my gaze traveled over his every dip and curve.

"Morning, sleepyhead." He grinned from the doorway of his closet as he reached for a pair of pants.

"Morning." Lazily, I stretched my arms out over my head and sighed at the soreness in my muscles.

Max's apartment was huge, but nearly empty. After Sarah left and took most of the furnishings with her, he never bothered to replace anything. In the living room, he had a television, a couch, and one table. He had a bed and one dresser in the bedroom, and only two cups, two plates, and a handful of silverware in the kitchen.

Jonathan's room, on the other hand, was packed with toys, books, and sports equipment. Max made sure his son's room would still feel like home, but he made no such efforts for himself. I didn't have much more at my own apartment, but something about Max's place made me sad. It also made me want to make a home for the both of us. Everyone should have a home filled with all the things that made up a full life.

"Up for another driving lesson today?" Max had pants on now, and he held a shirt loosely in his hand as he came to stand beside the bed.

I reached out and ran my fingers over the ridges of his stomach muscles. He sucked in a breath. Then I grasped his hand and tugged him down to me. He pretended I was strong enough to pull him onto the bed as he fell beside me and kissed my lips.

Our first time sleeping together could have been awkward or frightening since it had been so long for me, but Max put me at ease. He made me feel beautiful and desired, and I forgot to be scared or feel guilty. It was special, and so was each time that followed.

When I opened my eyes on the mornings we were together and turned to see Max's head on the pillow next to mine, there was an unexpected lightness inside my chest. It was foreign and slow to surface, like a shy turtle peeking out of its shell. Sometimes, I was still afraid to be happy, but I could admit that Max made me happy, and that was progress. Even though I couldn't put into words all that I was feeling, I could show him. Because I had so much to show him, we weren't dressed in time for breakfast, but we were ready by lunchtime. Just in time to go pick up Jonathan.

"Do you think I am ready to take the Mercury out on the city streets?" I asked Max as I turned the car into the parking lot of the diner. He drove most of the way here, only letting me drive when we left the gas station a block away.

"It's not much fun driving in the city. You mostly ride the brake."

"Ride the brake? You mean press the brake more than the gas?"

Max glanced around the lot, watching for Jonathan. "That's right. Nice parking job, by the way."

It was Max's weekend with Jonathan, and Sarah was meeting Max here to drop Jonathan off. Although I'd heard much about Sarah, this was my first time meeting her.

I was a bit anxious, which was silly, since she might not even get out of her car. But from what I'd heard, Sarah could be volatile, and for Max's sake and Jonathan's, I didn't want an uncomfortable scene. It was no mistake that Max planned this first meeting in a public location. He couldn't predict how Sarah might react to seeing me. Certainly, she'd heard about me by now from Jonathan.

"Relax." I turned off the motor and handed Max the key. "What is the worst that can happen?"

"She can make a spectacle of herself and embarrass Jonathan." He sighed. "She could also say any number of awful things to you."

I smiled at his nervousness and his worry for both Jonathan and me. "If she behaves that way, she will only embarrass herself."

Looking toward the diner, I could see the faces of customers sitting in booths by the windows. They might get a show they weren't expecting. I imagined our plan to eat lunch here once Jonathan arrived would be canceled if Sarah made a scene.

"Will it bother you if she's difficult?" he asked quietly. "My life can be complicated, Meira, especially when it comes to Sarah and issues that concern our son."

The hesitance in his voice surprised me. Did he really think I'd meet Sarah and run in the other direction?

"It will bother me if she bothers you. But she will not chase me away, if that is what you are worried about."

He smiled ruefully. "I might be a little worried."

"Well, do not be." I leaned over and kissed him.

Max kissed me back, but he seemed distracted. How worried about this first meeting was he?

"I always thought I'd have a few kids, or at least two, but then Sarah and I broke up, and I figured it wasn't in the cards. Have you ever thought about having more children, Meira?"

My gaze flew to his. "No." The word came out quickly.

Max opened his mouth to say something and then closed it again.

"What? You thought my answer would be different?" Unreasonable anger swept over me so suddenly, I blinked at the burning sensation in my stomach.

"I'm sorry. I didn't mean to upset you." His calming tone only made me more upset.

"You want another child?"

He nodded. "I don't just want a child, Meira. I want *our* child."

I pressed my lips together. "I am almost forty."

"My grandmother had my father when she was forty."

My eyes closed. "Please, Max. Do not ask this of me. How could I bring another child into the world? I cannot control what will happen now, any more than I could then. What if there is war again? I could not have another child, only to watch it suffer."

Max took my hand in his. I went to pull it away, but he held on tight. "I understand why you would feel that way. I can't predict the future either, but I do think the world learned from what happened. You're helping it to keep learning. If you want a child, don't let fear stop you. Don't let the people who took so much from you take one more thing away."

His words wrapped around my heart and squeezed it tight.

Did I want to be a mother again? I loved being a mother to Tovah, but I couldn't protect her. How selfish would I be to have another child that I couldn't protect? Unlike Max, I wasn't so sure the world had learned anything.

"Here's Sarah." Max got out of the car and went to meet the gray sedan that had parked in the spot across from us.

I took a deep breath as I pushed open the driver's side door, feeling more brittle than I would have liked while meeting Max's ex-wife for the first time.

Jonathan flew out of the back seat and ran to Max. After a quick hug, Jonathan began his usual nonstop chatter about what he'd done with his friends all week. A slim woman with long, sleek hair the color of chestnuts pushed open the driver's door and stepped out. She was beautiful, like a movie star with high heels and dark sunglasses.

I'd made an effort that morning with heels and a maroon dress that cinched at the waist, but Sarah was on an entirely different level. As a couple, Max and Sarah must have been stunning together, but there was an edge to her that I could sense from where I stood. Her deep red lips were turned down in a scowl, and her arms were held stiffly by her sides.

"Is that Mara?" she asked Max, jutting her chin in my direction, speaking as if I weren't standing right here.

"This is *Meira*," Max said, correcting her as he put out his arm and beckoned me to his side.

"Good to meet you, Sarah," I said.

Picking up on the tension, Jonathan stopped talking as he looked from his mother to me.

"Jonathan said you gave her my car." Sarah frowned in my direction without acknowledging my greeting.

Max stiffened. "I said you could keep the car if you wanted it."

"In that god-awful color? Are you serious?"

Max sighed, and Sarah's gaze traveled over me in an assessing way. I wasn't sure what she saw, but her scowl deepened.

"Make sure you get Jonathan to school on time Monday. He said you were late last time."

"I wasn't late," Max said.

"Mom gets me there at eight fifteen, and you dropped me off at eight twenty-five," Jonathan said.

"You have to be there by eight thirty, champ. You had five minutes to spare."

Sarah eyed me again before she motioned Jonathan over to her. She handed him a small duffel bag and pulled him into a hug before she slipped back into her car without bothering to say good-bye to us.

"That could have been worse," I said under my breath.

"She was rude, pretending like you weren't even standing here. Thank you for being so polite."

"You do not have to thank me for that. It is good she did not make a scene in front of Jonathan."

Jonathan walked over with his duffel bag over his shoulder.

"Are you okay?" Max said softly so Jonathan wouldn't hear.

"Of course. She does not bother me, but I am sorry she upsets you."

Max put his hands on my shoulders and turned me to him. "I don't mean about Sarah. I mean what we talked about before she arrived."

I wasn't okay, but I didn't want to talk about it again and risk crying in front of Jonathan. With a quick nod, I changed the subject.

"Why did you get that car in such a bright yellow color anyway?" I asked. "And it has that odd black stripe on the side. It does not seem like you to be so ostentatious."

The new topic surprised him as he looked from me to the car. "You think this car is ostentatious?"

"What's ostentatious mean?" Jonathan asked.

"It is when you want to be noticed," I said.

Max ran a hand over the bumper. "You're right. It's not my style. But I wanted an automatic transmission, and all the dealer had was Swallowtail Yellow or Laguna Blue. Now that I'm used to it, I think the yellow's kind of sharp."

"This color is called Swallowtail Yellow?"

Max nodded. "They named it after a kind of butterfly, the salesman said, a yellow one with black-tipped wings."

"A yellow butterfly with black-tipped wings," I whispered, staring at the car as my body went still.

Max's words repeated in my head, sinking deep inside me. The whole world seemed to stop except my own heart, which felt as if it might pound out of my chest as I pictured the small images carved into the floor.

"Butterflies," I said, tracing my hand over the carvings. "You're drawing butterflies."

Tovah nodded. "I saw one."

"Really? Where?"

"On my sleeve, when I was coming back from getting our rations with Papa. It landed on me, and when I tried to touch it, it flew away."

I ran my hand over her hair, gathering the unruly locks that had fallen into her eyes. "What color was it?"

"Yellow, and it was black on the tips of its wings. I thought maybe it was Zayde saying hello. I don't know why I thought that. Probably because I never saw a butterfly here before, and I haven't seen once since."

My throat tightened. "Maybe it was Zayde giving you a little butterfly kiss."

"Maybe there are lots of butterflies where Zayde went. If I die, Mama, I'll come back and give you a butterfly kiss too."

My gaze shifted from the car to Max. Was I crazy to think that his car was the sign from Tovah I'd been hoping for, the one I'd given up on? Him and that yellow car with the black pinstripe. Was Max my butterfly kiss? Had Tovah sent him to me?

When the world began to move again, it beamed in the sunlight. I blinked Max into focus. There he stood, smiling curiously at me, and I wondered what he saw in my expression.

What did someone having a revelation look like? I didn't know how to tell him all I was feeling in that moment, all the emotions bursting inside me.

Instead of struggling to find the right words, I put my arms around him and hugged him as tightly as I could. He wound his arms around me automatically like he always did because he loved me. All of me, even the parts that I didn't like very much. Max was a good man right down to his soul. After all the evil and hatred I'd experienced in the world, good was everything I needed. Maybe Tovah knew that better than I did.

"Are you okay?" Max asked.

"Yes." I smiled and held him close because for the first time in a very long time, I truly was okay.

Someday I'd tell Max the story of the butterfly kisses, but for now, it would be our secret. Tovah's and mine.

epilogue

Greenwich, Connecticut, 1966

Sometimes I imagine a fragile thread is all that connects us to everything else. That thread can bend and overlap in places, or it can unravel and give way. As forces pull on it, you can try to hold on, but once it's broken, that piece of thread can't be mended. All you can do is take hold of another thread or let yourself drift alone, untethered to the world around you.

I used to think that was what I wanted, to be alone, with no connections and no more losses. I thought the pain of loss was so great, that not loving anyone was better, but I was wrong. Feeling empty and alone wasn't better. It was just empty. Max helped me see that. He made me want to grab hold of life again, and each day I was thankful that he did.

As we sat together in the synagogue, I couldn't help thinking how handsome Max looked in his suit. His thick hair was now more gray at the temples, and laugh lines were etched into the skin around his eyes and mouth. I didn't think it was possible, but he only got better looking with time.

I wasn't aging quite so gracefully. My hair color now came from a bottle, and no amount of moisturizer could make my wrinkles disappear. My joints ached sometimes, especially my shoulders and back. The doctor said my time in the ghetto and the camp had likely taken a toll that was only revealing itself now, all these years later.

But I paid no mind to the mirror or my aches and pains. I had too much to be grateful for.

As everyone watched, Talia stood from her seat and took her place at the lectern on the *bima*. Max reached for my hand, seeming just as nervous as she was. After pulling in a shaky breath, Talia met Max's gaze where we sat in the first row, and I knew he'd given her his trademark wink when she smirked and relaxed her shoulders.

I'd done her hair that morning. Two twists pulled most of her hair back off her face, and they were fastened with barrettes just above her ears. The rest of her dark blond curls rested on her shoulders. Her dress was blue, her favorite color. Talia had my coloring, but she resembled Max more. Her temperament was similar to his, steady and thoughtful.

They were fast friends, Max and Talia, an unstoppable team, and I found myself ganged up on quite a bit, but I didn't mind. I'd carried her inside me. I named her after Tovah and Leah, and I loved her more than I thought I could love anyone or anything.

As Talia started to recite her half Torah portion, her voice soft but confident, I turned and looked around the synagogue at all the familiar and unfamiliar faces. Max and his family made up the majority of the guests at Talia's bat mitzvah. My only family was Zotia and the family she'd built here in America with Eli and their two sons, who now had families of their own.

Blanka was here with her husband, and David had flown in from Israel, much to my surprise. Unlike everyone else, he hadn't married or had children, but he was still a young man. David and I often exchanged letters, and I asked him once why he hadn't met a nice girl yet. There must have been plenty of girls to choose from. David was a hero, capturing escaped Nazi soldiers, working for Israeli intelligence, and now training to become a pilot in Israel's fledgling air force.

David always wrote back, *No girl can compare to my first love.*

I stared at those words because I knew he'd meant Tovah. I shed a tear and felt conflicted because he would have been a wonderful son-in-law, but I wanted him to find his own happiness. I always wrote back to tell him so.

At the back of the synagogue, standing on his own, was Mr. Diamond. I caught his eye, and he smiled. It didn't surprise me to see him here today. He showed up on occasion.

Now that we no longer lived in the city, Mr. Diamond joined me on the porch swing in front of our house late at night when it seemed the rest of the world was asleep. I had trouble sleeping sometimes, and so we'd listen to Chopin together and talk until I was ready to go back to bed. Real or not, he would always be my friend.

Facing forward again, I watched Talia as she chanted from the Torah in her high-pitched voice.

"Mama and Papa would have been so proud to see their granddaughter on this day," I whispered to Max.

He pressed a kiss to my temple and squeezed my hand. His parents were in the front row with us, beaming up at Talia. I had a polite but distant relationship with them. They never fully embraced the idea of their son marrying a penniless Polish immigrant, but they doted on their granddaughter. It was impossible not to love Talia with her easy smiles and quick mind. She loved them back, but she always had a soft spot for her brother.

From the day Talia was born, Jonathan declared himself her protector. He was thirteen, the same age Talia was now, when his baby sister came along. While I was pregnant, he griped and complained at the prospect of a baby in the house. He wrinkled his nose at all the baby furniture when it was delivered, but it was only an act. The first time he held her and she wrapped her tiny hand around his finger, he was lost to her. We all were.

Jonathan insisted on coming with me for her first day of preschool, and he interrogated her teacher until all his questions were answered to his satisfaction. It was no different for every grade she entered, right up until he left for college.

Now he was back in the city, attending graduate school. Like his father, he wanted to work in finance, and he had a girlfriend he seemed serious about. Dressed in a navy suit with a crimson tie, Jonathan sat on the other side of Max, looking much too mature for my liking.

Time passed too quickly. I wanted to keep the children small and protected under our roof, but that wasn't the nature of things. Naturally, children grew older and moved away to begin their own lives. That was exactly how it should be, and I'd always wish Tovah could have had that chance too.

Talia finished and smiled with relief when the rabbi walked over and patted her on the shoulder. After months of preparation, she was finally done with the most difficult Hebrew parts.

Next came her speech. I'd helped Talia with her half Torah, but Max helped her write the speech, and when I asked to hear it, they both said no. They were so serious about it that I didn't press them, but I did feel a bit anxious as Talia lifted the piece of paper with her speech written on it and glanced at me before she began to read.

"I want to thank all of you for being here today, especially those of you who traveled from a distance. I think Uncle David came the farthest, all the way from Tel Aviv." She glanced up and found him in the crowd. "I'd also like to thank my grandparents, my brother, and my parents. I couldn't have done this without their support."

Clearing her throat, Talia looked back at the paper. "When I sat down to write my bat mitzvah speech, I thought about my friends in my Hebrew class, and how different my family was from theirs. They took it for granted that they would be here someday, having their bar or bat mitzvahs. They wondered how much money they would get from their relatives, and thought about all the things they would spend it on. But I knew this day was not guaranteed. I knew that because my sister never got to have a bat mitzvah. She died in a concentration camp during the war when she was only ten years old. That's why I want to share this special day with Tovah, my big sister."

My lips parted in surprise as Talia glanced down at me.

Max put his arm around my shoulders. "I hope this is okay. It was her idea."

I nodded and smiled up at Talia. She pressed her lips together to keep her emotions under control. My daughter was strong and sweet, and knew more about the world than most children her age.

Talia continued with her speech. "The seat next to mine this morning is empty as a symbol of Tovah's presence. I know she is here today, and she's smiling down on us now, especially on my mom. My mother was in the concentration camp too. You may have heard her story. She's a kind of a celebrity now that she's been interviewed on television."

Talia grinned at me, and I could feel the attention in the room shift in my direction for a moment. I was still lecturing, but in larger venues now, and was often invited to speak at symposiums. One of the national news programs covered one of those symposiums, and I sat down to give an interview afterward. Now I had many requests for interviews.

"But for a long time," Talia said, "my mother didn't talk about what happened to her and the rest of our family. It was too hard. It's still hard, but she changed her mind about talking. She says silence only encourages hatred, and that she has to talk about it so people will never forget. I will never forget my sister or the grandparents I never got to meet. As part of my bat mitzvah, we are going to Israel next month to plant trees in their names."

Talia finished by thanking the rabbi and her Hebrew teachers, and when she finished, she rushed toward me and threw her arms around me.

"I am so proud of you," I said as tears fell onto my cheeks, my heart bursting with joy and pride.

"Daddy said it would be okay to share my bat mitzvah with Tovah, but I wanted it to be a surprise."

"It is a wonderful surprise."

Talia grinned at me and then went to hug Max next.

Family and friends gathered around us to congratulate Talia.

"That was beautiful, Meira." Zotia approached me with glassy eyes of her own. "Mama and Papa would have been overjoyed to see all this."

"I think they do see it."

As I stood smiling beside her, I couldn't have imagined any of this when I climbed out of that ditch in Poniatowa. The years that followed in the DP camps, I sometimes wondered what compelled me to keep going. It would have been easier if I'd lain there with Tovah and waited for the end to come. But then I wouldn't have found Max, and I wouldn't have Talia. Maybe some part of me knew that if my heart still beat, there was more to be done. There were truths to be told and stories to be passed on of those who were gone, but would never be forgotten.

"Ready to come dance with me?" Max asked softly by my ear. To celebrate Talia's day, we'd rented out a ballroom in a nearby hotel and hired a band to play.

I moved in closer to Max. "You know I am a terrible dancer."

"All you have to do is stand in my arms and move with me."

I smiled up at him. "That I can do."

author's note

Thank you for reading this story. I wrote it over several years, in bits and pieces, because it was difficult to stay with for too long. *Where Butterflies Go* is based on the life of my great-aunt, a Holocaust survivor. Her daughter died at the age of ten when she was made to lie in a ditch with hundreds of others while Nazi soldiers fired guns at them. A bullet passed through my great-aunt's arm and went into her daughter's head, instantly killing her. Somehow, my great-aunt climbed out of the ditch and survived to tell her story.

I wanted to mention that the word Holocaust never appears here because it was not used to describe what occurred in Europe during World War II until the 1970s. By the 1930s, the Jewish community was using the biblical term *Shoah* to describe the mass killings of Jews that was taking place. But Hitler and his Nazi forces always called it *the Final Solution*.

books by
debra doxer

Contemporary Romance
Harsh
Breaking Skin
Play of Light

Paranormal Romance
Keep You from Harm (Remedy #1)
To Have and to Harm (Remedy #2)
Harmful Rush (A Remedy Stand-Alone)

Young Adult
Like Candy (Candy #1)
Sweet Liar (Candy #2)

connect with the author

www.facebook.com/AuthorDebraDoxer

www.twitter.com/debradoxer

www.instagram.com/debradoxer

debradoxer@gmail.com

Printed in Dunstable, United Kingdom